Waking Tamara

Beverly Ovalle

Paranormal Dystopian Romance

Paranormal Dystopian Romance

Waking Tamara

ISBN: 978-1-952525-03-2

First E-book Publication: May 2024

First Print Publication: May 2024

Edited by Devil in the Details

Model Photo by 6:12 Photography

Cover by AAP

PUBLISHER

Midwest Dragon Press

www.beverlyovalleauthor.com

Dedication:

Thank you to Sam, Marty and Robin in your help getting this moving and your advice, assistance and cheerleading. This book took forever!

Thanks to Eric and 6:12 Photography for his wonderful photo and model and AAP for making the cover to showcase it.

And to my editor at Devil in the Details who had to deal with my nonsense!

As always thanks to my family for letting me have the time to finish it, though I am my own worst enemy!

TABLE OF CONTENTS

CHAPTER ONE

The smell of decay wafted in the wind. Indra circled the sky, looking at the devastation below. His heart ached over the destruction. His wings beat to keep him aloft, sending him gliding in the currents around the town.

Indra back-shifted his wings, hovering over the once bustling village. He blinked his second eyelids down, setting off his thermal imaging. He flew slowly over the town center, heading toward his aunt's house.

Set away from human towns and cities, this was a haven for the paranormal. Or it was. Most of his werewolf cousins lived here. A ball of grief tightened his gut. He was looking for anything with a heat signature. He'd thought—mistakenly—that they would be spared. None of the dragons were affected by the spreading diseases. He hadn't worried about the other shifters dying, but then found out he was wrong when his mother contacted him. The furry shifters were being hit hard.

Few though they were, no dragons had died, except those who took a direct hit from a missile. He knew a couple who were foolish enough to think they could stop one in mid-flight. Some might call it courage, but not him.

He settled on the perch on his aunt's house. The one his cousins added. He took a deep breath, then choked. The stench of death permeated his nostrils. Stifling the roar that wanted to erupt, Indra closed his eyes, ignoring the tears that rimmed his lashes. His talons gripped the wooden pole. The cracking of the wood had him loosening his grip. Chest aching, he shifted and stepped onto the stair landing. He automatically grabbed clothes from the basket at the top, quickly dressing, swinging his backpack on, and then headed down.

He stalled at the door. Dread at what he would find keeping him there, one hand on the door handle, the other pressing against the window. It was too quiet. Swallowing, Indra swiped at the wetness on his cheeks. He had to do this. Just in case.

Opening the door, he stepped through. The kitchen was empty. He glanced at the refrigerator. Pictures of him and his cousins hung on the front. Smiles, missing teeth, slicked up for church, graduation. Every occasion for all to see. It didn't matter if they were dragon, werewolf, bear, or human. Their grins marked each and every one as family.

It was truly unusual. His aunts and mother were all originally human. All of them became mates to paranormals. Family reunions were truly interesting. A desperate call from his mother to check on family had him winging his way here. He caught his breath, stifling a sob. The smell alone spoke volumes.

Nowhere in the village, even here, had he seen any signs of life. He grabbed a snapshot of him and his cousins at the last reunion that hung haphazardly and slid it into his backpack. Breathing shallowly, Indra turned toward the living room.

He grabbed the doorframe, a moan spilling from his lips. “No.” His aunt and uncle sat in a chair. Their bodies wrapped around each other, cuddling together in death as they often were in life. On the couch, three of his four cousins' bodies lounged. The stench of death permeated the air. The television played the news, looping on the same broadcast Indra had seen on every TV across the nation.

“No.” He stepped into the room. His throat worked, tight now that tears ran unchecked down his face. “No.” Indra clenched his hands. This couldn’t be. He couldn’t stop the whimpers emerging. He slid down against the wall, the lifeless bodies of his cousins, his closest friends all his life, decaying in front of him.

Curling up, rocking in place, Indra sobbed into his arms.

Wiping his swollen eyes, he sucked in a shuddering breath. From this angle, he saw an envelope on the coffee table. Standing, sniffling still, he moved closer. His name was sprawled on it in his aunt's handwriting. Indra grabbed it, carefully opening it.

Indra,

My child from another mother. (He chuckled. His aunt always referred to him this way.)

This human disease hit us hard and fast. There was nothing anyone could do. Not even you. Those not struck by it were sent away. No one knows if it is contagious or a result of the bomb that exploded nearby. Not everyone got sick at once. Or perhaps we just didn't realize the symptoms.

Randy left on a scouting trip before the bomb went off, but we don't know what happened to him. We marked the area around the town as quarantined. I don't know if he survived or not. None of the scouting party returned. We pray they saw the signs we posted, or got our messages and survived.

Our alpha tried to reach them too, but we don't know if they received the message. If they received any of our messages.

I know you won't like this part, but please, please, do as we beg. Burn everything. Those alive are gone. It is only the dead left. I'm sure you checked that on your way in.

Whatever this is, it is deadly. The young and old went first, then the healthy. Please, for the sake of any wolves left, get rid of everything. The whole village. We can't chance this spreading.

I love you. Tell my sisters and the rest of the family to stay away. I pray you are immune and that, hopefully, Randy will find you or you him. I pray he is still alive.

Make it burn, Indra. Even this letter.

Remember us.

Love from us all.

He crumpled the letter in his hand. His heart hurt. He swallowed. Sucked in a big breath and choked on it, his body shaking. Tossing the letter on the table, he headed outside. Stripping off the clothes, he shifted into his dragon, taking up much of the street in front of the house. He looked around, remembering playing soccer and stickball in the street. He hung his head, and a mournful cry escaped. He took one last look at the house. His second home. His family.

He filled his lungs and did as they asked. He breathed out and let it burn.

He double-checked before he burned the rest of the town. Just to make sure. But no heat signatures showed in the houses. The adults and the tiniest of babes had succumbed to the spread of disease. There was nothing he could do to save them. But he could ensure the sickness here didn't spread. Just like his family asked.

Landing in the center of town, Indra used his earth dragon magic, found the water throughout the town, and directed it away. Pushed it down and through the sediment, cleansing it deep underground before changing its direction back to the surface, forming a new path circling the town, keeping anyone away.

Indra shifted, his dragon giving away to his human form. He walked into the grocery store. The shelves were bare, with few items left. The disarray emphasized the panic of the last however many days. Finding what he needed, he grabbed the matches and lighters scattered on a shelf. Gathering any flammables, Indra piled them up, lit a match and watched them burn. If he'd been a fire dragon, he could scorch the town, but as an earth dragon, his fire had limits. He could burn, but not enough to encompass the area needed.

Using the bonfire he'd created, Indra carefully set each building on fire. Gasoline and lighter fluids found along the way assisted in erasing the town from the face of the earth. Leaving behind glowing ashes and emptiness. His stomach ached for the dead.

His last stop was the church they worshipped in. Indra's steps slowed. He didn't want to go in there, but he had little choice. This rampant disease had to be stopped.

Opening the door, Indra gagged. He could not let the smell stop him. Gazing around, lips pressed together, he swallowed a lump in his throat. Pews were filled. Young and old, sprawled out, graceless in death. Some were half-shifted as if to run. The disease didn't discriminate. Humans and shifters of all ages caved to its insidious destruction. Only the dragons seemed immune.

Blinking rapidly, Indra refused to pick out individuals. Refused to see faces he laughed with, babies he'd rocked in his arms. Wolves he'd run with as a youth. The town had been the center of the pack. One of the largest packs on this side of the country.

Choking back a sob, Indra closed his eyes and prayed to the gods. Unclenching his hands, he took hymnals, careful not to touch the bodies, and lit them. Dry paper and old wood fed the crackle of flames, greedily leaping from spot to spot until the whole of the church was sheeting in flame. The smell of rotten roasting meat filled the air.

Swallowing back his saliva, Indra backed out of the building. No longer a place of worship, the old wooden structure burned, the ashes spiraling into the sky. Tears filled his eyes, twisted his heart. Flames devoured the people he once knew, laughed with, and played with. He wondered if the pain would ever go away.

Unable to watch any longer, Indra shifted, pumping his wings to carry him away. But not far, no. He had a responsibility to make sure the fire didn't spread to the trees surrounding the small town, to gobble up the land like the diseases ravaged the people. Ravaged his four-footed family.

Circling once again in the currents, Indra watched. Watched the buildings turn to ash. Ensuring the last flickers of flame burnt out.

Calling to the earth, he hollowed the town out, sinking it down before summoning the water to cover it. He trumpeted out a last mournful cry for the denizens now wiped from the face of the earth. One last circle, ensuring nothing was left of the town, and Indra left a new lake behind.

He flew through the mountains. The stink of death following him. Through the peaks of the smoky mountains, he tried to outrun his grief.

Indra finally stopped, sides heaving, at a stream flowing down the mountain across a meadow into fields ripe with grain. Domesticated animals lowed and clucked and quacked below him. Dipping his head in the stream, Indra gulped down the refreshing water. A few fish helped stave off his hunger. An unwary rabbit hopped by and he quickly devoured it down.

Throat no longer dry, his stomach sated enough for the moment, Indra looked around. A chicken coop, stone walls to separate the animals, and gardens were below. He lifted his snout, sniffing the air. No decay. Closing his second lid, Indra checked for heat signatures. Only the animals showed around him. No humans, but the valley, lush, green, organized, and filled with animal life, proved they were there at one point, not so long ago.

Something drew him here. He looked up, spying a missile heading toward the mountain. Taking a last drink, he leapt up, speeding away. He reached the opposite mountain and turned back at the sound as part of the mountain behind him exploded. Rock rolled down, covering a cave entrance. He hoped nothing was living in there. A small crater covered the ground, changing the flow of the river he'd just visited. The chicken coops were gone. As for the chickens, they were probably blown up or buried in rubble. The cows were stampeding away. The ones who were not injured.

Indra considered grabbing an easy dinner from one of the wounded cattle but decided not to. He scanned the valley one more time. Despite the feeling he needed to be here, there was nothing to see. Nothing alive other than the fleeing cattle.

He sighed and flew away.

~

Mara took one last sip of her coffee, placing the drained cup in the sink. The cold room had no personality. None of the Doomsday Facilities did. This room, guarding the rear entrance, was quiet and rarely used except by her.

Just beyond the door lay apartments for one hundred families, equipment to start the world over, and food stores specially engineered to last a century or more. Beyond that, a state-of-the-art cryonics center and more.

Mara shivered. The thought of being immolated in a gel-like fluid while still alive had her hair standing on end. But the data predicted ninety percent of the world's population succumbing to the viruses unleashed, spreading around the globe. The airlines spread it to countries whether the bombs brought it or not. Ships replaced the planes, but it was too late.

Their government made the call. The chosen few responded. Their families gathered with them. Her father, herself, and her brother included. They were flown and dropped by helicopter into the meadow. The surrounding mountains hid what was happening. Drops of others she didn't know, whom the government deemed necessary, joined them.

Her brother planned and implemented the intricate solar panel system that powered the nearby town and the facility. Mara couldn't explain it, but her brother helped build it. He swore it would last a thousand years. Time would tell. She only cared that it lasted until they woke again.

A horn blew, once and again, calling all to the cryonic center to be put under.

A chill ran up her spine. Taking a deep breath, Mara stood straight. Her hand pressed against her racing heart. As a medical doctor, she knew this whole procedure was risky. On the other hand, they'd probably be dead in a matter of weeks if they didn't. Waves of viruses had been released. There was little guarantee any of them would survive. Each virus wave was mutated, taking out more survivors with each attack.

Pulling her shoulders back, Mara headed into the corridor to the cryonics lab. Her footsteps echoed down the long, empty hall. She tried not to think of them as steps to her doom. She didn't want to go under. She'd never thought it would come to this. But better to outlive the viruses unleashed and wake up when they were no longer viable. Hopefully, no longer viable.

She stopped outside the door. Took a deep breath and let it out. She would be one of the last ones going under. Her job as a medical doctor was to make sure all the participants were healthy enough to undergo the process.

They'd been checked previously, so it shouldn't be an issue. Each group had been quarantined in quarters for a month to ensure they were healthy. If anyone had any virus, it should have died by now. They couldn't afford to bring the diseases wiping out the world into the future.

The line of people stood waiting for her to get their vitals. She was the last one to the party.

"Dr. Phillip, are you ready?" Her father, also Doctor Phillip, spoke loud enough for everyone lining up to hear.

"Yes." Walking over to her exam area, Mara straightened her lab coat. "Place your arm here." She checked blood pressure, height, weight and drew two vials of blood from each person, carefully marking their information on it. She also took a DNA sample from everyone.

Once she had a tray of samples, she refrigerated them. Her assistant then checked one of the samples in the VirScan for viruses. Once the government discovered the machine's ability and money was thrown at the project to get it up and running, every facility had them installed.

A centrifuge, equipment for rapid blood testing, and any other medical need she could think of. Most of it was in a medical laboratory behind the cryonic chamber.

On the second floor of the facility, a complete medical unit was created. Everything from an MRI to an X-ray machine was installed to her specifications.

She wasn't the only doctor, of course. There were medical teachers, specialists, and scientists knowledgeable in cryonics and cloning already lying in their cryonics beds.

The first few hundred people had been cryonically frozen over the past couple of days. Today should be the final push to put everyone under.

Retesting seemed a waste of time since, regardless, they were being put under. The greatest minds in the country, the government deemed needed to restart the human population, were being processed in three facilities across the nation.

Each facility also had a cloning room. A cross-section of DNA from every person who had their DNA tested for their ethnicity was stored there. It would give humanity a chance to come back from near extinction. Those who had genetic anomalies with any type of disease were disposed of. The government wanted only the most viable DNA to repopulate the world. The samples she took today would join them.

In addition, DNA from as many species of animals as possible had been gathered. She had no doubt that if the government could have gotten its hands on dinosaurs, that DNA would be included also.

The room of insects gave her the creeps. Not one to play in the dirt, Mara never liked the creepy crawlies found there and in dark, damp spaces. Goosebumps ran up and down her arms. She knew they were essential, but she didn't have to like it.

"I'm getting hungry." Her assistant nudged her shoulder. "I think we could use a break."

Mara nodded and yawned. Her computer screen blinked back at her. One hundred people processed, at least one person from each of the one hundred families done this morning, with one hundred to go. One hundred and three, counting herself, her father, and assistant. She checked the time. It was a little after one o'clock. Her stomach growled in protest. Stretching her back, she followed the sound of her father's voice.

"Doctor Phillip, how many more do you want to process today?" Even though he was her father, he insisted on formal addressing when around other people, especially in what he considered a professional setting.

"Where are we at now?" He pressed a green button and closed the pod in front of him.

"One hundred people have checked in this morning. There are still one hundred to go, including essential people." She figured they would finish all but the essential personnel needed to fill the pods today.

Rows upon rows of pods filled the large room, a total of close to five hundred. There were extras, just in case of a technical glitch, but none had been encountered so far.

He looked at the clipboard in his hand. “I have seventy-five of those one hundred already in their cryonic pods. Another hour at the most and the people from this morning will be settled in their pods.” He looked at her. “Finish processing everyone. We need to complete the process today.”

Mara nodded, stomach sinking. That meant today was her last day until sometime in the future. If she dwelled on the thought, she’d be a basket case. Not an example she wanted anyone else to see. “I’m going to take a short break. I don’t want to make any mistakes with the data I’m loading. My assistant needs to, also. We’ll be back in half an hour.”

His scowl wouldn’t stop the hunger gnawing at her belly. It took him a moment to agree. Her father rolled his eyes. “Fine. Let everyone know they can head to lunch. Except the twenty-five I still need to process.” He turned toward the next person and began preparing them. “Be back in an hour. And bring me a turkey sandwich.”

She snorted and nodded. “Will do.”

Mara addressed the twenty-five people who had already checked in. “You can each go to the next open chamber. Please sit in the chair next to it and wait for further instructions.”

She turned to the rest of the people still in line. “We’re breaking for lunch for forty-five minutes. Please line up back here at that time. We plan on putting everyone into cryonic sleep today.”

She ignored the murmuring, turning instead to her assistant. “Henry, take an hour lunch and then you can get back to work.”

“I thought you told them forty-five?” His eyebrow raised, but his eyes twinkled.

“You know they won’t make it back on time. This group thinks too highly of themselves.” She shook her head. “I told them that so they’d be back in an hour.”

He laughed. “Fine. I’ll be back on time.”

Mara smiled, then headed to the laboratory in the rear. Her sack lunch was in there. And one for her father. She grabbed both, dropping her father’s off before heading out the door of the cryonic lab. A short walk took her to the door guarding the outside. Sliding out, she stepped quickly through the cave, protecting the front of the facility. Breaking free of the oppressive feel of the mountain, she smiled at the expanse of greenery in front of her. If only she could stay here forever.

One group of government employees was stationed in the closest town to maintain the solar and wind farms, setting up apprenticeships to keep the knowledge alive. Mara bet they had no idea the facility was here. People had to be trained to keep the power to the facility running. She imagined they were told it was set up just in case the major power plants were destroyed. Most probably had no idea it ran more than their town. They were probably even grateful the government was trying to save them by isolating them from the rest of humanity.

Like her, many didn't like the idea of being surrounded by gel and suspended in time. The children were the worst. Luckily, there were few young families. Most people here were single or had children in their teens or early twenties. But her responsibility was to her patients, and each and every person going under was her patient.

Settling down on a large rock conveniently next to a river, Mara took her lunch from her sack. From her pocket, she pulled out a transistor radio. Turning it on, she played around with the knob attempting to tune into a station.

"Yay." Smiling, Mara managed to find one. Her joy dipped upon hearing the news. Millions of people dead across the United States. Billions across the world. The missile strikes, hitting supposedly random spots in the US. Unfortunately, the devastation proved they weren't so random after all. Many of the diseases ravaging their country were cooked up by their own government and released in the explosions. The antidotes blown up along with the labs.

Eyes stinging, she turned it off, dropping it to the ground. Her appetite lost, she stared at her lunch. She didn't want the turkey on wheat anymore, but her body needed the energy. Choking down the sandwich, she stared around her. Filled her lungs with probably the last fresh air she'd be able to enjoy. Dipped her hands into the river, drinking from the water's edge. It was so cold her mouth went numb. The last time she'd drink fresh water, at least for the foreseeable future.

Waving her hands dry and getting her circulation going from the icy water, Mara gathered her radio and trash, ready to return to the cave hidden inside the mountain. Delaying wouldn't help anyone. Glancing around one more time, her fists clenched. Her heart stuttered. Her whole body rejected the idea of returning to be placed in a sleepy death. Taking a last deep breath, she ignored the dismay in her soul. Looked up into the clouds, taking one last moment of peace.

Her gaze caught the sight of a large bird soaring over the mountain. Mara squinted. It couldn't be what she thought. Clouds drifted across, obscuring the animal. It had to be a hawk or something. Dragons weren't real. Though she never thought the world would be dying either. She shook her head. She was seeing things. Ignoring what her head told her, she decided then and there to listen to her heart and believe dragons were real. Why not? Hoping on fairy tales wasn't any worse than acknowledging the world around her was dying.

Mara stretched, letting the sun bathe her in its warmth. Ignoring her inner cringing, she headed back inside. It was time to complete her task. She shut the door behind her, setting the seal and locking it.

A loud blast shook the mountain. Mara jumped, stifling a scream, while she fell to the floor. Rocks tumbled down, blocking the passage she had just been in. Shaken, she stood and headed to the cryonics room. It was time to finish her task, saving humanity and their way of life.

If a little niggle of doubt crossed her mind about how their way of life brought them to this point, she ruthlessly pushed it away. She could only hope that humanity would do better in the future.

CHAPTER TWO

Indra kept coming back to the valley he'd watched the missile hit. It definitely tugged at his soul. He couldn't, wouldn't believe there was no reason.

He looked around the valley and the mountains, checking for any heat signatures approaching. Nothing but the animals below and a goat herd higher up on the mountain. His stomach rumbled. The fish he'd eaten earlier were a decent snack, but his dragon needed more. Checking one more time for human signatures, Indra flew down across the valley. The cattle lowed, shuffling around in alarm when his shadow passed over them but didn't run. They weren't used to predators.

Snatching two of the herd, Indra flew away. His talons cut off the squeals of his prey, leaving them limp in his claws. Dropping them, they landed in his camp with a thud. Following them, Indra settled down to enjoy his meal.

He repeated that often enough in the days that passed. The solitude was mixed with a sense of longing. He would stay. Something here called to him. To his dragon. Unlike other dragons, earth dragons were perfectly happy living above the ground. He didn't need a cave to keep him happy.

Earth dragons didn't hoard treasure underground. Their treasure was in making sure the land around them thrived. This valley became his treasure.

His life became routine. Indra lost hope of his mate showing up in the valley and surrounding mountains. His wings took him away, searching for the one who would complete his heart, but he always returned to the valley. His dragon demanded it.

Occasionally, he'd check on the children he'd saved. Their parents had succumbed to whatever disease affected them, leaving the children alone. Stepping in, Indra cared for them until more of their family showed up. The little homestead grew, attracting humans who heard about it.

A town had grown up nearby, offering handmade products and services. Oddly enough, a tattoo parlor saw a lot of business. Indra had a tattoo commemorating his fallen wolf brethren, the spitting image of his cousin's wolf immortalized on his chest. He rubbed his chest, his heart clenching. Though wolves lived almost as long as dragons, no evidence of his missing cousin ever came to light. The pain of having lost a whole branch of his family never left him.

Years passed, and the earth covered the scars of humans. Buildings and towns crumbled, turning into ruins. The roads, the power plants, the huge edifices showing man's footprint on the earth all crumbled away. The humans used to have a saying, ashes to ashes and dust to dust. They never knew how true that was.

He searched for any sign of the wolf packs he knew of, but none ever showed themselves. He could only believe the human diseases affected the rest of the wolves the same way they had the town he'd burned. He ignored the ache in his heart and headed home.

Indra flew, enjoying the frigid air against his scales. The wind shifted, pushing against him. The beat of his wings changed, finding currents to make his journey faster, smoother. He lifted his snout, sniffing. His gaze sharpened. A throbbing entered his loins. Could it be? He sniffed again, filling his lungs. Oh yes, it could.

Indra arrowed down, following the scent. A dragon mating ritual and he was close enough to answer the call. His cock lengthened. The chill air barely cooled him off.

His gaze searched below, though the scent alone guided him. Below, two dark heads towered over a dainty figure. The mating pheromones rising from the male, her mate.

Indra hadn't been in a mating ceremony in a long time. It had been ages since any of his clan mated. Off to his left, Indra shifted due to mild turbulence. He glanced over but saw nothing, and then a blue dragon appeared. A sky dragon. He hadn't seen any since humans took to the skies. It made sense to see one again now that the skies were clear. Indra dipped his wings in acknowledgement.

They both spiraled down, drawn by the pheromones. He ignored the sky dragon, racing through the air, too intent on sinking his cock into a hot, tight pussy.

Indra watched the three below drop to the ground. They maneuvered the woman so she was spread between the two dark men. The small female writhed in a wild frenzy, her pheromones inciting him. He bugled, signaling his intent. Indra flew down, covering her, shifting to his human form to move into place, his cock aiming for her mouth. He hissed his name, the bare minimum of courtesy to the other dragons. Her fervor making him wild.

"Rog." Her mate spoke before immersing himself back to pleasuring his mate.

"Zeru," the sky dragon said. But Indra couldn't care less.

Indra moaned, hips rocking in place, head thrown back. He shook and let loose, cum coating her throat. He groaned. “Haven’t heard of a mating in years.”

Her eager cries had him hard again before he pulled out of her throat, easing down to worship her breasts, hands slipping down to tease her clit. He bumped the man humping her, ignoring the cum splashing over her body.

Indra moved again, easing home between her legs.

She writhed against him, against all of them. Screaming in joy, demanding more, she thrashed in ecstasy as another orgasm squeezed his cock.

Her scream of pleasure was cut off. A dick filled her mouth. She sucked frantically, the noises coming from her throat beautiful to hear. Hands massaged her breasts while her nipples were suckled. A head drew back, stretching her breast until her nipple popped from a mouth. The deep raspberry, hard and tight, pebbled in the air.

Indra groaned at the beauty beneath him. Hands were pulling at him, wanting a turn.

Her pussy spasmed again around his cock. Indra let loose a strangled cry, pumping harder. He was torn from her. His cum spilled across her stomach, coating the underside of her breasts.

“Thank you,” Indra grunted.

He couldn't release inside another dragon's mate. Especially during the change. The dragon's seed started the fertilization. It was a battle her mate would fight with all of them. Hissing, he moved to taste another part of her.

The next hour was filled with bringing gratification to the woman between them. Indra felt the bond forming, coalescing. Earth, air, and fire swirling together to bring forth the dragoness from her soul.

Exhausted, Indra lay back, the earth beneath him reviving his energy.

"She'll need food." Her mate's voice was hoarse.

"We'll hunt; bring enough for all of us." Indra stood.

"I'll restart the fire, then hunt," said the air dragon.

"What was your name again?" Indra smirked. "I wasn't paying attention."

The air dragon laughed. "Zeru. And yours?"

"Indra."

They shook hands and turned in opposite directions.

Indra shifted, a pump of his wings taking him into the sky. Now that the mating frenzy had left his blood, he realized where he was. He hadn't been here in a long while, on the hunt for the wolf packs, but he remembered everything. A sense of peace filled him. He was home.

He knew just where to go to get food for the newly made dragoness. Homing in on the cattle, he grabbed a couple, his talons silencing their cries. He dropped them close to the fire and left to get more.

Her appetite would be voracious.

Indra snatched one and quickly ate. He captured and carried two more back to the mating ground. Knowing she was human, he placed one on the spit to roast. It wouldn't cook fast enough, but the smell of the meat over the fire was sure to tempt her appetite.

He repeated the trip three more times. Hopefully, the pile of carcasses would be enough sustenance for the new dragoness. The effort of changing would be impossible to maintain without proper fuel.

Indra watched her, marveling at the beautiful dragon she became. When the pile of food became low, he left and brought back more.

From the snarl on her snout and smoke from her nostrils, they landed before her just in time.

Indra chuckled as she filled her belly and fell asleep. Only then were the males able to take their meals and nap.

Indra winced when a mechanical banging assaulted his ears. The sharp clang of metal on metal reminiscent of a blacksmith in his forge. Frowning, he looked around. The noise came from the cave entrance once buried under rock.

The newest dragoness woke up, grumbling. She'd changed back to human during her sleep. "What was the noise I heard? Sounded like metal hitting metal." She looked around. "Where did it come from?" She looked down, squealed, grabbed a dress, and tossed it over her nakedness.

"It must have been one of the other dragons." Her mate looked around.

"Not I." Indra shook his head. "Nor Zeru. We were napping after our hunt." Indra lay more in a daze than dozing. His thoughts centered once again on finding his mate. His dragon perked up, searching around them like he would find her under a rock. Every time he came here, it was the same sense of urgency. He'd stayed away longer and longer but was constantly drawn back—to his frustration. He searched the mountains and the valleys but never once found his mate. His dragon's aggravation worsened with every failure.

Both fire dragons turned toward the opening in the mountainside.

"Do you think?" One ran his hand through his hair. Hark, he believed from their conversation around the fire.

"What else could it be?" The other, Rog, glared at the door.

"Trouble?" Zeru followed his stare.

"We found people in individual coffins in some sort of liquid. There were directions on one of them, so we followed it," Rog's gruff voice answered.

"Coffins?" Indra wondered if they found a mass burial site. But how would they have known a missile would land there and plan for all the bodies to be stored? He frowned and shook his head. They couldn't have known. His curiosity sparked. He would check this out. His dragon urged him in.

"They were in a room marked cryonics," Grace said.

"Oh." Zeru hissed out. "Frozen. They put themselves into a freezing sleep, hoping they would be woken up once the war ended. I heard rumors of humans doing this. I don't know who they thought would wake them. I don't think they counted on the devastation or the loss of so many people." He shook his head. "I never heard of a success. Just humans being froze."

"It's probably some former government lab." Indra snorted. "It's probably filled with the type of humans that caused the destruction."

"We did seal up a couple of rooms. One for weapons development and the other something about diseases." Hark frowned.

"Sealed how?" Indra asked. "If they are part of the former government, they can't be trusted."

"We used our dragon fire. Melded the door into becoming one with the wall." Rog slid an arm around Grace, tugging her against his side. "If necessary, we can destroy everything in those rooms. Burn it all."

Indra shrugged. "Maybe sealing the rooms will keep them out, but I doubt it. Anything in there should be destroyed."

"How do you know all this?" Hark looked him in the eye. "Hearsay?"

"No. I've been around since before what the humans call the *apocalypse*. It was easy enough to camouflage. Earth dragons tended to congregate in the old National Parks. We could blend in easily. And we held down jobs. Usually in the forestry department."

"So, you lived when there were airplanes and automobiles?" The dragoness sounded fascinated.

Indra ignored her question. Hadn't he just said so? He was staring at the opening. His dragon begged him to check out where the noise was coming from. Something tugged him that way. Could it truly be his mate? Hidden from him all these years.

"I thought the humans were all gone from here." Indra didn't look away from the tunnel. "The human government must have filled this area with animals. Then left. I thought they left. I had no idea anything was here. No one has ever come here until you."

"Are you guys just going to stand around naked?" Grace interrupted, her face turning red.

"Don't be looking at them. The only one you need to see without clothes is me." Rog turned her away from us. "Get dressed."

Hark shook his head and went for his bag.

Zeru rolled his eyes. "Fine." And did the same.

Indra just grabbed his bag and pulled out jeans to put on.

"Were you the one taking care of the animals?" Grace asked. She waved her arms toward them. "You truly were here since the apocalypse?"

"They foraged for the most part. I didn't do much. I want to see this coffin room." Indra stepped forward, breaking the group's inertia. His dragon wriggled in glee, pushing him into the tunnel. He was intent on checking it out. He entered the exterior door, transitioning from cave to tunnel. Moving farther inside, he stopped at a door marked cryonics. The banging came from within. His dragon was practically salivating.

Rog, Hark, and Grace moved around him and entered the cryonics room.

Despite his eagerness, Indra took up the rear, letting even Zeru go ahead of him. His fingers twitched. His eyes scanned the room around him. Coffin-like pods lined the room. Hundreds of them. Each had blinking lights and shadowy figures inside. The distinct features of the occupants became clearer the closer he peered at them. He shivered. The thought of being suffocated yet still alive—horrifying.

A whirling sound followed, and a loud bang came from one of the pods in front of them. The lid lifted and banged back down. The source of the noise they'd heard outside. Loud enough to wake the dead. However, it didn't have any effect on the pods around it.

Rog and Hark hurried over and tried to lift the top of the pod. They weren't strong enough.

Indra and Zeru joined them. Their combined strength effectively opened the moving lid.

Inside was a man who began to choke and mumble.

They gathered around him. Rog read the directions he'd taken from the machine and pressed buttons.

Indra's attention wandered. From what he could hear, the man was some kind of doctor and had belonged to the now-defunct government. Indra circled the room, looking into more cryonic pods. His dragon kept repeating*, no, no, no* with each glance inside.

Sighing, resigned to checking each one at his dragon's insistence, Indra walked along the rows. His heart thrummed excitedly in his chest. He saw men, women, young adults, and children all floating in a gel-like liquid. Waxy in a living death. Indra shuttered. He didn't know if he would call them brave or foolish. He continued to check each pod. Meticulously going from one to another.

Mine. The glee of his dragon broke through.

Indra froze. He looked down. His heart raced in his chest. *Mine, mine, mine.* His dragon danced in excitement. Indra drank her in. Dark hair, a straight nose, rose-colored lips, and delicate eyebrows. He leaned against the glass, staring down. Beautiful and all his. This was why his dragon kept dragging him back.

"Open this one." He looked over at the others hovering over the noisy man. He couldn't believe it. All this wasted time. He stared down at the beauty in front of him. He clenched his fists, took a deep breath. Letting it out, he rubbed a hand over his aching heart. "Do her next."

He would never have guessed his mate had been sleeping beneath the mountain all these years. He would have torn away the rocks years ago if he'd known.

No, if she wasn't hidden from him, she might have succumbed to the diseases. Being frozen for unknown decades kept her alive. This was why he was here. This was what he and his dragon wanted. His mate. He shook his head, his gaze tracing the contours of her face. Sleeping Beauty. He wondered if a kiss would wake her.

He glanced at the other shifters. If he'd found her back then, he might not have been able to change her into a dragoness. Few dragons were living amongst the humans. Only with their fall had dragons started to come out of hiding. He might not have had enough dragons to complete the mating process, which is not how an earth dragon would prefer. Most successful earth dragon matings happened with different species of dragons, not just one. It allowed the dragoness to absorb the talents of the species who assisted in the mating. Earth, air, water, and fire dragons. There were three of the four here. Perhaps the other dragons knew of a water or ice dragon to complete the mating. It wasn't necessary, but it was optimal.

Indra stared down at her, shaking his head. All this time, she'd been right under his nose.

~

Mara slowly became aware of her surroundings. A chill shook her, raising goosebumps all over her body. Mara opened her eyes. Blinking, she tried to clear them, the world around her nothing but a blur. Her heart raced at seeing the edge of the cryo pod open above her. She was alive.

Mara tried to lift her arm, but shook from the effort. Medically, she knew her muscle tone would be diminished. It shouldn't take long to get back into shape, but it was disconcerting. The cryonics pod should have helped retain it. A few years shouldn't have had this effect. She should know; she'd helped design them. The main facility should have sent out personnel to awake the other facilities. It was right there in the SOP, the standard operating plan. Though nothing about the situation had been standard. The way she felt, she wondered how long it had been.

The gel coated all of her body. It dripped down, and she assumed it was draining out of the bottom of the bed. What she needed was a long, hot shower.

The pod tilted into a semi-upright position. She gasped, choking on the air tube in her throat. She tried to brace against the movement. Her hands grasped the handles beneath them, her fingers curling around them to hold her in place. She felt herself sliding. Millimeters, but it felt like she was going over a cliff. Mara's breath hitched when her feet met the lip and her legs held.

"Tamara! You're awake." Her father's voice assaulted her. Doctor Steven Phillip liked the sound of his own voice, sometimes too much. He pressed a button that undid the straps holding her in place. He slowly removed the tube from her throat. She choked. Sucking in air when it was removed. It should have been automatic. Why hadn't it worked?

"Dad." Her voice cracked. Her legs wobbled. Hibernating had taken more of a toll on her body than she'd planned for. She started sliding down, her legs no longer holding her up once the straps were removed.

"I've got you." A deep voice accompanied by strong arms. He swung her into his arms, holding her against a well-muscled chest.

Mara blinked and gazed, mesmerized, into green eyes. Dark lashes turned the emerald green into a deeper, darker green. She couldn't look away.

"I'm Indra." His eyes crinkled, amusement sparking in them.

"Mara," she whispered.

He frowned. "Your father called you Tamara."

"Mara is my nickname. The one I prefer. Only my parents called me Tamara." Her eyes roamed his face, admiring the angles. Classically handsome, Indra could have modeled any number of statues she'd seen in museums around the world.

"Then I will call you Mara."

Her breath hitched. The fluttering in her belly something she was going to ignore.

"Tamara, how are you feeling? Are you weak? I'd like to check your cognitive abilities after being in the pod for so many centuries." Her father's words didn't make sense.

Mara turned her head toward his voice. "What do you mean, centuries? We were scheduled for revival in no more than fifty years. At the absolute most. It was in the SOP." She struggled in the stranger's—Indra's—arms. "Please put me down." Her movements had her almost slipping from his arms. The gel. She'd forgotten about that. Ick. Now, it was all she could think of.

Indra lowered her legs, holding on to her.

Mara was glad he did. Her legs started to give out, but he held her up until she steadied herself. "Thank you." She turned to her father. "Dad, what do you mean? How can that many years have passed?"

"Evidently, we were never woken up. I don't know what happened. The government is no longer in place. Much of humanity is gone. At least in this area." Steven waved an arm at the people standing there watching. "They've taken me to the nearest town. The one that keeps the solar power plant working. There is nothing but local law and order." He harrumphed. "And not much of that."

A couple of the people were helping her brother, Christopher. He also appeared weak and needed assistance to stand. Two men helped him out of the room. Presumably to his quarters to get cleaned up.

Something she wanted to do. "Well, nothing we can do about that. I need to get cleaned up and something to eat. I assume we'll start waking everyone, and I can check statuses at that point." Mara took a step forward but grabbed Indra's arm. "Can you help me to my quarters?"

"Lead the way." Indra bent and swept Mara into his arms.

She could get used to this. "Thank you." Most of the men she knew used their brains rather than muscles. Mara doubted any of them could carry her. They wouldn't even think of it; their minds too busy trying to build a better mouse trap.

She directed him toward her lab.

He frowned, walking the way she indicated. "You don't live in the main area?"

Her quarters were located above the lab, adjacent to the medical facility built above them. Part of the facility maintained the information on the cryonics pods, keeping track of all the data. She'd argued that having the doctors near the medical facility made more sense. Reason had prevailed, and a separate section for the lab techs, medical doctors, and their families was built near there.

"No. This is a shortcut." Mara settled her head against his chest. A shiver slid through her when his arms tightened around her. A thin line of chest hair tickled her nose. Heat filled her cheeks. How did she not notice he wasn't wearing a shirt? His skin was warm against her, making her realize how chilled she was.

Mara reached her arm out, opening the door to her lab. She indicated the opposite door. "Through there." She coughed, catching a whiff of her body. The gel stank, which meant she stank and she was pretty sure Indra would stink too now.

Her hand settled against the pad and the door opened, leading to a corridor and a staircase. Fans began moving, circulating the stale, dusty air. Dim lights came on, illuminating the hallway. It would be pitch black here if they weren't. She'd have to thank her brother later for his design.

"Up, or right?" Indra asked.

"Up and then take a left." Mara sighed.

Indra's steps echoed up the stairs.

Mara shivered. There might be light, but the dank chill of the inside of a mountain reminded her they were, in fact, deep inside one. No matter how livable the government tried to make it, it was still just a cave. A fancy one, but a cave nonetheless.

Indra reached the top of the stairs and turned. "Where to?"

Mara looked at the corridor. It was huge. Using forklifts to build and bring in equipment made it more practical to have a large walkway. "First door on the left."

Mara reached out a hand, her print unlocking the door. "Thank you." She relaxed once they were inside, surrounded by her things. Most of the quarters on the lower level were generic. Hers was built on the same model, but she'd personalized it.

Her brother added more lighting and one of the builders added bookshelves. All of her personal favorites were there. She had a fully loaded ereader but worried future technology would make it obsolete. Now, she had to wonder if it would even work.

"This is nice." Indra was looking around. "Cozy."

"You can let me go now." Mara blinked, caught in his gaze.

"If I must." Indra let her slide down his body.

She opened and shut her mouth, not knowing what to say. Her body molded to his. Every hard muscle pressed against her soft ones. Her pulse fluttered. She gazed at his mouth, wondering if it was hard or soft. Her arms seemed to have wrapped themselves around him.

"Did you need help getting cleaned up?" His face broke into a wicked grin. "I'm more than willing to help."

Her scalp prickled, heat flashing from head to toe. Mara stepped back, reluctantly pulling her arms from him. "I got this." Maybe that shower would need to be cold.

"Do you want me to wait?" His words stopped her.

"You can clean up too. Shower off the mess I made on you." Mara wrinkled her nose at the gel on him.

His smirk curled her toes. "Together?"

"What? No." Flustered, Mara waved to another door. "You can use the shower there. I'm using mine." Mara wondered if all the men in this new life were like him. She'd be an embarrassed puddle in no time at all.

"You're sure? I can get any place you can't reach." He was laughing at her.

"No." Mara escaped into her bedroom, slamming her door. She leaned against the door, hands pressing to her burning cheeks. Grimacing at the feel of the gel still coating her, she stood and crossed to her bathroom.

Sighing at the welcome sight, Mara turned on her shower. Please let it be warm. The water shot a couple of bursts of air before settling in a steady stream. The water turned from brown to grey and finally clear. Her shoulders relaxed at the steam rising from it.

Stripping the shorts and sports bra off turned into more of a problem than she thought. It felt glued on. She supposed she should be glad they could wear something in the pod. Mara shrugged and stepped under the water. The water beat down, sloughing off the gel. She struggled but was finally able to remove her clothes. She kicked them to the side. They would have to be thrown out. She doubted the stench of the gel would ever be removed.

Grabbing her shampoo, she lathered her hair. It had grown long while she was frozen. Glancing at her nails, Mara realized those had too. Huh, not things she had thought about when this project commenced. She figured being cryonically frozen would have stopped all growth. She'd have to make a note of the changes. Do a complete physical of herself, her brother, and father. She sighed. Not to mention all the other people.

She rinsed her hair, grabbing her bar of soap next. She scrubbed, grimacing when her washcloth began to disintegrate. Maybe it had been centuries. The commercials denigrating plastics made her hope her scrubby stood the test of time better. She grabbed that. The rough surface felt good and it didn't fall apart.

Mara wondered if Indra was showering. Would he appreciate the heat of the water? Would it roll down his defined chest? Her breath sped up, body heating. She imagined the water catching in his glory trail, watching it slide down until his treasure was revealed.

She squeezed her legs together, took a deep breath, and switched the water to cold, yelping at the change. She didn't even know him. Her body wanted to, though.

Turning off the water, she grabbed a towel and dried her hair. Bending over, she carefully twisted it and tossed it over her head. Grunted at the sound of tearing. The natural fibers definitely hadn't stood up to time. But it stayed, barely. Taking another towel, she dried her body, wrapping and tucking it carefully in to cover up.

Mara glanced at the clothing in her shower. She didn't want to touch the garments. Mara picked them up and stared. Tilting to better examine the pieces. The pale khaki was stained in places with the faintest tint of blue.

She shuddered. The lighter the color of the gel, the more it had broken down. The fact it was barely showing blue at all wasn't a good sign. To her, it meant she needed to start the wake-up process for everyone. Mara took a deep breath. She could do this. She had to.

But it would be nice to have someone to lean on. Someone she could confide in. Someone to hold her. Someone like Indra. Mara grimaced, shaking those thoughts from her head. She couldn't afford to let a man distract her. The lives of everyone in the pods depended on her and her father, not some unknown man. No matter how her body responded to his.

Standing tall, she put her shoulders back and marched into her bedroom. It was empty. Her body sagged a bit. Mara shook her head. What was she expecting? Indra sprawled out naked on her bed? The dampness between her thighs and the prickling of her nipples indicated that's just what she hoped.

"Everything okay in there?" Indra's deep voice released more slipperiness between her legs.

"Yes. Just fine." Jeez, she'd squeaked. Mara pulled out her underwear and slipped it on. Going to her closet, she pulled out leggings and a tunic top. She had absolutely no idea what season it even was. Luckily, most clothing was synthetic. They'd stood the challenge of time.

Since the men appeared to not bother with shirts, Mara doubted it was winter. Even in the slight chill of the cavern from which the facility was built, she should be comfortable.

Sitting on her bed, nope, not imagining Indra in it with her, she pulled on socks. Standing, she put on her chosen outfit. Ready, Mara exited, closing her bedroom door behind her. In the living room, Indra sat in a chair. His damp hair evidence of a shower.

Mara shoved down the twinge of regret it hadn't been with her.

"You look beautiful." Indra's deep voice did *things* to her body.

"Thank you." Mara's eyes drank him in. "So do you." Her eyes widened, her stomach growling and echoing across the room.

A grin flashed across Indra's face. "There's barbeque outside by the fire."

"Outside?" Mara smiled. The thought of seeing green lifted her spirits. She'd dreaded the thought of being in the cryonic pod. She'd have preferred to stay outside and take her chances, but her father and brother were all in and insisted she join them. Her mother died from one of the diseases that swept the country. If she'd have stayed, she would have been all alone.

Her stomach rumbled again. Her cheeks heated at Indra's chuckle. "Lead the way. I've a lot of time to make up for. Decades? Centuries?"

"More than decades, I believe. How many years are nine or so generations?"

Mara's jaw dropped. "No way."

Indra nodded.

"It depends, but it could be close to a hundred or perhaps up to three hundred years. It just depends on the average age people have children."

Indra shrugged. "I don't know. I do know it's been a long time. I don't count the years like humans do."

Mara's cheeks heated. His gaze never seemed to leave her face. Her stomach rumbled again. "Well, let's worry about food. I could eat a horse."

Indra's brows raised. "I thought humans ate cattle and chicken. I didn't know you ate horses."

Mara laughed. "Just an expression. We don't eat horses."

"Hmm." Indra shook his head. "There is much I've forgotten about humans."

"Humans?" Mara rolled her eyes. He kept saying it like he wasn't one. "I guess you must have been pretty isolated to refer to other people that way."

"Humans. I'm not human, not entirely." Indra gazed into her eyes. "I'm a dragon. I can be man or dragon."

Mara sighed. Of course, the first man, the most attractive man she's met in a long time, is deranged. Perhaps he had spent too much time alone. She gave him a long look, taking in his ruggedly muscled form. Maybe it's reversible. "Let's go eat." She wouldn't keep her hopes up though.

CHAPTER THREE

Indra admired Mara as she headed toward the door. He could see she was skeptical of his claims, but soon enough, she would learn he spoke the truth. Her scent called to him, especially with the stink washed from her body. The light floral scent she wore masked her natural one. Even so, it was better than the chemical compound covering her when she was revived. The gel stung his nose, leaving an unpleasant flavor on his taste buds. Even after a quick shower, it lingered. He sneezed, just thinking of it.

"Bless you." Mara glanced at him. "You're not sick, are you?"

"No. The chemicals just burn my sinuses a bit." Indra chuckled. "It's not like I'm a fire dragon and can clear them with a flicker."

Mara slowed and Indra kept pace with her. A cute little frown brought her eyebrows together.

"There is no such thing as dragons."

"Are you sure? You've been asleep a long, long time." Indra slid a sly smile her way. Wouldn't she be surprised once he revealed himself?

Mara snorted. "I doubt a completely new species could have evolved in just a few centuries. Not something that big anyway."

"Maybe they are not a new species." Indra linked his arm through hers. "Maybe they've been here all along."

"Yeah, right. We would have found them long ago. Very few species could hide from us and none of any size. Unless, perhaps, they were only a few inches long." She laughed. "Those little geckos that live in the desert, maybe."

Indra smirked and glanced at Mara. Slid his arm in hers. He didn't miss the subtle shiver she tried to hide. "The world is a different place than you remember." Indra pulled Mara tighter against his side. She didn't pull away. This was going smoother than he'd expected.

Mara scoffed. "It might be more primitive, but it can't have changed that much. A couple of centuries is a small amount of time evolutionary-wise."

She was pale, too pale. The growls her stomach emitted spoke of her hunger. He'd have to make sure she took it easy. The noisy doctor, her father, had gorged himself when he'd woken up and was sick. Indra didn't want Tamara—Mara—to be ill. He'd feed her little meals throughout the day to keep her strength up.

Her footsteps echoed in the corridor. She was obviously very familiar with the facility's layout.

Indra followed, peering into the windows of the rooms they passed. This would make an excellent weyr for their hatchlings once Mara became a dragon.

"What year is it?" Mara turned to look at him.

He shrugged. "I do not know." He entwined his arm to hers. "I wish I'd have known you were here. I would have revived you years ago. Once the threat of the diseases finally died."

Mara stopped but didn't disengage from his arm. "And is it gone? Are the diseases all gone?"

Indra nodded. "Yes. Once all who were susceptible were dead, the world was burned. Erasing evidence of all diseases. It gave the survivors a chance to rebuild." Indra frowned, thinking of the town he'd burned. The loss of a whole branch of his family. "But not enough survivors." He hugged her arm, taking what comfort he could. "Not enough."

Mara wiped a tear from her eye. "It was a horrible time." She took a deep breath. "How many survived?"

Indra tugged her forward. "I don't know. Towns here and there grew. Mostly, where they had access to fresh water and food." She still needed to eat. It didn't matter how many were left. Some of humanity had survived.

Mara came with him. They made their way outside, stopping just beyond the edge of the tunnel. Mara's smile, when they stepped into the sunlight, eased his tension. Her face, lifting toward the sun, cheered his heart, despite her hands covering her eyes at the brightness.

"I thought I would never see the sun," she spun in a circle, dropping her hands "the mountains and the green grass ever again."

Indra smiled. Her joy was palpable. "But you were frozen. Why did you think that?"

She stopped, facing him. "I did it because it was my job. Because my father and brother were doing it and wanted me to. I never believed it would work." She grabbed his hands. "It was experimental. It had never been done successfully before."

"You didn't think it would work?" Indra's jaw dropped. "Then why?"

"I had nothing else left. I didn't want to live without what was left of my family."

Indra gathered her into his arms. "I understand." He did. His despair at losing so much of his family still hurt. "But I'm glad it worked since I found you."

Mara buried her nose into his chest, her arms sliding around his waist. "Me too." She laughed. "I just hope you're not crazy."

Indra's head reared back. "I am not crazy." He savored the feel of her arms around him. Shivered at the breath from her laugh against his chest. He laid his head against her soft hair on the top of her head. "I am not."

"That's what they all say." She snickered and stepped back, her hand rubbing her rumbling stomach. "I really do need to eat."

He knew going further outside might shock her. Hark, Rog, and Rog's new mate were probably in their scales rather than skin. Zeru might even be around. With Grace newly turned, she would practice flying as much as possible. So, scales.

He turned his head, lightly kissing the top of Mara's.

She stiffened beside him.

Indra stifled a chuckle. "Evolution may just surprise you."

Mara frowned, pulling away from him.

"Tamara, I need your advice." Doctor Phillip called from behind them, interrupting their progress. "Can you come take a look at this data?"

She shrugged. "Sure."

Indra reluctantly let her go back into the tunnel, ignoring the doctor's glare. Since a trip outside with her was no longer in the cards, Indra followed the pair.

Doctor Phillip handed her a sheaf of papers, pointing from them to the screen he had somehow managed to get running. He glared again at Indra, moving to block his view of Mara.

Indra understood the doctor wanted to protect his daughter. What he didn't know was that it was too late. He'd already identified her as his mate. Nothing would keep him from wooing her.

Mara's shoulders drooped. She turned toward him, rubbing her tummy as it rumbled. "This will take a while. Could you get me some of the barbeque you were talking about?"

He perked up. His mate needed him. "Certainly."

She smiled. "Thank you." She turned to her father. "Dad, are you hungry? Did you want anything?"

Doctor Phillip scowled, but his stomach betrayed him. "Yes, thank you."

Indra snickered. "It would be my pleasure."

Mara and Steven Phillip bent their heads together.

Looking at them, his lips quirked. Their hair blended together. The colors identical. In all other instances, they were opposites. Mara's slender grace was dwarfed by her father's stockier and taller build.

Steven's glance toward him, eyes narrowed and nostrils flared, told Indra his courting might not go according to plan. Or so he thought.

Giving the doctor a big grin, Indra departed. There was nothing Steven could do to stop what fate wrought. Mara would be his.

Leaving the doctor to his minor victory, Indra stepped outside. He raised his head, breathing deeply. The fresh breeze brought scents of wildflowers, water, and ashes. The earth called, welcoming him. The fingers of the breeze caressed his hair, relaxing him.

A beast was spitted over the fire, roasting slowly. His stomach growled at the flavors in the air.

Dragons flew above him. Their graceful acrobatics around the tiny female beautiful to watch. He chuckled when she wobbled, the males instantly coming to her rescue.

Geckos, indeed!

He couldn't wait to show his world to his mate.

The scent of the roasting meat and the growl of his belly brought his attention back to his purpose. Grabbing a flat rock nearby, he tore off plenty of meat. Piling it high, he made sure there was enough for Mara and her father. He didn't want his mate to be hungry.

~

Mara slid a glance at Indra as he walked away. His graceful moves, more stalking than walking, kept her eyes on him. She shivered. She would be willing to be his prey any day.

"Tamara, look at this," her father demanded. He never asked. She loved him but had no problem realizing he was a narcissist. The more she gave into his demands, the worse he'd get.

"Father. I'm hungry. I just woke up after who knows how many years." She stepped back. "An hour will not make a difference. I'm going to go outside, enjoy the air and eat." She spun around and headed in the direction Indra had taken. She couldn't stop the smirk from making its way to her lips. She'd bet he was grinding his teeth.

"We've wasted enough time. Get back here." Her dad seemed one step away from a tantrum. "Tamara."

Mara spun to face him. "Dad, the government, everything we've ever known is gone. I'm going to see this new world we've been lucky enough to wake up in." She continued backing out of the room. "I'm going to see the sun and breathe in fresh air. And hopefully, have some delicious barbeque." She turned around and left through the door.

When the door shut behind her, she grinned. Gave a fist pump and headed toward the door to the cave opening. Mara pushed it open and filled her lungs. She stood there, enjoying fresh, non-recycled air.

The chance of seeing the sun and eating food cooked over a fire drove her forward. The harsh sun had her squinting and stumbling, but she refused to let it stop her.

"Mara." An arm slid over her shoulders. "Come, I've got you."

Her stomach growled again. She let Indra lead her. Already, she knew the feel of him, the sound of his voice. It felt too fast, yet not fast enough.

"Let's get you fed."

Mara spread her fingers, letting in more light. She gasped and dropped her hands, grabbing Indra's arms. Her mouth dropped. She couldn't seem to speak.

Dragons. There were dragons in the sky. *Dragons!*

"Uh, uh." Mara stood there, staring. Watching two, no three, no, four dragons. Soaring in the sky above her. She shook her head and looked at Indra. "It's just birds." She scrunched her eyes, rubbed them. "Right?"

Indra laughed. "No. They're dragons. You're not seeing birds."

"How?" Mara dropped down on a rock near the fire. "How did dragons develop in a couple of centuries, or however long it's been?"

Indra sliced more meat from the spit over the fire, adding it to the pile he'd already cut for Mara. Since she'd come back outside, they could share, because he was hungry, too. "We've always been here. We were around when humans still lived in caves."

"How old are you?"

"I didn't personally see them." He rolled his eyes and sliced off another strip of meat with his talon. Indra handed the plate of meat to Mara. He then sliced a piece off and slid it into his mouth.

Mara gasped. She looked at the meat and again at Indra. Watched him slice another piece with a thick claw that extruded from his finger. "You have a claw."

Indra smiled, flicked it toward her. "Talon. I call it a talon." He winked at her. "Told you I was a dragon."

Mara giggled. She slapped a hand over her mouth. She never giggled. She lifted a piece of the meat to her mouth, eating quickly. She moaned and shoved another piece in her mouth.

"Slow down. You haven't had food for a long time. You don't want to make yourself sick."

She put the slice of meat in her hand on the makeshift plate and sighed. “I know you’re right.” She licked her fingers. “But it’s so good.” Mara picked at the meat. “So, what am I eating?”

Indra chuckled. “Beef. What did you think?”

She shrugged. “Well, I thought it was beef, but you never know. Maybe there was something else I’d never heard of—like dragons.”

“Nope. Well, there were. I don’t know how many other species survived. Wolves and bears have always preferred not to mix with other species.” He shrugged, his face reflecting a pain she couldn’t interpret.

“Wolves? Like, like werewolves? They’re real?” Was that her voice squeaking?

Indra looked at the ground, his visage filled with sorrow. “They were.” He sighed. “I don’t think any survived the apocalypse.”

Mara stared at his bowed head, the drop of his shoulders. She would bet he lost someone close to him. As much as she wanted to ask, Indra didn’t volunteer the information. “So, dragons are real.”

Indra smirked and looked at her from beneath lashes wasted on a man. “Yeeees.” He flashed a heart-stopping smile.

Mara caught her breath. He really was a handsome man. Er, dragon. She nibbled on the edge of her meat. It was hard to believe, but the creatures flying above her were real. “Wait. You said you’re a dragon.” She glanced above. “Are you saying you can change into a dragon? Those creatures can change into men?”

“Yes. Men and women. One of them is female.” He looked up and smiled. “A new dragoness.”

“Wait, wait, wait.” Mara shook her head. “How can she be new? Is she a baby? Did she just hatch?” She looked above. “She doesn’t appear small enough to be an infant.”

“She’s not an infant. She’s mated to one of the fire dragons. The black one with a hint of green.” Indra pointed toward Rog. “Him.”

“So, how is she new?” Somehow, Mara needed to know this information. Not for science but for herself. “Can you explain it?”

Indra looked into her eyes. The glint told her she wasn’t wrong. This was information she needed. “I can.” His gaze caressed her.

“Will you?” Her breath caught. Her temperature rose just from his eyes on her body.

“I will.” He reached out a hand, a finger sliding down her cheek.

She shivered, the touch of his skin against hers electrifying.

"Tamara." Her father's angry voice made her wince. "You need to see these results."

Mara sighed and sat back. When had she leaned into Indra's touch? The man drew her like no other had before. "I'm almost done, Dad." She took the last few bites of her meat and handed her improvised dish back to Indra. "Thank you." Her whisper pulled a smile from his face. She placed a hand over her heart. That man was potent.

"You're welcome." He grabbed her rock plate and headed to the river with it.

"Wait. Our discussion." Mara stood, reaching toward him.

"Will happen later. See what has Dr. Phillip so worked up. I'll be here." His grin sent her heart into a crazy pitter-patter.

"Okay." Her voice was so breathy she was shocked he heard her.

His tilted head and the look in his eyes told her he had.

Mara spun toward her father. "All right, now what is it that has you so worked up?"

Her father sliced a bit of meat off the spit with a knife she hadn't even noticed next to it. He shoved it in his mouth and waved her back toward the tunnel. At least he didn't speak with his mouth full.

Glancing from Indra to the tunnel opening, Mara's shoulders drooped. She hated going back in. The last time she'd set foot in the tunnel to return, there was a cave-in. At the mouth of the cave, she peered around. Boulders and rocks now littered the ground. Nothing like the smooth surface the government had created. She could see someone had cleared the blockage from the tunnel's interior to the outside. So, someone had been in there and done it. She wondered who had made their way into the facility. No one authorized or they would have been woken up sooner. Much sooner.

"There are anomalies in the blood work on some of the pods." Her father must have finished his bite of food. "I'd like you to take a look at them."

"Is it on any of the pods that failed?" She frowned. That would only make sense.

"No. Not the ones I'm concerned with. The ones that failed succumbed to the diseases I had programmed it to look out for."

Mara turned to him in shock. "Did you set up the pods to fail if certain diseases were found in their blood? But we checked them before we froze everyone."

"Of course. We couldn't afford to carry them into the future with us. We didn't know the incubation period of all the diseases. It even covered infectious diseases we hadn't been bombarded with." He shook his head. "We were trying to save mankind. Why on earth would we try to save anyone carrying the diseases that killed the rest of the world? It was a failsafe programed in at all the sites." He pushed open the door of the cryonics chamber. "It only went into effect if the disease continued to develop. We hoped being in the pods would cure the diseases and provide us with antibodies. Those that perished never developed antibodies."

She had no words. No words. But she shouldn't have been surprised. It was logical. What good would it have done to bring back the thing they were running from? Mara rubbed her stomach, looking around the chamber at the number of failed units.

How on earth was mankind going to ever come back?

"Never mind that. We can't do anything about them now. Come take a look at the anomalies. This last group has extra chromosomes." He snatched her arm and towed her over to the computer. "It doesn't make sense. I'd like to wake this group up next."

“How have you been waking people up? What criteria are you using?” She quickly shifted right back into her normal personality. With no Indra to distract her, it was easy.

“I started with the essential personnel. You, of course. Though that dragon was insistent on making sure you were woken. I had to make sure it was done properly. Your brother, since he was in charge of the engineering systems to keep this place running. The other medical personnel to assist in waking everyone up and the rest of the engineers. We need to make sure the power, water, and waste systems are in place. There appears to be missile damage to the exterior. It’s what blocked the tunnel in the first place.” He tapped the counter. “Luckily, this place was built to withstand a hit.”

Mara shivered. “I had just come back in when the missile hit. I was outside having lunch. It was scary.”

“No wonder no one made it in here to wake us up. They couldn’t get in.” He scowled. “Those dragons cleared it out.”

“How did they get in here?” She peered at the screen. “Did they just decide to dig out the cave? And how do you know about dragons?”

"No, Grace found it. She was scavenging. Rog and his brother helped her break down a door. A secondary exit was created, just in case." She noticed he ignored her last question.

"Who is Grace..." her voice petered out. "Dad, this blood work is not normal. What do you think it is?"

"See? It was important. I don't know. Nothing out of the ordinary showed on the initial tests. They can't be infected with anything, or they would have died in the pods." He grabbed the mouse and clicked. He showed the original bloodwork. "Look, no anomalies."

"What test were you running?" She grabbed the mouse back, scrolling through the results. "These aren't the tests we performed."

"No, I was checking the DNA on the survivors. Most of it was normal. I know no one with abnormal markers was brought in. I just happened to notice a couple of dozen with the additional DNA strand. I went back and checked them against the rest."

"Hmmm. Let me look." She typed in some information, pulling up her records along with her father's and brother's. Then she added the information for additional markers. "Dad, look. There is more than one DNA anomaly." She frowned. "I don't remember processing so many people."

"What? Print them out. I want to see if we can figure this out before we wake them up." He paced back and forth. "Bring up all the files we have on those people. There must be an explanation." He grumbled, "This is why I should have been in charge."

She ignored his last comment. Her father acted like he was in charge of everything, but even if he had to answer to someone, it annoyed him to no end.

Mara was already tagging files to print. She didn't need him to tell her. Excitement raced through her veins. Could people have developed additional abilities while sleeping in the pods? She shook her head. That wasn't a possibility. But there was a mystery here, and she couldn't wait to find out what it was.

CHAPTER FOUR

Indra watched his mate walk away. The sway of her hips mesmerized him until she disappeared.

A splash and the spray of water against his back had him whipping around. He snickered. Behind him, upside down in the river, thrashed the new dragoness. “Need some help?”

She growled at him and continued to spray water everywhere, wiggling until she was upright. “No.” She raised her snout, sniffing the air. Ignoring him, she paddled to the river's edge and right up to the fire. With a quick bite, she snapped the rest of the cow roasting over the fire.

Indra blew out a breath. Luckily, he’d been able to feed Mara before Grace snagged the rest of the meat. “I think you need to learn how to hunt.”

Her harrumph and glare had him chuckling.

“You know you can speak while you’re a dragon.”

“Fine. It just feels weird. I’m this big beast, and yet, my normal voice comes out of me. Plus, I was flying. The landing didn’t go so well, though. And now I’m really hungry, and there’s no more food.” Grace wailed the end. Big, fat tears formed in her eyes.

A cow landed in front of her snout and she squeaked, jumping back.

Indra laughed.

She scowled and grabbed the cow, pulling it toward her.

"Don't worry, I won't take any." She watched Indra while she ate. "Want more?"

She slowly nodded while chewing.

Indra dropped the rock he was holding into the river. There were plenty of other suitable rocks around for plates. He quickly removed his pants and shifted, flying into the sky. A deep breath brought the faint scent of his mate to him. Indra didn't want to go too far from her. However, a hungry new dragoness wasn't a good idea. Dragons knew not to eat humans, but a new one might not be so choosy. Especially if the good Doctor Phillip opened his mouth.

Indra chuckled. Even he might be tempted.

Spying the herd they'd been eating, he swooped down and grabbed a cow in each claw. His talons pierced their necks, instantly killing them. He dropped them in front of Grace. He heard the crunch and snap of bones while he went to get more.

A push of air next to him told him another dragon was nearby. "Zeru," he acknowledged. Since he saw no form, he figured it was the air dragon. A chuckle let him know he was correct.

"Indra. I see you found your mate." Zeru came into focus. "Lucky. I hope to one day find mine." He was silent, gliding along beside him. "I'll stick around if that's okay with you."

Indra nodded. "Thank you." He dove, grabbing two more cows. "Grab a couple. I need to put another on the fire. Grace even ate the spit." He rumbled in amusement. He grabbed one more in his teeth. Crunching and letting it work deeper into his throat. Better he ate now, while hungry than have to come back a third time. Feeding the new dragoness was everyone's priority. Especially when he hoped to make another in the near future.

Zeru nodded. Quickly rending a steer in his mouth before grabbing a couple more cattle to follow Indra back.

Indra dropped his pair by Grace as did Zeru.

Indra flew off toward the trees, pulling up a couple of saplings and returning to the fire. Shifting, Indra carved the green trees to fit over the fire to roast another cow. "Are you full?".

Grace lay half on one carcass, with her talons tapping another.

She glanced at him and back to the cattle lying on their sides. She pushed a talon into the cow, shaking it a bit.

"Don't play with your food." Rog settled next to her. He grabbed the one her claw was in and ate it, ignoring her hissing. "You were done." He nodded at the third body. "This one is for the humans since you ate theirs on the fire."

"I like them cooked." She snorted at her mate.

"But your dragon prefers them raw." Rog grinned, nuzzling her jaw. "I saw the face you made when you ate it."

"I was hungry. And the toothpick in it was annoying."

Indra snorted. "That was the spit and you know it."

Grace huffed, then grinned. "I was hungry."

Indra laughed. "Well, just don't eat the next one. Your mate can show you how to hunt next." He slid a sly grin Rog's way. "Of course, he should have taught you how to land."

Grace blew smoke his way. "Jerk."

Indra smirked and returned to his task. He quickly stripped the cow and put it on a spit. It would take a while to cook. Unless...

"Rog, care to get it started?"

Rog nodded and sent a concentrated flame over the cow. A fire dragon could easily change his flames to get the result he wanted. With a flap of wings and his flame aimed at the meat, he took hours off the cooking time. "There you go."

"Thanks." This way, Mara wouldn't go hungry. He pulled a thin rock from the river and sliced some more meat. He'd take it to his mate. If she was anything like her father, she would forget. It was his job to take care of her.

"I'll make sure Hark stays around the area," Rog hollered at Indra's retreating figure.

"Thank you." He turned toward him, walking backward. "Do you know of any water or ice dragons?"

"As a matter of fact, I do." Rog tilted his head, a frown between his brows. "Why?"

"Earth, fire, water, air. Earth dragons prefer all four elements involved in our matings. It's how we ensure our mates maintain proper balance with the earth." He shrugged. "It's traditional."

"I'll let my brother Ari know. He can get in touch with one." Rog put his wing over his mate, turning his attention away from Indra.

"Many thanks." Indra headed back into the manmade cave.

He opened the door, checking out the interior. He hadn't spent much time in the facility, mainly keeping an eye on Mara. Doctor Phillip's voice carried into the hall, even through the closed door of the cryonics room.

Indra shook his head.

"Tamara, look at this data. Who were these people? Where are these people?"

Indra frowned. Why would the doctor not know everyone? Not know where some of the people were? He had told us he was in charge of putting everyone in pods. Indra stood outside the door, cracked it open and listened. Perhaps he shouldn't interrupt just yet. He might hear some truths they needed to know.

"Dad, look at the numbers. Is there another room with pods in it? These are not the numbers of the ones in this room." Mara tapped her finger on the computer screen. "Were there more rooms?"

Doctor Phillip swore. "There was another room."

"Where?"

"There shouldn't be anyone in them. My orders were to get everyone in pods and seal the facility."

"Dad, who put you in a pod?" She turned and leaned against the desk. "I know you said you'd do it yourself, but was that even really feasible?"

"I did it myself. My pod was slightly different. My controls were on the inside." He smacked his hand with the papers he was carrying. "But I don't want you involved with this group. Not if what I think is going on, happened."

"Tell me." Mara's face hardened. "What the hell did the government do, Dad?"

Doctor Phillip twisted the papers in his hands hard enough to rip. “If it’s the group I think, I told them not to even approach them.” He swore again. “Humans are at the top of the food chain. Hell, I never even knew about dragons. But why should we save anyone who is not human?”

“Dad, what did they do?”

He threw the papers at the desk. “I don’t know. Not for sure.”

Indra stayed frozen, listening. He knew the government knew about the paranormal population. Could some of them have been saved? Or were they deliberately targeted?

“Explain.” Mara grabbed the doctor’s shoulder and shook it. “Now.”

He sighed. “Dragons, which I didn’t know about, weren’t the only shifters on the planet. The government knew of them. It was proposed that one of these facilities be created just for them. They refused to have anything to do with it. Their scientists and engineers helped mastermind the three facilities, but they refused to *freeze to death,* as they put it.” He shook his head. “They were dying just as fast as the humans, it turned out. Still, they refused.”

“But that doesn’t explain the DNA readings, Dad.” Mara sounded exasperated.

Indra scrunched his face. Perhaps the doctor needed a bit of reminding of the power dragons held.

"Well, the shifters were faster and stronger than humans. I was against including them in the process. Humanity would face enough challenges rebuilding without having to compete against them. They were still dirty animals when you get down to it." The petulance in his voice spoke volumes.

"Dad!" Mara shrieked. "That is outrageous. You just said they helped design and build this place." She paced back and forth, glaring at her father. Indra smiled. Mara would make an excellent dragon when the time came.

"You don't know everything. They mate with human women. That would mean taking women from repopulating the human race."

Indra glared at the doctor. Sounded like he only cared about breeding, not the women themselves. He began to step inside the door.

He stopped at Mara's shriek. "Maybe we shouldn't if everyone thought like you." She grabbed her father's shirt, shaking him. "Where are these pods? Take me there, right now."

Indra stepped all the way in. "Yes, where are they? And who are they?"

Doctor Phillip growled at him.

Indra smirked. The puny man could try to intimidate him, but it wouldn't work.

"They're probably non-viable." The doctor's chin went in the air.

"Then you won't have a problem taking me to them." Mara stuck her nose in her father's face. "Will you?"

Doctor Phillip tossed his hands in the air. "Fine. But if they didn't volunteer, I guarantee they won't be happy when they wake up." He walked over to the computer and scrolled through some information. "I didn't think this section was completed, but let's go look. It was planned for each facility but never built, as far as I knew. Supposedly, there wasn't time."

He led them not back into the main hallway but across the room. He punched in a series of numbers on a lock and it cracked open, moving slowly with a groan. "Hmm. Here goes nothing." He glanced at them. "This will be a wild goose chase. The abnormal DNA markers are probably just a mistake. Maybe DNA for people that were rejected for the program."

"Then why do they have pod ID numbers, Dad?"

He didn't answer; he just tightened his lips and led them to a hallway much rougher than the rest of the facility. Farther down the hall, they passed a couple of other doors. A locked door sealed off the end of the hallway.

Doctor Phillip input another code, and the door was unlocked with a woosh.

He pushed it open.

Indra crowded Mara in behind the doctor. In front of him were more cryonic pods. Each filled and blinking.

Doctor Phillip cursed. “Those idiots.”

Mara gasped.

Indra grabbed the door so hard the metal groaned. He sniffed but couldn’t tell if shifters truly were in the pods. He looked at the sea of pods. Double the amount in the chamber above. Hope rose in his chest. Could this be what he thought? Could the missing wolves, bears, and other paranormal species he’d looked for across the globe be here? Looking at the number of pods, his heart sank a bit. Even if they were, too many had died.

“Start waking them up,” Indra demanded.

“I doubt they’ll be happy,” Dr. Phillip muttered.

He stared at the number of pods. “If you’re right, and they were put here under duress, you could be at risk. Show us how to remove them safely. The other dragons and I will handle this.”

Mara was shaking her head. “They need to be monitored while they wake up to ensure nothing goes wrong.”

“No, I cannot allow you to put yourself at risk.” Indra caressed her cheek. “You are too precious.”

Her cheeks flooded with color. Her gaze softened. “I should be safe with you, though.”

“Always.” The gruffness in his voice had him clearing his throat. “I would protect you with my life.” He glanced at her father. “Him, I wouldn’t.”

Mara gasped, her hand rising to her throat. “Indra.”

Indra snickered. If she had pearls on, she’d be clutching them. He leaned over and kissed her forehead. “Maybe if you asked nicely, I would. Grudgingly.”

“I never had a hand in this. Everyone was supposed to be a volunteer and *human*,” Steven Phillip grumbled. “I need to get the people above who are viable out. They were trained to run this facility.” The doctor shook his head with a scowl. “We set the facility up for the people above, not more. It will stretch our resources unless accommodations were made for *them* down here. I’ll have to have all the rooms searched and an inventory done.”

Indra watched him go to the first pod in line.

"Here, it's really simple." He pointed to the flashing numbers. "Mara can monitor their vitals on the computer, and you can manually open them." He pointed. "Press this button to open the lid hatches. You'll see the gel receding. Press this button and the pod will tilt and extract the hose from their throats automatically. Their airways will clear, and they'll be able to breathe on their own. This button will unlock the restraining straps and they can get out when ready."

He straightened up. "Simple. Just remember, it takes hours. Mainly for the gel to drain and the B12 to be injected into their system. The pod will regulate it. Just enough to start waking them up. If necessary, it will give them a shot of adrenaline or zolpidem."

"Only if medically necessary," Mara interjected. "I strongly discouraged either of them."

Her father shrugged.

"Anything else?" Indra started pushing the buttons on the coffin-like pod near him. He would not have chosen a living death like this, either. It angered him to see them so helpless when they had not chosen this.

"Hey, I'm just the messenger." Doctor Phillip put his hands up, trying to show his innocence. "But, if it managed to save a different species, was it a bad thing?"

"A species you didn't want to save." Indra growled at him, flashing his sharpened teeth. His dragon wasn't happy. "No choice is always a bad thing."

The doctor shrugged. "It wasn't my decision. They're here now. Nothing can be done except wake them up. Or not. The men who ordered this are probably dead or still sleeping in cryonic chambers across the country." He turned away. "Tamara, I'll leave you to help Indra monitor these animals. I'll use your assistant to continue reviving the *people* upstairs."

"Doctor." Indra cleared his throat. "Please send the dragons down here to assist." He tamped down his fury. The doctor was right, nothing could be done about it. Indra just hoped along the way, he would find some familiar faces.

Doctor Phillip nodded and left the room.

Mara moved to monitor the computer. "I'll keep an eye on their vitals."

"Thank you." Indra grimaced and began pressing buttons and unlocking the hatches on the pods. "This is going to be a long day." He moved from pod to pod. He tried to ignore the resemblance to coffins. At least these people had a chance.

He lifted his face and sniffed. So far, he didn't smell any decay. It didn't subtly permeate the room like the area upstairs did. Of course, he couldn't smell too much of anything. The chemical gel blocked almost everything. Almost.

Indra's eye drifted to Mara. Even covered in chemicals, her scent drew him in. His gaze raked over her, admiring her messy dark hair all the way down to her rubber-soled shoes. He snorted. In the last few minutes, Mara had donned a white doctor's coat. Lord knows where she found it. Only she made science geek look sexy. He was so smitten.

Turning back to his job, he pressed the button and flipped open the hatch locks, still stealing glances at his soon-to-be mate. He looked back at the man in the pod. "Fuck!"

"What's wrong?" Mara checked the computer, looking frantic. "I don't see anything wrong." She rushed over.

Indra laid his hand on the glass, tears slipping from the corner of his eyes. "I don't care if they didn't give consent. I thought I'd never find him again." He waited for the gel to drain. Pressed the button to activate the breathing tube removal. Once the lid was up and the gel gone from the face, the tube would slide out. "Come on, come on."

Mara grabbed his arm. “It’s obvious you know him. But you know it will take hours for him to wake up.” She shook his arm. “Let’s get everyone started.”

He wiped his eyes with his arm. “I thought he was dead.”

“Who is he?” Her hand slid down and entwined their fingers. “Obviously, someone important.”

“My cousin. I looked all over the world for him.” He tightened his hold on her hand. “I can’t believe it. When your father hinted about paranormals involuntarily being here, I hoped. My family lived not far from here.” He choked. “I’d given up hope.”

Mara gasped. “They managed to take dragons unaware?”

He chuckled. “No, my cousin is a wolf.”

“What?” She shook her head. “How is your cousin a *wolf*?”

“Our mothers were sisters. My mom mated a dragon and his mom mated a wolf. Another of my aunts mated a bear. Rumors in the family whispered of other types of shifters introduced into our bloodline, but we never met them.” Indra laughed. “Our families were really close. My wolf cousins were brothers to me.”

“And now you’ve found him.” Mara leaned against his side, staring at the slowly opening pod.

“And now I’ve found him.” He shook his head. “Randy is so going to give me shit. He pointed at his chest. See this tattoo? It’s of his wolf.” His grin split his face. Randulf could give him shit now until forever. It was worth it knowing he would once again have part of his family.

“Found who?” Rog crowded in the door, elbowing by Hark and Zeru. Ushering Grace in past them.

“My cousin.” He couldn’t stop the joy on his face.

“How the hell did a dragon get here?” Hark frowned, shoving Rog away.

Indra smiled, shaking his head. “Not a dragon. A wolf.”

“Well, they are slower.” Hark shrugged. “You needed help?”

“Yes. If the doctor is correct, these pods contain shifters. And they weren’t put here voluntarily.” Indra finally left Randy’s side and went to the next pod. “I’ll show you what to do.” He went through each of the steps Doctor Phillip had shown him.

“Easy enough. We can each take a row.” Zeru started on the next line of pods, quickly moving from one container to another.

“Sounds good.” Rog dragged Grace with him. “Stay near me.”

Grace rolled her eyes and pulled away from Rog. “I’m perfectly capable of managing this. I’ll do the next row.” She sent him a flirty look and winked. “Just try to keep up.”

Hark chuckled, slapped Rog on the back, and moved to the row just past Grace. “Yeah, bro. Keep up.”

He grinned because, well, why not? Indra had part of his family back, and hopefully, more of the people he’d grown up with would be in here. Plenty of hands to get started, bringing them back to life, and a beautiful, intelligent woman to build a life with. Things were definitely looking up. He couldn’t help but whistle, getting back to the job at hand.

~

It was hard to believe these people could really change into dragons, or so they said. She’d seen dragons. She’d seen them. She had yet to see if they could really shift. It was more than her brain could wrap around. Glancing at the people joking around in the room, Mara just stared. She’d never seen so much happiness in this building before.

Maybe no one had believed being cryonically frozen would work. She certainly hadn't. It was a Hail Mary to survive. Even the few who'd been reactivated above acted cautiously. Like it was a dream. Glancing back at Indra, Mara really hoped it wasn't. Maybe, just maybe, the future would include more than just surviving.

Sighing, she monitored the information coming in from the pods. So far, everything looked normal. Minimizing the screen, she opened up the results her father had been looking at. When he said he saw extra chromosomes. In her world, that was bad. Birth defect, bad. Learning disabilities and physical limitations bad. She was a doctor. Not just another scientist with a PhD. She'd worked at the hospital for years in the emergency room before joining a family-med practice.

Her dad had dragged her into this. It piqued her curiosity, and she started working for the government to find a cure for the diseases ravaging the country. But it was too many, too fast. Before a cure could be found, the diseases mutated. Killing even more people. It turned into a hopeless task. Then, she was brought in as a physician to test for diseases in an isolated group. A group scheduled for the cryonic pods. Guess the government knew there were no cures.

Now, here she was. In the future, without a clue how the world around her worked. So far, she'd met people who were shifters. Found out her father set up pods to eliminate people to prevent bringing diseases forward. And, glancing again at Indra, fighting an insane attraction to a man who just might be crazy.

Running her hands through her hair, Mara concentrated on the screen. None of the pods have had issues so far, thank goodness. She looked at the DNA information. Her dad was right. They all had extra chromosomes. Nothing she'd seen before. It wasn't extra chromosomes, like a duplicate that shouldn't be there or half a chromosome. These were totally new. She blinked, moving closer to the screen. They were additional. Not repeated. Not broken or missing. Not any type of trisomy she'd ever seen. Just extra. She glanced at the faces of the people she could see nearby.

No physical deformities showed. She looked from the numbers to the pods. She was a doctor, and this was stunning. Unimaginable. Mara cracked her knuckles, tapped a pencil against the desk top. Huh? When did she pick that up? Whatever. She looked between the results and the pods again.

She stood. "Are you really all dragons?"

Indra winked at her.

Her stupid heart fluttered. The man had game. She really hoped he wasn't a player. "Well?"

"We certainly are, sweet cheeks," the dragon man on the far side of the room hollered, wagging his eyebrows.

Indra scowled at him. It was kind of sweet. "Yes. I told you this right away."

"Can you prove it? Can you change?"

"If you'd like." Indra moved closer to her.

"Now. Here." Mara cocked her head. "I want to see."

Indra looked around. "I wouldn't want to knock over any of the coffins."

"Pods."

"Pods." He grabbed her hand, pulling her toward him. "The hall is big enough. They all look like they were made for dragons."

"More like equipment." Mara rolled her eyes. "Okay, let's go. Right now." She really hoped he was telling the truth. Then, to see if he would agree to what she wanted.

Indra ushered her into the hall. "I've got to remove my clothes." He gave her a come-hither look. "You can watch if you want."

"I will." Not because she wanted to see him naked... Who was she kidding? She totally did. But more because she had to see it from beginning to end. She had to see with her own eyes if he could shift into another creature, making sure there was no sleight of hand.

Mara flattened herself against the wall. She didn't want to be stepped on and she wanted a clear view.

"I can come out and get naked too." The flirty man was at the door with a big grin.

"Shut up, Hark." The man who looked so much like him, he had to be his brother, swatted him in the back of his head.

"I'm just saying," Hark grumbled, elbowing his brother.

Mara ignored him. He seemed like the type that if you reacted to him, he'd just get worse. She kept her eyes on Indra. Her cheeks heated. He really was spectacular. Or maybe she was just used to scrawny geeks. Nah, he was gorgeous. She waved her hands in front of her face.

Indra winked. "Don't be afraid." He dropped his trousers and kicked them by her.

Mara blinked and there was a large dragon in front of her. She shut her mouth and slowly approached him.

Indra stared at her. It was just a little creepy. He cocked his head and pushed it forward under her hand. His scales were warm to the touch.

Mara rubbed her hand along his jawline, avoiding the large teeth.

His eyes blinked, showing multiple eyelids.

Mara walked along his side, running her hands along his limbs, the edge of a wing, and along his tail. "I never believed in fairy tales." She avoided the deadly-looking claws with the talons on each of his four limbs. The spikes on his back looked deadly also. Contrary to anything she expected, his whole body was warm to the touch. "Are you cold-blooded or warm-blooded?"

"Warm-blooded, though the temperature change doesn't really bother us." The man—dragon— stepped forward. Nodded at her. "I'm Zeru. I'm an air dragon. Indra here is an earth dragon." He gestured to the two men. "Rog and Hark are fire dragons, as is the little dragoness, Grace."

"That is so cool." She couldn't stop touching Indra.

He preened beneath her hands, a slight rumble coming from him. Do dragons purr?

Mara gasped; suddenly, she was running her hands along a very naked man. She peeked lower. A very well-endowed, excited man. She squeaked, jumping back.

Indra chuckled and moved until she was pressed between the wall and his body.

"Don't need to watch that," Grace chirped.

Her stomach twisted, her loins tingling. Mara realized her hands were running along Indra's back. She didn't want to stop and Indra sure didn't seem to mind. He was solid against her hands and so warm.

His firmness pressing into her made her ache.

He looked into her eyes and lowered his head, nuzzling her hair. He ran his nose along her throat sending shivers along her body.

She gasped, leaning her head against the wall and arching against him. Wordlessly offering her body to him. "Indra."

"Mara." His lips locked against her neck. His arms lifted her up the wall, settling her groin against his cock. He pumped against her, drawing a moan from her. He sucked her neck, goosebumps flaring across her skin.

Indra dry-humped her, his naked cock rubbing her clit with each pass, and the pull of his mouth against her neck, sent her spinning from the sensations. Mara cried out, convulsing against him. Her pussy pulsed, clenching on nothing. "Holy crap."

Indra grunted, humping faster until he jerked, his cum spurting on her clothes. "Fuck."

Mara sniggered, her hands gripping him to her. "Not quite."

Indra barked out a laugh. "I think you'll need to change."

"Yeah, I think you're right." Mara slid her hand down and caressed his penis. "I'll go now."

Indra lowered her to the ground, leaned over, and kissed her.

She still held his cock, now rising from the unconscious squeeze she'd given him when he fried her brain from his kiss. She didn't really want to let go.

"Are you two done yet? We have people to revive." Hark. It had to be.

Mara tugged one more time. He was so soft, yet hard. She just wanted to continue touching him.

"I'm willing to fuck you right here if you don't stop." Indra thrust into her hands. "If you want, that is."

Mara shook her head. "No." She took a breath and stepped to the side, releasing him.

Indra groaned. "Look at what you do to me."

Mara looked. He was tempting enough to almost ignore the audience behind them.

His cock, risen to his belly, was long and thick.

Mara licked her lips. She could imagine it inside her mouth. Inside her vagina, pounding away. She gasped. What had got into her? She snorted. Unfortunately, nothing had gotten into her. Her nipples were diamond hard and her pussy dripped, ready for Indra to enter her.

"Go now, or I won't be able to control myself." Indra ran a finger down her throat, unerringly across a peaked nipple, and down to cover her mound.

Mara whimpered and nodded. Her voice cracked. "Okay." She turned and stumbled toward the door down the hall that led to the medical housing. She opened it and stepped in. Her pussy ached for what Indra had to offer. Mara grabbed the railing, squeezing it until she could breathe evenly again. She headed toward her quarters, needing a quick cold shower before returning to face the dragons below.

The possibilities in this new life made her giddy.

CHAPTER FIVE

Indra couldn't wipe the grin off his face. He watched Mara rush toward the door, her heavy breathing telling him he affected her as much as she did to him. The door closed behind her, masking her enticing scent. He stayed there one more moment. Just in case she returned, or stuck her head back out the door, inviting him to follow.

Nothing.

He grabbed his pants and slid them on.

Back in the room, he sent a glare Hark's way. "If you weren't the only fire dragon around, I'd be tempted to wring your neck."

"We're fire dragons," Grace spoke up. "You can totally send him away."

Hark laughed. "No, he can't. Not if he plans on changing Mara anytime soon."

"What do you mean?" Grace turned to Rog. "What does he mean?"

"Do you not remember us turning you?" Rog placed a kiss on his mate's forehead.

"That's what made me a dragon?" She gasped. "You are *not* helping change Tamara." Her flashing eyes could singe her mate.

If fire dragons were susceptible to another dragon's fire, Indra was sure he'd be crispy around the edges right now.

"No, only unmated dragons participate." Rog grabbed Grace, pulling her against his body. "Hope you enjoyed it because I'll be the only dragon mounting you from now on."

Indra watched Grace's face soften and melt against Rog. He wanted that. So much his body ached with it. His imagination didn't need much help. The feeling of Mara against him a short time ago made him want to search her out. He needed to give her time. She didn't realize she was it for him. Forever.

"Sounds good to me," Grace whispered.

Indra looked around. "Let's get back to getting these people out of here."

He checked on his cousin. The gel was still receding. He reluctantly left him, heading back to the next closed pod in his line. Looking at all the pods, Indra knew they probably had days ahead of them. There were only five of them, after all.

He continued pressing buttons and opening hatches. It was a monotonous chore. But if these were shifters, and he knew at least his cousin was, the probably illegal action of the now defunct government was a blessing in disguise.

The opening of the door stole his attention. Mara's fresh scent, unfortunately washed clean of his, heralded her reappearance.

"Wow, you guys are really making progress." She hurried over to the computer. A few touches to the mouse on the desk. "Everything looks good."

As she clicked and scrolled, Indra wondered what had her attention so completely engrossed.

She stopped and turned to look at him. "I was wondering…" She cleared her throat. "Wondering if you'd be willing to give me a vial of blood."

"Oh my god, she's a vampire." Hark's voice lifted in a falsetto. "Bring out the stakes, stoke the fire." He lifted a hand over his brow while he draped himself over a closed pod.

Indra rolled his eyes. Hark would take some getting used to. He really hoped they wouldn't establish a weyr near here. Of course, he wasn't mated, so he could end up anywhere. "Why do you need blood?"

"Well," she glanced at her computer. "If these markers indicate shifters, I'd like to see if any of yours match. What kind of markers indicate shifters." She leaned forward. "Normally, additional chromosomes indicate some kind of birth defect. But I've never seen extra chromosomes like this." She waved her hand at the computer.

Indra looked over to Rog, Hark, and Zeru. The latter was ignoring the conversation and continued opening pods. "What do you think? I don't plan on going back to hiding from the humans."

"Do you think there's any danger?" Zeru spoke up. Obviously, he could multitask.

At the thought, Indra continued to work. He could do both, too. "I don't see how. They already knew we existed, or we wouldn't be waking up fellow shifters." He moved on to the next pod. He ignored Mara, bouncing up and down on her toes. He doubted she even realized it. Mara struck him as always being in control, or at least trying to be. He stood and moved in front of her. "I'll do it."

"Thank you." She flung her arms around him, turned pink, and stepped back. "Let me get what I need." She skipped over to a door farther in the room, flinging it open. "Aha!"

She disappeared inside, and a light flickered on, followed by a lot of muttering and rustling around. Her triumphant look when she came back out suffused him with happiness.

"Got it." She hurried over to the desk, opening plastic-wrapped items. She carefully set them on a tray he hadn't noticed before.

Indra peeked over her shoulder, watching her.

"You can stand right here." Mara pointed next to the tray. "I have to find a vein." She grabbed his right arm and ran her fingers along the bend of his elbow. "Squeeze your hand for me. Make a fist and keep tightening it."

Indra shivered at the touch of her fingers.

"You've got a perfect one, right here." She grabbed a plastic strip and tied it off above his elbow. "You can release your fist." She took the needle out of the plastic and smoothly inserted it into his arm, removing the tourniquet as she did so.

Indra barely noticed the needle going in. He was concentrating on the feel of her fingers tickling the sensitive flesh of his arm.

The needle had an attachment. Then she stuck a tube into the end of the vacutainer, and the tube filled with blood. She switched the tube out to another one and then removed it. Mara used a bandage square and tape to cover the tiny hole as she removed the needle.

"Now me." Zeru stood next to Mara. He'd come over when she started the procedure. "I'd like to see if I have an anomaly."

Mara laughed. "Sure. Let me just label these tubes so I don't get them mixed up." She printed out little labels and attached them to each tube. "Thank you, Indra."

Zeru held out his arm to Mara.

Indra growled while she ran her fingers up and down the crease of Zeru's elbow.

Mara rolled her eyes but continued. "You could keep opening the pods. The sooner we wake everyone up, the better. I'm just checking for the vein in his cubital fossa."

Indra snorted, figuring out she meant the bend in his elbow. Still, despite wanting to push Zeru away from Mara, he figured she wouldn't appreciate it. "All right." He couldn't stop from giving Zeru a warning glance to leave Mara alone.

It only got him rolled eyes from both of them.

He stomped back over to the pods and continued to free those enclosed.

He was the only one still working. Indra pursed his lips but stayed quiet. Rog, Hark, and Grace were lined up behind Zeru. The joy on Mara's face stopped him from objecting. Watching Mara handle each of the dragons and their blood, he saw how professional she was, doing what she knew.

He supposed it would be interesting to see if other dragons had been captured and frozen. He doubted it. Most hid from humans, and as far as he could tell, none of the dragons he'd met had been sick. Most had been busy helping the humans survive.

The human apocalypse had brought dragons out. There was no more hiding from the few left. Most people realized that if the dragons hadn't brought those they could find together and to locations where food was available, the humans would be in worse shape than they were. In some cases, teaching them how to grow and hunt food. Most of them were used to grocery stores to purchase food someone else had grown or butchered. Luckily, it wasn't too hard to teach them.

Of course, there were places where the humans gathered without the dragons helping them. They weren't helpless. The more rural communities already had that knowledge. But many of them were not populated well enough to meet all of their needs. Many dragons transported those alone together.

Not that dragons flaunted themselves. They had no need. Indra puffed his chest out. Dragons were too awesome to need to do that.

Indra jumped at a touch on his arm. Mara was standing next to him, smiling.

"Thank you. If you hadn't let me draw blood, I doubt the rest of them would have."

The slight weight of her hand on him and the affection in her eyes warmed his blood.

"Anything for you." He drew her closer, wrapping his arms around her.

She hummed and tightened her embrace before stepping back. “Well, thank you.”

Indra reluctantly released her. She fit perfectly in his arms. “Now, what will you do with the blood?”

Mara perked up. “I’ll run DNA tests to check chromosome markers. Compare them to the ones we have on file. It’ll be interesting to see the differences.” She grinned. “Maybe there will be markers that make you resistant to all diseases and illnesses or how similar you are to humans. The possibilities are enormous.”

“Hmmm. Sounds interesting.” It sounded dangerous. Humans were not their enemies, but they were a fickle race. They could be truly underhanded if they wanted something. “I don’t know if that information should be shared. It could be dangerous for us.”

Mara cocked her head, tapping her lip. “Yes, I could see that. Let me check out the information. I can share it with all of you and no one else if you don’t want me to.”

Indra wanted to grab her up and squeeze. Instead, he huffed. “Thank you.” The look in her eyes, smiling at him, had him rethink. He quickly reeled her into his arms, holding her against him. Every soft curve cushioned his body. Indra sighed and rested his cheek against her hair.

Mara molded to his body. Her arms squeezed him to her.

Why had he even hesitated? She belonged with him.

"Let's get this going, you two," Hark sang out.

Indra tightened his arms, then released Mara. He whispered in her ear. "I'm beginning to not like that dragon."

She giggled and pulled away. "He's right, though." She looked at the number of pods. "It may take more than one day."

Indra frowned. "You said there were different markers in the groups. Were there only two different ones?"

"Hmm. Let me check. I think there were at least three." Mara headed back to her computer. She clicked around, looking at the data. "I see three for sure. There are a couple odd ones, though."

Indra leaned against a pod. "Are they marked so we can match them to the pods?"

"Oh yes." She checked the screen in front of her again. "Huh. They were put into groups. I can pull up the numbers and we can do each group in a day."

Indra looked at the others. "What do you think? Do what looks like groups together?"

Zeru said, "I think that makes the most sense. If it is different groups of shifters, that would be better. Prevent any fighting."

Everyone nodded. “You’re right,” Rog added. “We have no clue what we have here.”

“Wolves for sure.” Indra pointed to one pod. “My cousin is one of them.”

Grace’s jaw dropped. “Your cousin is a werewolf?”

Hark snickered. “I’ll start calling you a weredragon.”

“They don’t use that term. Well, the young ones think it’s funny.” Indra smirked. “Or if we want to insult them.”

“You know, there are some commonality markers in the groups. A bit of crossover. Do you think they could be related somehow?” Mara was checking out the papers printing and tapping on the keyboard again. “I could see if any of them are related.”

“Probably.” Indra shrugged. “I’m a dragon and my cousin’s a wolf. Pretty sure we have all sorts of shifters in the family. My mother’s family seemed to attract the paranormal.”

“Hmmm. Seems a bit unusual.” A smile flitted across Zeru’s face. “I’d like to hear that story sometime.”

“Later. Mara, did the list finish printing?” Indra wondered if he’d know any of the other shifters. Perhaps more were saved in the other locations. It would give them a chance of viability.

"Just about." She pulled a stack of papers from the printer. "Here. These numbers on top correspond to the number on the pod." She walked to the pod, and the numbers were on the lid. "These are all the ones that match." Mara looked through the papers and glanced at the pods. "Thank goodness. It looks like they grouped them together. Let's see..." She shuffled through the papers. "Yes, they are in order." Mara took the last page and walked around the pods. "Here. This is the last one that corresponds to the genetic markers of the rest."

"Rog, you want to start from there and work toward the rest? So, we know not to go beyond those today?" Indra stared at all the pods in between. "We have a lot to do just to get there."

"I think we need to keep going all night if necessary." Zeru nodded. "Wolves, you say?"

"Yes." Indra nodded.

"All the markers match the pod Indra's cousin is in, so I guess?" Mara responded. "I can help, too. The computer will beep if there is a problem opening a pod. I can open a pod in about ten minutes."

"They just take hours to drain." Indra stared at his cousin's pod.

"Yes, but our part is over fast," Zeru added. "If it takes ten minutes a pod, the six of us could have over a hundred done in three hours." He turned to Mara. "How many pods are in this group?"

Mara flipped through the pages. "This group has one hundred." She set the pile of papers on the desk and started opening one of the pods.

"Great, we can be done by dinner time." Hark smiled and, whistling, turned back to opening the pods.

Everyone went back to work.

Indra tucked in a groan. He'd hoped to corner Mara and explain mating to her. If he could just get her outside, he'd bet his pheromones would take over. He wanted to explain it to her. How it worked. Mara was a doctor. She would want to know first. He didn't want her to be unhappy if he changed her without her consent. Not that he would. He knew better than that. Plus, his sisters would make sure he'd regret it the rest of his life. The curse of being the only male in a clutch.

She responded beautifully to him. Just thinking of their encounter in the hall, tightened his pants. Her gorgeous curves and the feel of her silken skin. "Shit." He needed to stop thinking of it. He didn't want to be walking around in pain for the next couple of hours. Indra adjusted himself and tried to tame his thoughts.

~

“So, Mara, do you want to be a dragon?” Grace called over to her.

“What? I’m human. I can’t be a dragon. Though it must be wonderful to fly through the skies.” Mara looked over and smiled at Grace. “Why would you ask that?”

Grace laughed. “Oh, I was human, too. My mate changed me. Along with the rest of them.”

“What do you mean?” Mara frowned at Grace.

“Rog, control your mate,” Indra spat at him.

Rog chuckled. “Oh, no. You’ll learn. You can’t control a dragoness.”

“Yeah,” Hark said, “she controls you. Grabs those balls and you’re done for.”

Rog threw his hands up. “I can’t wait for you to find your mate.”

“Me either.” Hark snickered. “I’ll hand her my balls. She can do anything she wants.”

Zeru snorted, shook his head, and kept working.

"I think, having just been through it, I'm the best one to know what happens." Grace stuck her nose in the air. "Have you been changed from a human to a shifter? Have you? NO. I. Don't. Think. So." She put her hands on her hips and stuck out her tongue at Indra.

Mara swallowed a laugh. You could see the sassy in every wiggle of her body. Grace definitely was amusing, if not a bit delusional. There was no way to change a human to anything else. She was a doctor. People just couldn't become something else. She'd be happy to play along.

"Well, if I could choose to be anything, I think being a dragon would be awesome. I'd love to fly and see the world."

"And shoot fire at assholes. That's fun."

Mara choked down a laugh. "Oh, I'm sure that is."

Indra was just shaking his head. The rest of the men were chuckling at Grace's antics. Everyone continued to work. After Zeru's assessment of the time, no one stopped. She heard them murmuring to each other until Grace started talking. At least she had her mate and his brother to take care of her if her delusions became worse.

"It is. So, you wouldn't mind being a dragon? You wouldn't want to be a wolf or a bear or a cat? Maybe even a mythological creature?" Grace was persistent.

"Well, like, what kind of mythological figure? Like a gorgon?" Mara shivered. "I wouldn't want to turn anyone to stone."

"You know, Grace, many consider dragons mythological creatures." Zeru looked at her, arching a brow. He seemed the calmest to Mara, not a jokester like the two brothers. Not nearly as sexy as Indra, either, though he was extremely attractive.

"But we're real!" Grace turned toward her again. "I'm serious. I was human a couple of days ago. Let me tell you, you'll love being changed. All those sexy dragons up in your business."

Mara swore she could hear Indra grinding his teeth. "Just leave it, Grace."

Mara looked around. None of the men seemed concerned with what Grace was saying. Indra seemed downright disturbed, though.

"I don't think this is the time to discuss it, Grace." Rog looked over at her. "If Mara has questions, she can ask you. Right now, we need to complete this task."

"Fine." Grace huffed. "I can do more than one thing at a time, you know."

Rog laughed. "I know. How about after supper we go check on your mom?"

Grace perked right up. Her whole face seemed to glow. "Yes, please."

Indra moved to the pod next to her. "After dinner, would you go for a walk with me? Or would you rather go for a flight?"

"Fly? How?" Mara's head whipped toward him.

"I can put you in my claws. You'll be safe there."

"Not on your back? I read books about dragon riders when I was a kid. They mounted and rode near the neck."

Indra looked alarmed. "I'd have no way to protect you. And my spine is covered in spikes. You wouldn't be able to sit there safely."

"Oh." It was stupid to feel disappointed. She smiled at Indra, ignoring her thoughts. "I would love to go flying with you." She was sure it would be a wonderful experience.

His smile, complete with dimples, made the room seem brighter. This man was lethal. Mara could fall for him so hard. She tried to reign in her feelings but decided, why bother. It was a whole new world for her. Why not enjoy it?

"It's a date then." Indra's smile shone from his eyes.

Mara couldn't help but return it. She was beginning to think being woken up so many years later was meant to be. "Yes. It's a date." She didn't know if he meant it the same way, but his smoldering glances made her think so.

Mara fanned herself and ignored his chuckle. If she could be a dragoness to his dragon, sign her up.

"I guess I shouldn't have even tried. Before you know it, you'll be wearing scales." Grace grinned at her. "They are lethal, aren't they? So hot." She shook her head and pressed a button before moving on to the next pod.

Mara had to agree. They were all swoon-worthy. Indra, especially so. She hoped he followed her back to her rooms after supper. If their encounter in the hallway was anything to go by, she couldn't wait for them both to be naked.

The electronic clicking and the clank of the hasps disengaging became a monotony of sounds. The repetitive actions and noises felt like they'd never end. Mara sighed and wished they were almost done.

"That's it." Rog broke the silence.

Mara finished the pod she was working on and stretched. Yawning, she looked around. "Wow. I can't believe we finished."

"The first group." Indra blew out a breath. "Two more days. At least."

"Do you think we should leave a day in between?" Zeru wandered over to join the others. "Give them a chance to acclimate?"

"Well, it might not be a bad idea. Wolves can be a bit emotional, especially if they were detained here against their will." Indra glanced over at the pod holding his cousin. "Randulf can be a bit of a hot head."

"We've only Steven's word that they were not voluntary." Hark peered into the face of one of the people in the pod near him. "He didn't even know they were here."

Indra prowled the room. "I would hope they knew. Especially with so many of them here."

"I wonder if the rest of the facilities had shifters?" Mara sighed. "Despite my father acting like he was in charge, he was not. He was involved in a lot of the planning, but mostly in the cryonics lab." She laughed. "If you listen to him, it was all his idea."

Rog, Hark, and Grace were nodding. Obviously, they'd been dealing with her father.

"How long do you think it will be before they wake up?" Indra stood in front of his cousin.

"The capsules are set up to drain over a several hour period. It all depends on each individual. They are being monitored for oxygen levels, nutrient levels, and brain activity. Whether they need zolpidem or wake up on their own. The machine keeps track of all of it."

"So, we need to make sure we are here in about five hours at the most." Indra nodded.

Grace groaned. "That's the middle of the night."

Indra laughed. "Yeah. Maybe we need to make sure the next group is started earlier in the day."

Grace enthusiastically nodded her head. "Yes. Definitely."

Rog chuckled and hugged her. "Have I been keeping you up?"

"Yes!" Grace tipped her head back and smiled. "But I didn't mind too much."

Hark snorted. "Time to eat. That cow should be nice and tender by now." He headed out the door.

Everyone followed.

He turned to go back through the door to take them to the upper level.

"Wait. There's a passage directly outside from here. If it wasn't blocked from the rock slide." Mara headed straight. The door led to another, rougher passage. It angled up, the floor carved out, but not as nice as the rest of them. "I wanted a more direct passage outside from my quarters. They put this in so I didn't have to go in and out through the cryonics lab."

She slowed, and Indra came abreast of her. He grabbed her hand, lacing his fingers through hers. Zings shot from her hand straight to her heart, joy simmering through her.

The others chatted around her. Mara held her excitement in. With Indra, hopefully, by her side, her future teased her with a glory of happiness. She couldn't wait.

CHAPTER SIX

Mara hadn't pulled away when he grabbed her hand. Indra tightened his fingers on hers. He'd get her fed and see if she would sneak away from the rest of them. He'd been ready to wring Grace's neck, but Indra could tell Mara hadn't believed anything Grace said. Of course, she didn't explain it well. If Indra hadn't known how a mating worked, he'd never have understood what Grace meant.

He would have to see if Rog had contacted his brother about sending one more dragon out. As a mated male, Rog couldn't participate. His female would kill Mara if he so much as looked at her. Luckily, unlike some human males with no honor, dragons didn't stray from their mates once they were mated.

He could barely contain his excitement. He didn't want any other female and would be happy to start the mating frenzy right now. If only the other dragon would arrive soon.

The walk up to the passage led to another door. Mara slipped her fingers from his and pushed against the handle. "It won't move." Disappointment rang in her words.

“Let me try.” Indra carefully moved her away. He shoved against the door. It shifted slightly.

Hark and Zeru lent their strength and the door slowly moved open. Stones clattered on the opposite side of the door. Finally, they had it open enough to go through.

“Let me make sure it’s safe.” Zeru moved through first. He grunted and rocks hit against each other. “We need to clear the way out. It appears to exit to the other passage going to the exterior.”

“It does. It’s just a faster way outside.” Mara beamed in pleasure. “Hopefully, we can clear it up easily.”

Indra went through the door, Hark behind him.

“You two stay here while we clean the rocks out of the way.” Rog kissed Grace, smiled at Mara, and joined them outside. “I didn’t even see this doorway.”

“The rocks covered it. I think we may have to take them outside by the fire.” Indra grunted, hefting a large rock into his arms. No need to expend his earth dragon powers when the rocks could be used.

“It will give us places to sit if we arrange them around the fire.” Zeru lifted a large rock and headed outside with it.

Rog and Hark followed with their own. They placed them in a circle, leaving room for more.

"We're going to need more cattle. I can go harvest a few and bring them back if you can handle clearing the cave out." Hark's teeth gleamed in the waning light.

"Please. I'm surprised Grace hasn't been complaining about her empty belly. I heard it making demands already." Rog shooed him away.

They all laughed. Grace had already shown she was a bit impatient when it came to being fed. None of them needed to mention a new dragoness's appetite.

And hopefully, there would soon be another. Indra wondered what Mara would look like as a dragon. Her main undertones, as his mate, would be green, as most earth dragons tend to be. No matter, she would be spectacular. He just knew she would love flying. He could hardly wait to take her up.

"This would be easier if we could use a bulldozer." Mara peeked out the door.

Indra caught the words, but it took a moment to remember what she meant. "Those types of equipment are few and far between," he mumbled. If any were still in service, which he doubted.

"Bulldozers? What good would sleepy bulls do?" Grace sounded puzzled.

Indra stifled a laugh and continued to move rocks. He'd leave Mara to answer that. She had brought it up. It had been so long since he'd seen any type of large equipment working, he'd forgotten about it. To Mara, he imagined it felt like yesterday.

They cleaned up the major rocks in the way, taking them to use by the fire. The rest were shoved against the cave walls. Indra quickly incorporated them into the mountain, not wanting the debris left in the tunnel everyone used. They also checked to make sure there were no other surprise doors hiding behind the rocks. Not easy if more doors were disguised like this one.

It had been covered in the rock face to match the cave walls. They would never have known it was there if they hadn't walked through it from the inside.

Grace and Mara continued to peek out the door, exiting before the men completely cleared the way. But it was good enough.

"I'm so hungry."

Ah, there it was. Grace, once again starving. Hopefully she wasn't too possessive of food still. It could get awkward.

"I could eat, too." Mara smiled at Indra, sending his heart thumping even harder.

He guessed he couldn't steal her away before feeding her. He could eat on the fly, just scoop up dinner while he flew her around. He'd just have to remember to close her in his claws when he grabbed an animal. She didn't need to see him devouring his prey up close and personal. Not before he explained what Grace had so thoroughly butchered when trying to describe a mating.

"Let's get you two fed." Rog brought the flat rocks we'd used for plates to the fire when they served up the cooked meat.

Zeru sliced meat from the spit and deposited it on the plates.

Rog passed out servings to the humans in the area.

Indra saw the outline of a few cows on the ground beyond the fire. "For us?"

Hark nodded. He was munching on a carcass on the opposite side of the fire, away from the humans hanging around outside. Doctor Phillip conversed with a few humans awakened around the same time as Mara. They murmured thanks when Rog presented them with the food.

"Thank you. I figured I'd eat along the way while I took Mara for a flight. This is better." Indra checked on Mara.

She was wandering toward her father, munching on the meat from her plate.

Indra moved away, shifting and settling down for a quick bite. He gobbled up a cow, crunching and finishing it before Mara returned to the fire. He didn't want the reality of life as a dragon to be up in her face. He'd worked and lived with humans for years before the apocalypse and he knew seeing him devour his meal would upset her. Humans had no problem eating a cow cooked over a fire, but show them a dragon utilizing every bit of an animal would gross them out. They would rather waste half of it, only going after the tenderest bits.

Not a dragon. Every bit of their prey strengthened them. Grabbing a second carcass, he bit off the head and legs. With a talon, he sliced it open and removed the insides. Then, Indra used a talon and carefully removed the skin. He ate the pieces he removed and then shifted. Diving into the river, he washed the blood evidence away.

Clean, he slipped his pants back on. He walked over to Hark and slapped a hand on his tail. "Thank you. I'll get this one on a spit ready to cook."

Hark grunted and went back to his meal.

Indra lifted the meat and took it to the fire.

Rog gave him a hand, holding the spit off of the supports so Indra could slide the large body on. "I don't think I'll have to precook this yet. It can roast until the morning."

"Agreed. Though there should be more humans ready to eat by then." Indra helped Rog put the spit back on the supports.

Zeru snorted behind them. "I won't be eating humans. Not enough meat on their bones."

Indra laughed. "Not what I meant."

Zeru smirked and walked off, heading away from the fire. "There are getting to be too many people here. I'll be back in the morning." He shifted and flew toward the mountain peaks.

Rog quirked a brow at Indra. "So, will you be mating tonight?"

Indra sighed. "I doubt it. I would prefer to explain it to Mara first. The humans back then, when Mara lived, didn't believe in dragons. Didn't believe in anything but science." He shrugged. "She may not believe me, but I'd like to give her the chance."

"I think I had it a lot easier. I didn't get stabbed by my mate like my brother. I didn't beg for my mate like my other brother. I tried to learn from their mistakes." He chuckled. "Good luck finding new problems to overcome."

Indra slapped him on the back. "Thanks. I'm sure I will." He walked toward Mara. He frowned at her posture. She looked shrunken in on herself, her face pinched and unhappy. Her father appeared to be lecturing her.

"Mara." He had no problem interrupting her father. The man never stopped talking. "Are you ready?"

She glanced at her father and turned to Indra. "Yes." She handed her plate, still with plenty of meat, to her father and walked off. "Thank you," she whispered.

"You are most welcome." Indra slid his arm over her shoulder, pulling her to his body while they walked. "Did you need more to eat?"

"No." She sighed. "I'd rather fly away." She smiled up at him, relaxing the farther from her father they got. "If it's still on offer."

Indra grinned, slipping his arm down to her waist. His dragon hummed, loving having his mate so close. "Oh, it definitely is."

They walked past the fire. Indra ignored Grace's thumbs up, though Mara giggled. He circled far enough around Hark, still munching his supper.

Mara slowed, looking at Hark.

Indra ground his teeth. He didn't want Mara to see how they ate, at least not yet, but she surprised him.

"Do dragons eat every bit of their food?" She cocked her head, watching Hark crunch right through the animal. "Hmm."

"Yes. The bones strengthen our teeth as we bite. Our bodies completely process our prey."

"Efficient. Too bad humans can't do that." She nodded, then turned back to Indra. "How far do we have to go to be able to fly out? Do you need a runway?"

"What?"

"You know, space to get moving before you fly into the sky, like an airplane?"

"No, not really. I can take flight from almost a standstill, though a little room to maneuver my wings is necessary." Mara didn't seem bothered at all. He'd worried about her reaction, and it hadn't been at all like he expected. "It didn't bother you to see a dragon eating?"

"Well, no. Did it bother you?"

He sputtered. "No, of course not."

"Well, me either." She slid her arm back around his waist. "I wouldn't expect another person to eat a cow like that, but seeing a dragon isn't a big deal. It's just how an animal would eat."

"But he's not an animal." Indra glowered. He didn't like Mara thinking of him as an animal.

"No, but he's not a person when he's a dragon. I don't think I'd want to see him eat like that when he looked like a man. But scales ought to be scary, don't you think?" She grinned impishly at him, fluttering her eyelashes wildly while she leaned into him.

Indra snorted, shaking his head. Mara kept his emotions topsy-turvy. “I think you’ll be trouble.”

She laughed. “I think I will be too.”

“Let’s go for that flight.” Indra released her, then grabbed her back, giving her a quick kiss on her forehead. “Give me some room to shift.” He stepped back and dropped his pants. He chuckled at her widened eyes.

~

Holy cow. The man didn’t even give her any warning. Just dropped trou and stood there letting it all hang out. It didn’t matter that she’d seen it before. In the flickering firelight, Indra looked primitive, savage even. All hard muscles and lickable bits. Mara swallowed, wetting her lips. Oh, how she wanted to lick him.

Indra moved back and within a blink of an eye, a dragon sat in his place. “Are you ready?”

Mara yelped. “I didn’t realize you could talk in this form.”

Indra showed his teeth. She supposed it was a dragon grin. “Yes. Would you still like to fly?”

“Of course. But, can I touch you?”

“Yes. You’ll have to if you want to go with me.” Indra moved, gliding forward within her reach.

She'd swear he looked eager to get her hands on him. She touched his snout and, soon enough, was running her hands along his flanks.

He shivered when her hands caressed his wings.

"You're gorgeous." She didn't want to stop. He was warm to the touch. His scales smooth and seemingly seamless.

"I'd be happy to let you pet me all night long if you like." His voice rumbled. He leaned into her touch.

Mara rested her head against his. "That sounds wonderful. You're magnificent in your dragon form." Her arms circled as much of his neck as she could reach.

"Only my dragon form?" He circled his tail around, caressing her back.

Mara shivered. A dragon really shouldn't make her want to jump him. "So, how about that flight? How will it work?"

Indra chuckled. "Easy. I'll put you in my claws. Just let me get in the air."

Mara reluctantly let go of him. She watched in awe as he spread his wings, hovering above the ground.

"Don't be alarmed." He reached out and scooped her up in his claws. "You might want to sit."

She muffled a shriek and curled her legs underneath her, grabbing onto one of his digits. Luckily, his talons remained on the outside of his claws. Mara kneeled forward, peeking through the gaps. She gasped. Below her, the moon shimmered off the river and the fire flickered in the distance. “It’s beautiful.”

“Let me take you over the nearby settlement.” Indra banked and headed toward the mountain peak.

Mara was amazed at how warm she was. Though the temperatures weren’t cold, she was sure the higher they flew, the colder it was. Sitting in Indra’s claws was nice and toasty. Wanting to get more comfortable, she moved, lying down to peek at the world below. “Is this, okay?”

“Yes. I can shift my claws if you want to see more.”

“Oh no, this is just fine.” Mara wiggled a bit before settling. “I have a perfect view.” She gazed around. It was getting darker, and she couldn’t see much, but the moon painted a beautiful picture.

They crossed the mountain peak and flew beyond it. This new world, and to her it was, was haunting. She remembered the path to the facility. Roads led to it, with a manned fence line to keep people out. Well, people that didn't know about what was happening inside. Until there was no one left to guard the gates. Now there was no evidence left of any of that. No roads, no fences. She closed her eyes and said a prayer. Nothing was as she remembered it. Only remnants of her world remained.

How many people survived the rash of diseases and missiles? Below, she saw a slight glow. "There's lights." Maybe not as much was lost as she'd feared.

"Yes, the solar storage units run the lights at night. Well, certain ones." Indra flew lower, the closer the town came.

"Do they not have electricity?"

"Whatever the sun provides." Indra soared over the town. "It's a nice enough place. Grace's family lives here. Her mother, grandparents, and uncles."

"I didn't know dragons lived in town." She laughed. "Truth be told, I never knew dragons lived." Mara eagerly peered below. "Do they usually stay in human form?"

"Her family aren't dragons." Indra sighed and his ribs expanded above her.

"I'm a doctor. People just can't change into another species." Mara rolled over, looking up at Indra. All she could see was the scales over his abdomen and his legs in a small gap. She would prefer to look into his face. This conversation wasn't making any sense. She had to be missing something.

"Let me land. I'll explain and I'd prefer to do it face to face."

Mara moved, sitting back on her heels. She flinched. The ground was coming up faster than she expected. She grabbed Indra's hand, claw, whatever, and held on. She jerked a bit when he came to a halt.

"I'm going to open my claws. Hold on and let me know when you're steady on your feet."

Mara tightened her grip.

Indra opened his claws, letting her legs slide down.

She felt the ground beneath her feet and clung to his digit while she tested her weight. "I'm good." Mara relaxed her grip and watched as Indra flew up above her. She shook her head. He moved like a helicopter, able to go up and down.

Once his talons were clear of her, he settled to the ground nearby and shifted.

At least, she thought he did. Even with the moonlight, almost everything around her was dark. He was a study in light and shadows, mainly shadows. She could see him doing something but couldn't determine what it was.

He stood and walked toward her. "I thought we could talk here." He gestured, "We can sit on the benches."

Mara hadn't even noticed the benches. All her attention had been on Indra. They appeared to be in a park. Underneath her feet was a path. To the sides of it, spread apart, were benches. She'd like to see it in the daylight. See what else was there. In the distance were a few lights. They must be near the settlement Indra had mentioned.

"Shall we sit?" Indra held his hand out to her.

Mara smiled and took his hand. The feel of his skin against hers sent shivers through her body. Moisture slicked between her legs.

He sat and wrapped his arm around her, settling her against him.

Mara snuggled in with a happy sigh. "What did you want to talk about?"

"What Grace was trying to say." He nuzzled her hair. "You smell good."

"What she said made no sense." Mara cleared her throat. "It's good she has the brothers to take care of her. They don't mind when she seems a bit... well, crazy. She seems happy though."

Indra snorted. "She is happy. And she's not crazy. Well, she might be. I don't know her that well. But here's the thing about dragons. We take humans as mates. Well, unless a female dragon is our fated mate. But there are not as many female dragons. Most clutches are male, with rare exceptions. We've been taking human mates for as long as there have been dragons. Honestly, I think it's why we're shifters."

"That makes no sense. You'd always have to have been shifters. Women would not have wanted to mate with beasts."

"Uh, you'd be surprised. Humans can be a perverse bunch." Indra felt Mara stiffen beside him. "Not most. Not at all. I just meant that humans didn't have to be willing. Dragons are magical beasts and the mixing of genes could have created the first shifters."

Mara harrumphed. "Let's just skip how shifters came about."

Indra chuckled. "Good idea." He turned and pulled her onto his lap. "I want to see you while I explain."

"Or try to."

"Yes, that." He exhaled. "Mara, I believe you are my mate. I can't keep my hands off of you. Every bit of my body cries out for yours. If I could keep you in my arms forever, I would."

A grin spread across her face. "I've never been attracted to anyone like I am to you. It's like a compulsion."

"Yes." Indra nodded, resting his forehead against hers. "An obsession. Until we complete the mating, it will get harder and harder to ignore," he whispered, nudging his nose against hers.

His breath caressed her lips.

Mara licked her lips and leaned forward. His lips were soft.

"Be my mate, Mara. I want you by my side forever." He deepened the kiss, leaning her over his arm.

Mara wrapped her arms around his neck, opening for the silken caress of his tongue against hers. Heat roared through her. She wanted nothing more than to sink into Indra until they became one. Time lost all meaning. The feel of his lips, his strong arms wrapped around her, became her world. She would give up everything to be in his arms forever.

Indra pulled his head back.

Mara followed his lips, not letting him escape.

Indra lifted her and set her against the bench, pulling away from her. "Wait. I need to explain."

Mara crossed her arms and glared. She'd enjoyed losing herself in him. Her body was not happy. Neither was the rest of her. "Fine. Explain."

Indra stood and paced in front of her, running his hands through his hair. "Mating sets off special pheromones, letting other dragons know a mating is happening. Humans can be, and *are*, changed into dragons. The pheromones call the other dragons. It requires at least three dragons to power the change. Four is best, especially if the mix of dragons are earth, water, fire, and air."

Mara pressed her lips together. "So, what does this pheromone do?"

"It starts the reaction in the female so the change can happen." Indra stared at her. "When a dragon... when we mate, the four elements gather and help the change."

"When you say four elements, you create some type of spell? I don't understand what the elements do." This was getting a bit woo-woo for her even having seen him change into a dragon. She was a doctor. She dealt with facts.

Indra shook his head, crouched in front of her, grabbed and held her hands. "I'm not explaining this well." He shifted his weight. "When we kiss, I lose all sense."

"Me too." Mara was thrilled he had lost himself in her. It boosted her confidence.

"When I lose all sense, I start emitting the mating pheromone. My desire for you sends the pheromones out and attracts other dragons. The closest dragons will answer the call. I'm an earth dragon. When an air dragon, a fire dragon, and a water dragon are nearby, I will start the mating process and they will assist. The four of us will combine our bodies and pheromones with yours. The culmination of my seed and their seed will jump-start your body change to become a dragoness."

Mara jerked back against the bench, yanking her hands away. "Whoa. So, you're saying I will be in the middle of a dragon gang bang?" She shook her head, snapping her mouth closed. She ignored the wetness flooding her pussy and the hard tips of her breasts. Her mind rebelled at the thought, but her body didn't.

"Gang bang?" Indra looked bewildered. "What is a gang bang? It doesn't sound good."

"It's when multiple people have sex with one person, either one after the other or all together."

"It has to be all together. If we don't cover and fill you with our seed, you won't change."

Mara squirmed. The naughty thoughts racing through her mind had her body charged. “I see.” What she saw was even if Indra was as deluded as Grace, just trying, it had her ready to jump Indra right now. “And how often do you have to do this? All the time, every month, once a year?” Mara lifted a brow in inquiry.

“Only the first time we mate. Dragons are very territorial. We don’t share except to create a new dragon.” He grabbed her hands in his, kissing each one. “A mated dragon never participates. I will never be part of a mating change again if you agree to mate me.”

“And we would be mated, even if I don’t change? If I agree to do this?” Mara’s heart raced, her breathing speeding up at the thought. Even though she knew changing from a human to basically another race was an impossibility, the thought of being on the receiving end of four men turned her on. Who knew she would be interested in a menage? Who said she would have to abide by the rules and mores of the old world?

Indra’s face lit up. “Yes. We will belong together forever.” He slid to his knees in front of her. Sniffed the air and dove his face between her legs, nuzzling her. “You like that thought.”

“Indra!” Mara pulled at his hair, trying to tug him up. Her legs spread without her permission, his breath heating her vagina. She moaned, bucking up.

Indra nuzzled her.

She felt his mouth against her, his teeth scraping her mound.

He pushed her dress up, nuzzling against her panties, and then her panties tore.

His mouth was on her bare pussy, his tongue dove into her opening, slurping up the wetness. His teeth found her clit, nibbling and then sucking. Ravishing her.

Mara bucked, pushing deeper into his face. She yanked him against her, fucking his face.

Indra’s hands slid around her ass, pulling her into his face. One finger slid, teasing her anus.

She tightened her hands, spreading her legs farther. Groaning when his finger inched into her back hole. Her body tightened, then exploded. “Indra!”

He pulled his finger from her hole, swiped his tongue from her asshole to her clit, making her shiver. “Delicious.” His voice was hoarse. His hands pulled her to his face, nibbling on her lower lips. “I could eat you forever.”

Mara puffed out a laugh. “Yeah. I’d be okay with that.” She caressed his head, enjoying the silkiness of his hair. She could barely move. Her body wanted to melt where she was.

Indra looked pagen, like a god of old, sitting there on the ground, smacking his lips. The moonlight glistened off of his face, covered in her fluids.

“Yes.” The thought of Indra servicing her body, concentrating on her pleasure, overwhelmed her, but in a good way. A fantastic way. In a way she’d never dreamed of.

“Yes?” Indra cocked his head.

“Yes, I’ll be your mate.”

A grin spread across his face. He dragged her down to him and ravished her mouth until she couldn’t do anything but drape across his body.

Mara could hardly wait for more.

CHAPTER SEVEN

Indra pulled Mara across his body. He ignored the stones digging into his back. His only thought was of her. She agreed even after he explained what would happen. From the scent of her body, she would relish it. He was a lucky dragon.

Indra thrust up. His pants now too tight. Mara wiggled and had him straining up, his cock seeking her warmth.

She moved across him, pulling her dress to her waist.

Indra yanked the top down, frustrated to see her in a bra. He groaned and forced a talon out. He sliced the bra down the center and grinned at Mara's gasp.

Mara stiffened and scrambled off him. "Shit."

He groaned when her knee made contact with his dick. "Why?" Then he heard the beating of wings, large wings.

"Yoo-hoo! Hope we didn't interrupt," Grace's voice teased.

Of course, they interrupted. Indra dropped his head to the ground with a thud. He knew damn well they could see the two of them and knew exactly what was happening. He also knew if they came close enough, he'd want to strangle them. Sucking in a breath, he ignored his blue balls and stood.

Mara had shoved herself back into her top. Her sliced bra tucked neatly back in place. Her torn panties were under the bench where they fell. She looked delectable.

Indra pulled her to him, turning them to face Grace and Rog, hovering over them. "What are you doing here?" He grimaced, not able to smile at their intrusion.

"We're going to see my mom." Grace practically bounced in place. She had recently found out that who she thought were her parents were actually her grandparents. She'd found and reconciled with her real mother. Who'd given her up to protect her from her uncle. Even though her grandparents weren't the warmest, Grace could safely grow up at least. If she had lived with her mother, her uncle would have abused them both instead of just her mother.

"Maybe go somewhere private." Rog laughed at Indra's expression.

"Good idea," Indra ground out. His jaw ached from not snapping at the pair. He still sported a mammoth erection. Knowing Mara was without panties and ready to be mounted aroused his senses. He slid his hand down, cupping her ass. One finger slid between her cheeks, seeking her warmth.

Mara squeaked but snuggled in closer to his side.

Indra grinned. He'd spent too much time talking to Rog and Grace. It was time for them to leave. He turned, pulling Mara into his arms.

Her arms slid around him, cupping his ass in both her hands. She pinched his cheek, her eyes sparkling.

He jumped. *The little devil.*

Indra chuckled and brushed his nose against hers. "Shall we go somewhere more private?"

"I guess you're done talking to us." Rog snorted. "Grace, let's go see your dam."

"Fine." Grace flapped her wings, stirring up grass clippings and dust.

Indra ignored them both. "Once they are gone, I'll shift, and we'll fly over the settlement and then somewhere private."

"It's called a town," Grace shouted and flew off.

Rog followed her, chortling as he left them behind.

Indra rolled his eyes. “Ready?”

Mara nodded. She didn’t release him though.

He lowered his head and nuzzled her breast. He slipped his tongue inside her top, laving the tip of her breast.

Her nipple hardened while he tickled it. Shifting his hands to her waist, he tugged her dress, dragging it down until her breasts popped out.

Indra teased it a bit more, then engulfed her nipple into his mouth. His hand grasped her breast, holding it while he suckled. He slid his other hand down, caressing the lips of her vagina through her dress. Her warmth tantalized him. The dampness calling to him.

Indra dropped his hands and unbuckled his pants, yanking them to his knees. Letting go of Mara’s hard nipple, Indra spun and plopped on the bench. He yanked her to him and straddled her on him. It had the wonderful effect of bunching up her dress around her waist.

Indra moaned at the sight. Her spread legs showcased her glistening womanhood, lips spread and weeping. Her clit peeked out from beneath her hood, begging to be loved. Her breasts were framed by her dress, pushing them up for his perusal. Her nipples were hard, one shiny and deep red from his attention.

He couldn't resist. Indra latched onto her neglected nipple, sucking while he manipulated her against his cock.

Mara slid, rocking her vagina against his penis, moaning each time his head bumped her clit.

Indra lifted her and drove his cock into her pussy.

She screamed and melted against him.

Indra flexed, groaning at the tight, silken strangulation of her passage. He increased his speed. Glided in and out, holding her body in place while he fucked her. His hands gripped her hips, moving her body to fulfill his desire.

Mara bowed back and shoved a breast into his mouth, her pulse racing beneath his fingertips.

Indra ignored the sweat dripping down his back. His whole concentration was on making Mara explode. He suckled the offered breast. The pull of his mouth synced with the thrust of his cock inside her tight depths. They came together easily, her juices easing each deep impalement.

Mara tightened on his cock, keening into the air. Her body arched, beautiful to his eyes.

He grunted, erratically jackhammering deeper, then cried out.

Her pussy tightened on his cock, demanding he explode.

His cum burst out, filling the depths of her delicious cunt.

Their arms wrapped around each other.

Indra's blood beat in his ears. His erratic pulse blocked everything but the heaving breaths from Mara. He gasped, his penis buried within her still, pulsing with any cum left inside him.

Mara's body massaged his length, not letting him leave her.

Not that he wanted to. His cock was at home inside her. "Guess we didn't make it anywhere private."

Mara snorted. Her choked laugh against his neck sent tingles down his spine. "'Sokay." She fidgeted, perking up his cock. "Down, boy. Not sure my body can handle any more today. At least, not yet."

Indra smirked, puffing out his chest. He pulled Mara even tighter. He rubbed his cheek against her hair. The feel of her in his arms, on his cock, filled him with excitement and contentment. He was exactly where he was supposed to be. With exactly the person he was supposed to be with. His mate. Soon enough, the beauty of her transformation would bind them together for the rest of their long lives. He couldn't wait.

Squeezing her again, Indra sighed. Her silken skin against his lulled him into a stupor from their detonation together. He didn't want to let her go.

Mara moved, sliding off his cock.

He whined; the warm air chilly on his penis. Indra pulled her toward him, intent on burrowing back inside her warmth.

Mara giggled and slid off his legs, plopping next to him on the bench, sprawling on the seat.

“Why?” Indra couldn’t stop his whimper. He snorted at his foolishness. His eyes took in the delectable sight of Mara’s dishevelment.

Her spread legs were barely covered by her dress, teasing him with a glimpse of her treasure. Her plump breasts pink from his handling, delivered up to be devoured by the support of her top baring all. Her nipples, deep red and begging to be nibbled.

Indra’s penis hardened, cum dribbling from the tip. “More?”

Mara spread her legs imperceptibly. Her pussy now on display.

Indra stared unabashedly. He licked his lips, imagining her taste. He reached out, swiped a finger between her lips, and brought it to his mouth. “Mmm. Delicious.”

Mara squirmed, moisture leaking from her depths.

His nostrils flared. The evidence of his possession mixed with her essence evident for anyone to see. He leaned over her, spearing her with his fingers. He nibbled on her neck while she rode his hand. “Mine.”

She gasped. “That caveman crap shouldn’t be so hot.”

Indra grinned. But not once did she stop riding his drenched hand. He nibbled his way down to her nipple and bit. His thumb ground against her clit.

Mara whined, increasing her grinding.

Indra dragged back her nipple with his teeth, letting it pop free, then seeking the other. He suckled her nipple and areola into his mouth. He slid his other hand down her ass and slid a finger into her anus.

Her pussy sucked his fingers in. She screamed, humping his fingers, and grabbed his head, practically smothering him. “More.”

He added a second finger to her ass. Pulled her back over him and impaled her. He groaned. Her heated canal took every inch of him. He pinched her clit, tugged on it and nibbled on her nipple.

Mara screamed. Locked down on his cock and humped him.

Indra swore and thrust, slamming Mara down on him. She screamed her release while he shuddered and emptied into her.

Mara fell back, supported by his knees and immediately by his hands. She lay limp across his lap, gasping for air. Her head hanging toward the ground.

Indra spread his legs, forcing Mara's farther apart. He admired the slick wet pussy speared with his cock. He watched their combined cum leak out, the thick white liquid trickling from between her lips, coating his cock, and down between her butt cheeks. He slid a finger down her pussy, tickling her clit, and watched her shiver. "All mine." He tasted their combination and slid his finger through it again and offered it to Mara.

She opened her mouth, sucking his finger and moaned.

His cock twitched. The erotic sight stiffened him inside her again. But she was obviously too sore. He didn't want to make her worse, but his erection wasn't listening. He shifted and froze at her moan. It wasn't a good moan.

~

It was so good. Hypersensitivity and satisfaction sent goosebumps racing across her body.

But his movement, just a quick flex, made her wince. Maybe too good. It had been a long time since she'd been involved with anyone. She swallowed a laugh, at least a century, if she could believe it.

"Hmmm." Indra pulled out of her body, sending a cascade of their fluids gushing down the crack of her ass.

"Ick." Mara wrinkled her nose. She raised her hands to Indra.

He tugged her up, enfolding her in his arms.

Mara slumped forward, nuzzling him, and snaked her arms around his neck. She didn't want to move. She didn't care that her bottom was hanging out for anyone to see. She was enjoying the caress of Indra's hands along her curves. Loving the press of his hard chest against her soft breast. It didn't matter they were sitting on a park bench where anyone could come along. Plus, it was dark. Of course, she had no clue if anyone was even nearby.

"How about we go back to your rooms?" Indra whispered. His breath sent delicious tingles through her.

"I could..." Mara cleared her throat. It was just a bit rough from her screaming. "Take a shower."

"So could I." Indra moved her to the bench from his warm lap. "Let's go." He slid his pants the rest of the way off his legs.

How could she not have realized he was still partially dressed? Fair play, she guessed, since she still wore her dress.

Indra stepped back, and his dragon was in his place. His head loomed over hers. His tongue came out and licked her from toe to head. “Mmm.”

“Eww.” She wrinkled her nose at him. “I have to stink.”

“My seed and your essence.” He rubbed his snout against her cheek. “Delicious.”

“Well, you are a dragon. I suppose you like the smell of different things than a human would.”

“I like the smell even when I’m not a dragon.” Indra ran his nose along her body, sniffing and snorting.

“Stop.” Mara squirmed and pushed his snout away. “Let’s head out.”

Indra let out a huge sigh. “I suppose.” He hopped in the air, closed his claws around Mara’s waist, and cupped his claws to enclose her.

She snuggled into the safety of his claws and laid down to peek between his digits. “It’s beautiful. No constant noise, no light pollution. It’s like the earth has been reborn.”

Indra moved swiftly through the sky.

She was warm because he generated so much heat. The little bit of cool air coming through his claws couldn’t compete.

"We're almost there."

Mara watched the fire get closer. She didn't really want this night to end. "Will you stay with me?"

"I never intended to stay anywhere else."

Mara raised a brow. That seemed a little pushy. "Without an invite?" She felt rather than heard his chuckle. It vibrated his body and sent tingles through her.

"I was hoping to persuade you." Indra hovered in place. "Get ready to stand."

He opened his claws, letting her legs slide down. Once she was steady, he shifted into a man.

She didn't think she'd ever get used to seeing him shift. It kind of blew her mind. Everything he was went against the laws of science. The blood she took from him should have results by now. She wanted to check but was so tired. She didn't want to mess up any of the results.

"Shall we stop by the lab?" Indra took her hand, pulling her into his arms. "I'd like to check on my cousin."

Wrapping her arms around him, Mara hugged him back, taking a deep breath. She loved the smell of him. Maybe it wasn't so farfetched that he loved the smell of her too. "Sure. It's on the way to my rooms."

Indra walked them over to the fire. He snagged a plate and piled it high with meat. He slid one arm around her waist, moving them toward the cave.

Mara stared at the door disguised in rock. “I think the door uses a badge reader, not a bioscan.” She yawned. “But I’m too tired to figure it out.”

“It’s okay. We can look at it in the morning.” Indra steered her toward the doors leading into the main facility. He pushed it open, waving her through.

Mara blinked, trying to keep her eyes open. She entered the cryo lab and cut across to the door opposite.

“Mara.” Arms wrapped around her, lifting her into the air.

She squealed and looked up. She hadn’t even noticed her brother. She smothered another yawn. “Didn’t see you.”

Christopher laughed. “No kidding. Go to bed. I’ll see you in the morning.” He set her down. “Not too early.”

Mara smiled and shuffled off. Bed was sounding really good. She shook her head. She was almost there.

The door opened in front of her and she kept moving through. It swooshed shut behind her and then she was swept over Indra's shoulder. She thought about protesting, but it wasn't worth it. She didn't want to keep walking. She lay her head and arms down Indra's back and tried not to drool.

His chest vibrated beneath her. "Go to sleep."

If only it was that easy. But his warmth made her drowsy. She blinked, seeing the floor go by between bits of darkness. Huh, guess she was ready to drop off.

A door opened. Indra stepped into the lower cryo facility. "Hark."

"I see you've captured a fair maiden. I don't believe they like to be carried off and stolen away." Hark grinned. "Not that they ever really did."

Mara waved an arm. "Is okay. Tired."

Hark barked out a sharp laugh. "My bad. I guess I was wrong."

"What are you doing here?" Indra's voice rumbled through her.

"I thought I'd stay in here tonight. Make sure no one woke up and freaked out." Hark lifted and dropped Mara's arm.

She grumbled and tried to swat him. Halfheartedly, but still.

"Leave her be." Indra shook his head. "I wore her out." His chest expanded and his posture straightened. "She needs to recuperate."

Mara narrowed her eyes and pinched his ass.

"Ouch."

Hark laughed. "So, I see. Take her to bed. I'll come get you if any of them start moving around."

"Thank you." Indra moved in front of a pod.

Mara figured it must be his cousin.

He turned and left out of the door. His hand smacked down on her ass as soon as the door shut. "That's for pinching me."

"Ouch." It hadn't really hurt her, no more than her pinch hurt him. Mara giggled.

Indra laughed and took her back to her quarters. Mara lifted her hand, pressing her finger against the biometric lock to open the door.

"Did you want a shower or just fall into bed?"

"Shower, I guess."

Indra set her down, steadying her, then slipped her clothes off. "Want help?" His pants followed.

"Sure." She wanted to lay down, right there, and sleep. But she smelled like dragon and was sticky in places she thought only the cryo gel would ever get into. Indra had proved that theory wrong. She still didn't move though. The thought of walking didn't do it for her.

Indra chuckled and swung her up in his arms. "Let's get clean and get to bed."

Mara nodded her head and laid it on his shoulder. "Okay."

CHAPTER EIGHT

He enjoyed the feel of Mara's soft curves against his hard body. Her delectable scent, especially covered in his. Soon enough, she would carry his scent forever. He ignored the erection that thought brought. Mara was too tired. He wasn't sure she was still awake in his arms.

Once in the bathroom, he set her on the toilet. She almost fell off. "Mara, wake up, just a bit."

She roused and he was able to let her go.

Indra turned on the shower, and once the temperature was warm without scalding, he picked her back up. "We're getting in the shower now."

Mara buried her head in Indra's chest. Her arms loosely hooked over his shoulders. She groaned as he slid her legs down until she was forced to take her own weight. "Wanna sleep."

"In a bit. Let me wash you." Indra ran a soapy cloth along her body, arms, legs, boobs, and butt. Even the bottoms of her feet.

If she was more awake, she would have enjoyed it. The nylon poof cleaned every crevasse of her body. Then she saw Indra cleaning his. She moved back and leaned against the shower stall so he could at least get his legs. Especially his feet. He hadn't worn shoes at all, so they probably needed it.

"Hair?" The shampoo bottle was in his hand.

"No." She shook her head. "Sleep."

Indra laughed and the shower shut off. He stepped out, grabbed a towel, and wrapped it around her. He wrapped another one around his waist. Then he lifted her.

He pulled the blankets back from the bed and deposited her in it, pulling the towel from around her.

Mara grumbled but rolled over and buried her head in a pillow. She was gorgeous, all warm and sleepy.

Indra slid in beside her, pulled the covers over them both, and wrapped his arms around her, loving the feel of her next to him.

She snuggled into him and drifted to sleep.

Indra stroked her cheek and pulled her closer. He took a deep breath and savored her scent. Contentment spread through him.

He settled down, happier than he'd been in years. He understood why he continued to return to this area. He must have sensed his mate here. He pulled Mara close and sunk into sleep.

Indra groaned. He was warm and had Mara cuddled up next to him. Her head pillowed on his chest. Something woke him, though. He listened and didn't hear a thing. It didn't feel like he'd been asleep long. He laid his head back down when it started again. A tap, tap, tap.

"Indra," came Hark's voice through the door. "Indra, they're starting to wake."

He dropped his head back, sighed, and eased away from Mara. Sliding out of bed, he laid Mara onto the pillow. She needed her sleep. He quickly cracked the door before Hark woke her.

"I'm up. You're sure?"

"Yeah. They are starting to stir like the humans did when we first woke them up. I figured you'd want to be there." Hark headed back toward the lab. "I'll meet you there."

"Let me get dressed." Indra left the door open and grabbed his pants, sliding them on. He closed the door. It locked behind him. Glancing at it, he realized he wouldn't be able to open it. He didn't have access. He shrugged. It was a problem for later.

He quickly made his way to the cryo lab. Hark had been right. Maybe, being shifters, they were able to metabolize waking up faster. Depending on their reactions, it was better Mara, being human, wasn't here.

"What should we do?" Hark leaned against the wall, looking at the pods.

Indra shrugged and scratched his head, a yawn breaking free. "Wait, I guess."

A choking sound from one of the pods, followed by more. Stirring from the first ones, and soon enough, the rest followed. The first pod they'd started the process of waking up suddenly jerked.

Indra made his way over to it.

A man glared at him, his face shifting from human to wolf and back again. He coughed, grabbed his stomach, and stumbled from the pod.

Indra clasped his arm, helping him stand.

Hark lent an arm to the next person.

Rog and Grace stumbled through the door.

"We're here to help." Rog looked around. "Grace, get some water to help clear their throats."

Grace rummaged in the cabinets at the sink. She held up a plastic-wrapped package of disposable cups. "Found them." She opened and started filling cups and setting them on the counter before passing them out. Once done, she continued opening cabinets. "Aha."

Indra lifted the cup to the man's mouth he was assisting. "Do you know how you got here?"

The man grabbed the cup, tilted it, and drained it. He cleared his throat. "More?"

Grace scurried over and refilled it from a pitcher she'd found. That must have been her *aha* moment.

Indra waited.

Once the man was finished, he handed the cup to Indra. "We walked, dragon." He smirked.

"Were you taken by force?" Indra figured from the man's nonchalance; they'd come here voluntarily. He would like to know why, though.

"Manners." The man bared his teeth in a very fake smile.

Indra sighed. "Indra." He held out his hand to him.

"Morgan." He shook Indra's hand. "No, we walked here. There was a Skype meeting with all the packs. The illness was decimating our numbers. One of the packs near here was contacted by the military about the facility and cryonically freezing some of us."

Indra sagged in relief. They wouldn't be facing hostile wolves anytime soon. "How did you decide from the packs who would come?"

Morgan grimaced. "Everyone from all the packs in the eastern United States that could, came. Those not showing signs of illness." His voice broke. "This is all that is left of us, as far as I know."

Indra grabbed his shoulder, squeezing it. "I'm sorry." He blinked, willing the tears to stay hidden. He pulled Morgan into a hug.

Morgan hugged him before stepping back, stumbling into the pod.

"Sorry." Indra grasped Morgan's arm, steadying him. "Well, everyone should wake up within the next few hours."

"I'll help." Morgon's stomach growled. "Maybe after I get something to eat."

Zeru strode through the door, a large tray filled with meat in his arms. "Thought this might come in handy about now."

Indra grinned. Maybe being around these other dragons wouldn't be too aggravating. He'd wait and see.

The newly awoken wolves—and they were all wolves, Indra could scent their fur—surrounded the meat Zeru had dumped on the counter along the wall.

"I'll get more." Zeru carried the empty tray and left again.

Indra and the other dragons helped each wolf one by one. Zeru kept them fed.

Suddenly, Indra was looking into the surprised eyes of his cousin. “Randy.” Unlike the other wolves he’d helped, he pulled him into a hug. Indra just wanted to shake him. He’d feared he would never see him again.

Randy coughed and Grace handed him a cup of water. He chugged it. “Indy.” He held out his cup for more and swallowed it down. “What the hell are you doing here?”

“I could say the same to you.” A short laugh burst from Indra. “Do you know how long I looked for your mangy ass?” He shook his head and grinned at him. He’d found his mate. Now, Randy was here and Indra had part of his family back. The world had just gotten brighter.

“We were dying.” Randy grimaced. “It may have been hit or miss for the humans, but almost all the wolves got sick.” He shook his head. “Like we were targeted.” Sorrow filled his eyes. “We were sent out in a hunting party, and the sickness hit the village while we were gone. There was a message from the alpha. We should go to the coordinates he’d sent if we weren't sick. So, we did.” Randy grabbed his arm. “What happened to them, Indy? Do you know?”

Indra ducked his head. His lips tightened. “I do.” His voice was hoarse. “They were all dead. Every last one of them. The whole village.” He embraced Randy, tears slipping down his face. “They’d left me a message too. I did as they asked and burned the village. Pulled a lake to cover the area so none of the illness lingered.” He looked into Randy’s eyes. His vision blurred. “I made sure no one was alive first.” He choked. “A couple of times. I couldn’t bear the thought of burning anyone alive.”

Randy pulled him tighter. Tears dripped from both their eyes until Randy’s belly protested. He stepped back, wiping his eyes. “Thank you.”

“No thanks needed. I’m glad you’re alive.” Indra pushed him toward the meat. “Now go fill your pit.” He dried his face. “I’ve work to do and your needy ass will have to wait.”

He laughed, slugged Indra on the arm and beelined toward the food. “Get moving, then.”

His heart filled with joy. Indra turned to the next pod and continued helping the men and women wake up.

It took a few hours, but soon enough, all the wolves were awake. The realization on their faces of how little of their species had survived was heartbreaking.

“Maybe some survived on the outside. Or around the world,” one wolf spoke.

"Indra? You searched for me. Did you find any packs?" Randy's solemn face was so unlike what Indra was used to.

Indra sighed. He didn't want to tell them, but they deserved to know. "No. I searched all over the US. I even flew through what was once Canada and Mexico. I didn't find traces of any shifters. No wolves, no bears, no cats." He grimaced. "Only dragons and we were few to begin with."

The silence spoke of the horror the news was received with.

"What about Europe and Asia?"

"Africa?"

Questions abounded. But he didn't have the answers. "I don't know."

"Would the dragons be willing to help us find out? Could you take us there?"

Before Indra could answer, the door opened. It may have just been a whisper of sound, but everyone turned toward it. The perils of a roomful of shifters.

"Oh my god! Everyone in the first group is awake." Mara stepped in, smiled, and slid her arms around Indra. "I wondered where you'd gone. But I figured you were checking on your cousin."

~

Silence filled the room. Mara wondered why. Everyone stared at her. It was a bit disconcerting, considering most of them were naked.

"Cousins?" One of the men just awakened looked at Indra. "How is this?"

Indra's cousin raised his hand with a grin on his face. "Because our mothers were sisters. That whole human family was claimed by different types of shifters. My mom mated a wolf. His mom mated a dragon." He shrugged. "They were just a lucky group."

Mara figured this must be Randy.

"One even found a bear. Poor thing." Randy shook his head in exaggerated sorrow.

A snigger, then a chuckle rang out. Soon enough, the room was filled with people who were getting acquainted. Her father must have been wrong. These people didn't look like they had been kidnapped and put under. None of them exhibited any signs of anger.

Mara slipped away from Indra's arm, intent on checking the data from those awakened. According to the information on the computer, they'd woken up hours earlier than expected. She glanced back and saw Indra looking at her. She smiled, warm fuzzies filling her.

When she'd woken up alone, Mara thought maybe it had all been a dream. But the evidence of a person sharing her bed, the towels in the bathroom, and a strange backpack in her rooms assured her it wasn't. Not to mention the well-used feel of her body. Then she'd worried that she'd just been a convenience. But his bag showed he intended to return.

Once her brain went back online, she realized he was probably checking on his cousin, and she settled into her new reality. Seeing him again firmed her belief. Her new future was wonderful.

Since they planned not to wake a new group until this group had settled, Mara decided to check the dragons' bloodwork results. She typed in her parameters and waited.

Arms slid around her waist, pulling her against a warm body. She'd know Indra's touch anywhere.

She dropped her head to his chest and looked up. "Just checking everything went right with the pods waking everyone up."

"It did, as you can see." Indra kissed the top of her head.

"Indeed." Mara smiled up at him. "So, are they all wolf shifters, as you thought?"

"Uh-huh." Indra peered at the computer screen. It beeped. "What does it tell you?"

“Nothing, yet. I wanted to see if the dragon DNA results were done.” Mara scowled at the monitor.

“How long does it usually take?” Indra peered over her head at the screen. “Why are the numbers running across the screen like that?”

Mara shrugged. “I don’t know how long it takes. I’ve never run one from the start before.” She sighed. “I could ask my father.” She didn’t really want to. He’d lecture without giving an answer. Or it would take him a good, long time to answer while he trapped her into listening to him.

Don’t get her wrong. Her father was a brilliant scientist but extremely verbose. She often thought he talked over everyone because he didn’t want to hear anyone else’s opinions. It was why she went into the medical sciences rather than follow in his footsteps. She was pretty sure it was why her brother went into engineering.

How they both managed to get wrapped up in one of their father’s projects didn’t even make sense to her, but they had. Of course, thanks to Dad, she and Christopher were alive.

“Well, no offense, but he’s the last man I want to talk to. That is a man who loves the sound of his own voice.” Indra grunted.

Mara giggled. “I was thinking the same thing.”

She snuggled in his arms. Seeing her father was the last thing she wanted to do.

"Indy, get your butt over here," Randy hollered.

Indra tugged Mara behind. "What?"

"We need to discuss a few things." Many of the people were sitting on the ground.

"Like what?" He leaned against an open pod, arm still holding her to him.

"Maybe, like clothes?" Mara tried to keep her gaze above their necks. It was hard when most were naked.

Snickers broke out.

Mara felt her face heat and kept looking up.

"Nudity is normal for shifters," a man said.

"Not for humans. But I don't mind if you don't. Lots of eye candy." Grace smiled, her eyes twinkling.

Rog's growl filled the room. "Clothes for everyone."

Hark laughed, smacking Rog on his shoulder. "Or fur."

"You dragons and humans won't understand us if we're in fur." An older man stood. "If it takes clothing to get this discussion moving, find us some." He glared around the room. "I want a shower, more food, and to know how the world fared."

"Our belongings should still be in lockers near the shower rooms." Randy waved to a door on the same wall where Mara had found the blood-drawing equipment. "I'll go look."

Grace whistled at him, and Randy grinned over his shoulder, adding a bit more swagger.

Rog growled while a few wolves cackled.

Mara rolled her eyes. Randy didn't mind stirring up the dragons. She would have thought he wouldn't mess with them since his animal was so much smaller. She guessed she thought wrong.

"One day…" Indra chuckled.

She couldn't help but nod in agreement.

Suddenly, the group stood up and followed Randy.

"What? What happened?" Mara watched the group walk away, chatting among themselves.

Indra looked surprised. "Randy called them over."

"He did? I didn't hear a thing." Mara frowned. "Are you sure?"

"Yes. He whistled, but I doubt you'd have heard it." He spoke a bit louder. "It sounded like a dog whistle."

The last man going through the door looked back and rolled his eyes. "Woof." He laughed and the sound of water cut off as the door closed behind him.

It was just Mara and the dragons. The room seemed awfully quiet. “So, when do you want to wake up the next group?”

“Let’s get this group settled. They’ll have to figure out where to live. Wolves aren’t much for living in caves,” Hark added.

The door flew back open. Randy stood in the opening.

“Wrong. Most wolves have dens. Dens are in caves. Of course, we’re modern wolves and prefer running water and stoves rather than cooking over an open fire and peeing in the grass.” Randy sauntered back in, jeans hanging low on his hips and towel-drying his hair. He snapped the towel at Indra, making him jump. “Unlike dragons.”

Indra pursed his lips, looking like he was holding in a laugh. “Too bad things have changed. It’s back to the forests for you furbearers.” He elbowed Randy and the two began tussling.

The affection between them was obvious. She was glad Indra had found his cousin. She was sure waking up to family would help to ease the pain of so much loss. Even though her father could be aggravating, she would miss him if he weren’t around.

The group around Indra grew. He hugged a few of the men and women, obviously they knew each other. Soon enough, the room's capacity had once again swelled.

"Why don't we go outside if everyone is back." Zeru stretched. "There is more food and the air is much fresher." He led the way outside. No one argued. The wolves, in particular, seemed eager.

Once outside, they all settled around the fire. They made quick work of passing out more food to everyone. One of the wolves stood. He seemed to think he was in charge.

"How many years have passed?" He looked around, pulling in a breath of air. "It seems more than the fifty years the government told us."

Indra shrugged. "I'm not sure when you were all frozen, Morgan. It has been, what…" He looked at the other dragons. "Nine or ten generations? Once most of the humans died away, no one seemed to keep track of the years."

"It didn't matter anymore," Zeru added. "What difference did it make? The humans are in small groups across the country. The animals roam freely once more. And the dragons are once again ruling the skies." He nodded like he agreed with himself. Pride infused in every line of his body.

"Why were we not woken up?" Morgan scowled. "We were told we would be. Did they just forget about us?"

"No. We, the other humans you see here, were just woken also," Mara said. "We were all forgotten about." She frowned. "I'm not even sure what happened."

"We found you," Grace piped up. "I'd been trying to get in a locked door and met up with Rog and Hark. They helped me open it. We were exploring and found all the coffins. Well, we thought they were coffins. One of them had instructions, so we followed them." She made a face. "It was Doctor Phillip's pod."

Mara stifled a laugh. She was surprised they'd opened more after her father started talking.

"He opened the human's pods. While checking the information on the computer, he discovered the pods on the lower level. He didn't even know shifters were down there." Rog scratched his chin. "He wasn't even part of it. He thought the lower section had never been completed."

"His papers showed pod numbers that weren't with the ones in the upper cryo chamber. And the DNA readings were..." Mara's scrunched up her face, trying to be diplomatic, "different."

A woman laughed, one of the wolves. "Emma, here. I think you're trying not to say abnormal." She looked amused. "I'm a doctor. I know what our DNA looks like to humans. I'm surprised you woke us up."

Mara spread her hands. "I might not have, but Indra recognized his cousin, so I figured the abnormal DNA possibly pertained to a gene sequence for shifters." She smiled at him.

"Why did you not wake up the rest of the wolves?" one man asked. "There are lots of pods still filled."

"Because we don't believe they are wolves. There are three different DNA abnormalities." Mara tipped her head toward the dragons. "They believe one is for you, the wolves, and the others, possibly bears and felines."

A few grumbles were heard.

"Not cats."

"Damn cats."

Mara laughed. So, cats and dogs didn't get along. Not too much had changed.

Morgan hushed the groans. "We need to find a way to survive and thrive in this world. We'll have to establish homes and hunting groups to feed ourselves. I don't intend to live off the dragons' good graces." He looked around the group. "How many packs do we want to establish?"

"Did we want first to find out if any other groups survived?" Emma moved closer to Morgan.

"I found no shifters other than dragons loose on the continent," Indra added.

"No, but how many other facilities were there in the US? Maybe they have shifters too. And maybe they need to be unfrozen." Emma raised her hands. "Maybe we need to find them." She turned to Mara. "Do you know where they are located?"

Mara slowly shook her head. "No, but I'm sure my father and brother do. My dad was instrumental in the development of the pods. My brother was the chief engineer who designed the power for the facilities. There were three facilities in the US that I know of." Mara shrugged. "There could be more, but I was only one of the physicians in this facility. I had no need to know about any others."

"I can get your brother or your father." Rog stood. "Your father is probably still working on the pods. Your brother is around somewhere."

"We'll both go look for them." Grace wound her arm around Rog's. "I'm sure you don't need us."

They headed back into the cave, Rog's head bent to listen to Grace. Watching them, Mara hoped Indra's claim to change her into a dragon was true. The depth of devotion between the two was something she'd always wished for in a spouse.

"We can grab more cattle. With the number of humans and shifters being unfrozen, we will need more meat." Zeru left with Hark scrambling after him. "I doubt we'd be able to help with any information."

Morgan inclined his head. "Thank you." He looked around. "Did anyone want to hunt? Or would you all prefer to continue this discussion?"

Randy faced the wolves. "Do you all want a say, or are you willing to go along with what your designated alphas decide?"

Voices rang out over each other.

"Alpha."

"I'll stay."

"I want to hunt."

Morgan, Randy, Emma, and a few others stayed. They began by introducing themselves and what Mara assumed was their pack affiliation. For the most part, it was the alphas left. The others were the doctor, Emma, two wolf scientists, and five scouts.

Mara wasn't sure what a scout was, but hopefully, it would be self-explanatory once the discussion began.

Morgan asked Emma, “Why do you want to find the other facilities?”

She blinked at him. “There are maybe one hundred of us. Suppose there are no other wolf shifters left. In that case, we will no longer be viable as a population within a couple of generations because of inbreeding. If there are five hundred, occasionally mixing with humans, we will continue to be viable and able to rebuild our species. It’s as simple as that.”

“If we bring all the wolves together, we can have a mating ceremony. The more, the better. Then we can split all the wolves into packs. I think we need to remake ourselves.” Randy squeezed his eyes shut. “None of our children survived. What is a pack without a future? I vote we look for the other facilities. To give ourselves a future.”

Sorrow washed across all their features.

They all had lost loved ones. Mara supposed she was one of the lucky ones. Her family was small and the three of them had survived.

“I agree.”

“To our future.”

“Blessings of the moon for our people.”

“I believe this is the correct decision.” The scientists nodded.

“We stand ready.” The scouts pounded their chests once and sat.

Morgan sat, with the rest following suit. “Now we need to decide who to send. Besides the scouts, of course.”

“We should have doctors. There might be some amongst the other shifters.”

“Plus, me. I’m willing to go with, so we have two for sure,” Mara said. “And I know the systems. I can brief everyone on them before we leave.”

Emma smiled. “Good. I’ll help with unfreezing the rest of the shifters.”

“That will give us a few days to plan.” To the scouts, Morgan said, “In the meantime, each of you take a different direction. We’ll need to find a place to house the packs. At least one in this area.”

A scout stood and nodded. “We can go now.” The rest followed.

As one, they shifted and took off in different directions.

Mara’s jaw dropped, watching them change. She pressed her hand to her heart, her eyes following them. Seeing them move and flow into a new creature was amazing.

Indra whispered in her ear. “The wolves are lucky. When they transform back, they’ll be wearing the clothes they had on. Dragons, not so much.”

Randy laughed. “We have many advantages over the dragons.” He wagged his brows at Mara. “We can keep you warm at night. We’re like having your own living fur blanket.”

Indra scowled.

Randy grinned.

Mara guessed the taunting had gone on their whole lives and ignored them both. She jumped and screamed at a loud thump behind her. A couple of cattle and bison lay on the ground, dust and dirt flying around them. Pools of blood seeping out of them. In the sky, two dragons flew off.

She shuddered when Indra's stomach rumbled. He might like the smell, but she would prefer her meat roasted over the fire.

"There's not much for us to do until Doctor Phillip arrives." Indra stood. "Perhaps the wolves and humans would prefer more than meat tonight. I know where we can harvest some corn if anyone wants to assist."

Mara hurriedly stood. Anything to get away from the carcasses. "We can roast it in the coals." She shrugged. "Or use the large cafeteria inside to cook them." She was sure there were staples available to make more food, but it seemed the wolves and dragons preferred fresh food. From the grimaces at her suggestion, they were an outdoorsy people.

Indra led the way down the river, crossing in a shallow spot. Soon enough, they came to rows and rows of corn.

"I can't believe they survived." Mara laughed. "When the facility was built, they were just planted." She looked at them. "It's amazing."

"Without being picked, they tend to reseed. They move from season to season with the wind. Nature's own rotation. The animals that wander through keep the ground fertilized." Indra pointed farther out. "Usually, wild carrots can be found there. Along with turnips and parsnips. They're all intermingled. If you hunt around the valley and into the lower slopes, you'll find many of the crops originally planted here thrived."

"This is amazing." Mara touched the ears in front of her. "They even carry more than one ear per stalk."

"The bioengineering of the crops ended a long time ago. What survived has been by Mother Nature's blessing." Indra started tearing ears off the stalks, walking outside of the rows. "We can pile what we pick here and return to the fire. I'll fly out with something to carry them back to roast."

Mara started down a row parallel to Indra's. She plucked and dropped them to the ground at her feet. When she thought she'd gotten as much as she could carry, she picked them up. Arms full, she deposited them in a growing pile and finished getting the rest she'd picked off the ground.

"Do you think that's enough?" Indra stood, arms akimbo, at the pile.

"I suppose it depends on how many humans there are." Morgan looked at Mara.

She tossed up her arms. "I've no idea. I've been helping with the shifters."

"Let's head back then." Indra said to Randy, "I'm assuming you can find your way back?"

"Of course." Randy headed back the way they came. The rest followed him.

Indra wrapped his arms around Mara. "Care to fly with me? I have something I can carry the corn in. You can help me put them in the container."

"Sounds good." He stripped and shifted. Mara picked up his pants and bundled them in her arms.

Indra rose and grabbed her, quickly enclosing her in his curled-up claws.

To her surprise, he flew into the mountains, where the trees grew thick. Mara watched the different trees and suddenly, they were over a clearing with a small cabin and a couple of outbuildings.

Indra set her down and shifted. He strode over to one of the outbuildings and opened it. He tugged out a wire container holding a white plastic tank into the center of the clearing. He shifted and sliced the top of the white container off. He flicked it away, tossed it back to the building, and shut the doors. “Can you latch the doors?” He wiggled his talons. “These are too clumsy.”

Shocked into movement, Mara latched the doors.

Indra was magnificent in the daylight. His dark scales shimmered with different shades of green and brown. If you didn’t know he was there, he blended into the earth and surroundings. She licked her lips. If she didn’t know it was Indra, she’d be wet-her-pants scared right now. “Now what?” As a dragon, he was a bit intimidating.

“Now this.” Mischief sparkled in his eyes. He leaped and grabbed her. Then set her in the IBC container. His talons hooked through the metal grating surrounding what was left of the white plastic tank. He soared up and Mara’s feet slid.

She quickly sank down to sit against the container wall. She used Indra's pants to cushion her bottom. From the shape it was in, she would have to agree that plastic didn't degrade. She doubted anyone was still producing them. Which meant this container was close to a couple hundred years old. Maybe. The date stamped into the plastic bottom was 2007. Ironically, a number five recycling symbol was also pressed into the bottom, yet it was still around. Her race had done their best to destroy their world without even trying. Hopefully, they would do better this time around.

She really wished she had a way of telling how much time had passed. Nine generations would indicate a minimum time of around one hundred eighty years. If you counted twenty years as a generation. Her brain hurt thinking about it.

Mara laughed to herself. It didn't even matter in the scheme of things. It wasn't like the waking up of a few hundred people from before the apocalypse would rebuild the world.

She felt it would be a huge culture shock for the majority of those they were waking. Then, once they met shifters, their world would be turned on edge. The dragons had no intention of going back into hiding. It didn't seem like the wolves would either. She had to wonder where the population percentages stood.

The basket stopped moving and jarred her slightly as it hit the ground. She threw Indra's pants out of the basket and stood.

Indra shifted and lifted her out and dressed. "Thanks. Let's get the corn in the basket."

They leaned over and started tossing the ears in the plastic container. It was tedious. Mara and Indra groaned and stretched out their backs.

Indra pulled her in for a hug and tugged her off the ground with a bit of a shake.

"Oh." Her back cracked. Mara dropped her head forward onto Indra's chest. "Thank you."

"We should get back. Hopefully, they found your dad or your brother." He squeezed her, then tilted her face toward him. "Or we could stay here for a while." His lips descended on hers.

Her knees wobbled, and she leaned against him to keep from falling. "That sounds nice."

"Just nice?" He chuckled against her lips. "I must not be doing it right."

"Are you done yet?" Randy's voice pulled a groan from Indra. "I came to help, but I see nothing I can help with." He wrapped his arms around both of them.

Indra shrugged him off, baring his teeth.

Randy just laughed.

"We might as well go." Mara climbed over the container wall and wiggled down among the corn.

Indra tossed his pants at Randy and shifted, stirring up the dirt and chaff in the area.

"Dammit, Indy." Randy ran and leaped into the container just as Indra lifted it into the air. "Fly, Indy, fly!" He whooped and burrowed next to Mara.

She chuckled and shook her head.

"So, are you boning my cousin?" He wagged his eyebrows. "Tell me all."

Indra growled above them and Randy snorted.

Mara dropped her head into her hands. This flight couldn't land soon enough.

CHAPTER NINE

Indra was tempted to dump the container just to see Randy scramble. Except Mara was in there. She was already suffering enough with his cousin next to her. Though from her giggles, he was pretty sure Randy was embellishing tales of their youth.

He gritted his teeth and tried not to growl all the way back to the fire. He didn't succeed. He hovered near the fire and let the basket drop, snatching Mara so she didn't hit the ground.

She clung to his digits the instant he snatched her. "Indra. That wasn't nice."

He snorted and gently set her on the ground. If he didn't know his cousin was a wolf, he'd swear he was a hyena from his laughing. Indra shifted and grabbed his pants from the corn.

Mara's cheeks pinked nicely, gazing at him.

He strutted to her and pulled her close. Indra tossed his pants over his shoulder. "We could head inside." He took a page from his cousin's book and wagged his eyebrows at her. "We can play hide the wiener in the bun."

She choked, laughing at him. "Good lord. Don't get any cheesier." She hugged him to her, snuggling with her face against his chest. Her embrace soothed him, making him rumble. "You're purring."

Indra snorted. “Dragons don’t purr.”

“Hmm. It sure feels like it.” She rubbed against him.

His body tightened with desire. His penis hardened even more. He whispered in her ear. “If I keep holding you, I’ll have you flat on your back right here.” He licked her ear, loving her shiver.

“Well, you better put your pants on then because that is not happening.”

“It could.” He flexed his hips, pulling her curves against him.

Mara hummed, then pushed out of his arms. “Pants on. We’re not putting on dinner and a show.”

“Thank you!” Of course, it was Randy. “I’ve seen quite enough of my cousin’s ass today.”

Indra dropped his head back, gritting his teeth. Why had he wanted to find him? Just wait until Randy found his mate. He’d become the cockblocker. He yanked his pants from his shoulder and slid them on without turning around. After his cousin’s interruption, they fit easily.

Mara trailed her hand across his chest and headed to the fire. “Do we have a pot for the corn? Or should we just bury them in the coals?”

Indra stared into the clear sky and sucked in the fresh air. He spied Hark heading to the fire.

"I can bury them." Hark scooped out coals, ignoring Mara's gasp. He was a fire dragon. The flames wouldn't hurt him. "Go ahead and dump some in there and I'll spread the coals over them."

Mara, Randy, and a couple of others grabbed armfuls of corn and dropped them in the hole he'd created.

Indra put an armload in.

"That ought to be enough for a while." Hark tossed the coals over the ears of corn.

"Maybe I should find a kettle." Mara looked at the large number of ears left in the container. "Might make it easier."

Indra grabbed her hand. "I'll help you look." He ignored Randy's snort and Hark's sniffing of the air. He must be putting out some pheromones if Hark smelled them. He tried to ruthlessly shove his arousal down.

Hark put a hand on Indra's shoulder. "Blanc, the ice dragon, should be here tomorrow."

Indra inclined his head, excitement sparking in his veins. "Thank you." He tightened his hand on Mara's. Tomorrow, she would be his. He tried to imagine what she'd look like. But it didn't really matter. She'd be magnificent.

"You know, all the new dragonesses are small." Hark grinned. "My brother calls them pocket dragons."

Indra's eyes widened. "Pocket dragons? Truly, Grace is tinier than most dragonesses, but surely, they're not all that small."

Hark nodded. "Yes. My brothers all have tiny mates. Of course, Hope and Faith are sisters, and Grace wasn't huge either." He shrugged. "Mara is small. I imagine she'll be a pocket size too."

"Hmm. Is there a problem with that?" He grimaced. "I just assumed the females were naturally smaller."

"My sisters are close to my size. A bit smaller, but not as much as the new ones." Hark scratched his head. "Maybe they grow with age."

Indra moved toward the cave, Mara gliding beside him. "Maybe." It didn't matter to him. Mara could be any size she wanted. It was the spark within her that attracted him. He glanced at her. Heat swirled in his body. She was gorgeous too, and all his. He hoped neither Randy nor Hark would follow and that maybe he could take her back to her room. Get to know her even better.

"I think a kettle might be in one of the larger storerooms." Mara headed to the larger door that led to the main facility.

Indra hadn't really explored that area like Rog, Grace, and Hark had. He had shown up after scenting the mating pheromones. Mara appeared to know her way around. He snorted. Of course she did. She worked and lived there. He wondered how long she'd been here.

"How long did you spend here?" He might as well ask.

"I was here for about six months. This place had been here a long time before. I believe it was built sometime in the 1950s and updated when it looked like we were losing."

"Losing what?"

"The war."

Indra shook his head. "There was no war. We were attacked. They took out most of our military and we called the rest home. The whole world succumbed to various viruses released across the world." He cleared his throat. "No one knows for sure who started it. It didn't matter in the end. Everyone was affected."

"But our military was fighting. There were stories and pictures on the news." Mara opened a door into a huge storeroom.

Indra snorted. "Lies. Old footage. I think it started in the Middle East, but that is now just a wasteland. Nothing survived. A nomad or two, but without a way to get food and water in and out, they died out."

"I thought Russia attacked."

"I'm sure they took advantage of it. However, air traffic in and out of each country was more damaging than any bombs and missiles. The illness hit most countries before they realized it. Then it was too late." Indra followed Mara down the aisles. "This is huge."

"This is for *extra* things. Each of the apartments above was filled with the basic items. There is a storeroom with food basics. I imagine most of the food items are stale by now. Probably edible, but I'd rather have fresh."

"Me too." Indra looked around the shelves. "A lot of this will be useless. There isn't a ton of electricity around."

"They'll run off the solar electricity. And once the hydroelectric power is hooked up, it should be fine."

"You know, we won't let humans ruin the world again."

Mara stilled, her body stiffening. "We did not ruin the world." Then she drooped, whispering, "Maybe we did."

He snorted. "You wiped each other clean off the face of the earth."

She whirled around and glared at him. "We survived. You said there were still people out there. We planned for all eventualities."

Indra grimaced. “No. You have no idea what the world is like. There are pockets of humans. Some good, some bad. Most just worried about surviving the next day, week, or year.”

“Yeah, well, what did dragons do?” Her jaw jutted out, eyes angry slits.

“We saved humans. We transported them together where there was food, water, and shelter. Company. Your government abandoned them. Hid away in these fancy facilities.” He waved his arm at the items stored. “This could have meant survival for some that didn’t make it. Shelters that weren’t blown up. Medical facilities to help cure the sick. We did what we could.” He laughed. “But your government forgot about even their own. Otherwise, you wouldn’t be waking up now, generations after it fell.”

“They couldn’t save everyone. They didn’t have enough resources.” Her voice raised, making him wince.

“No, they couldn’t.” Indra shrugged. This might not have been a good subject to bring up. “They collapsed. Every government did. All we did was help pick up the pieces.”

Mara huffed. “I’m sure they didn’t foresee that.” She turned, moving down the aisle again. “Let’s find a couple of pots for the fire.”

“You know, even though the government set up these facilities, they have no control anymore.”

Mara ignored him. He would have to take her to some of the human settlements. Let her see what the world was like now. He caught up to her and slid his arm around her shoulder.

She shrugged it off.

He tightened his lips. Yup, he'd screwed up. "I'll look on the higher shelves." Keeping his gaze on the upper shelves, he looked for the pots. They wandered down one aisle, then another.

"Here we go." Mara sounded a lot happier. "There are quite a few here. How many do you think we should grab?"

Indra stuck his head down, perusing the huge pots. "Four? We can cook the corn in them. Should be enough for everyone."

Mara grabbed one, struggling to lift it. "It's heavy."

"Let me." Indra grabbed one in each hand. "I'll just make two trips. It would be awkward carrying all four."

Her jaw dropped, and she closed it with an audible click. "Okay. I'll hold the doors open."

Indra grunted. "That would be helpful." He followed her out, bringing the large vessels. They returned for two more, and he set them near the corn container.

A couple of people came to see what was going on. "What are these for?"

"We've corn roasting in the coals, but figured we can boil a lot more so everyone can have some." Mara waved at the huge stack of corn.

"We can help shuck them." They grabbed armfuls of corn, stripping them efficiently and dumping them in the pots. A couple more came over to help.

Indra sidled up next to Mara. "Let's see if they found your father."

She nodded.

He slipped his arm through hers, relieved when she didn't move away. He guided her toward the group of alpha wolves.

"Did you find my father or brother?"

"Your father is still working in the lab and wouldn't leave. Your brother will speak to us this evening. He was working on the hydropower and needed help. Some of the wolves are assisting your father and brother. Doctor Emma was most eager to help." Morgan chuckled. "I'm sure she'll regret it. Your father—" He looked at her.

Mara sighed. "My father loves the sound of his own voice. Don't get me wrong, he's brilliant. But he loves a captive audience."

The chuckles around the group seemed to relax everyone.

"I should go help him out. There are a lot of people to still wake up." Mara tugged her arm, trying to disengage his.

"I'll help." Indra entwined his fingers with hers. "I can press buttons." He smiled into her wary eyes. "Look at how many shifters we woke up."

Mara tightened her fingers around his. "Okay. I'm sure he'd appreciate the help."

They headed to the cave entrance. Indra tugged Mara closer. He was happy she didn't pull away again. He regretted upsetting her. He wondered if his words were true. Perhaps the government had a plan and they hadn't intended on abandoning their people. It had been a horrific time. He doubted anyone had a plan.

He knew he was bitter about losing his family. But the government's actions had given him back his cousin and his mate. Perhaps it was time to let it go.

~

His words had stung. But it wasn't Indra's fault the truth hurt. It did appear their government had abandoned the people.

It wasn't like that though. Or was it? They'd gathered the best minds and frozen them for the future. If the best minds had stayed, would it have been different? Would a solution to the spreading illnesses have been found?

But plenty of brilliant people refused to go into cryosleep. They'd stayed, hoping to help.

Her father had assured her these people were the logical choice. For all she knew, they had the deepest wallets.

She'd never know. Until they woke up. She was pretty sure if they bought their way in, it would become apparent in short order.

Indra's warmth next to her soothed her fears. It was as if he could conquer anything. Look at when he carried the pots. Two large, heavy, cast-iron kettles she could barely lift. She couldn't stop staring; he didn't even struggle with the weight. She wanted to run her fingers along each defined muscle. Lick him all over. Wallow in his arms.

What had she said as a kid? *I licked it, so it's mine.* She wanted Indra to be hers. She worried she had scared him off with her over-the-top reaction. He looked wary but still reached out.

"I'm sorry. For what I said earlier." She kicked a small rock out of her path, not looking at him. "I didn't want to go into cryo. But I didn't want to be left by myself. I guess I always felt like we were trying to escape."

"I didn't mean to upset you. It was so long ago. I guess to you, it seems like it just happened." He pulled her into his arms, tilting her chin to look at him. "I've lived it." His eyes twinkled. "I even remember the missile hitting this mountain. I was flying over the valley when it exploded. I've always assumed it was a bit of a dud because it did such little damage."

Mara gasped. "I swore I saw a dragon in the sky. I thought I was just seeing things. I had just gone back inside when the missile hit. That was one of the last days we put everyone in the cryogenic pods. After the hit, we worked all night to get everyone under. Dad was worried it carried some type of new disease and wanted to avoid anyone catching it."

Mara was beginning to believe in fate. Maybe Indra was meant to be hers. Maybe she was meant to be his. It felt right, being in his arms.

"No wonder I kept returning here, year after year. I tried to stay away. I wandered the world looking for my cousin. But I always returned here. Somehow, my dragon knew." Indra wrapped his arms around her even tighter. "I'm glad I didn't find you then. It was a bad time for humans. So many died."

"I wish I had met you then."

"Then you would still have been conflicted. You'd have had to choose to be with your family or me. I would never want to make you choose." He smiled, sending heat through her body. "Now you can have both."

Mara stood on her tiptoes and pulled his head down, wanting his lips against hers. The heat in his eyes said he wanted the same. She lost herself in the firmness and warmth of his mouth.

He yanked her up, her toes now dangling and his arms beneath her butt. His lips devoured hers. Her world settled. This was where and when she was supposed to be. She believed this with her whole heart.

"Shall we head back to your rooms?" Indra's voice was rough. Filled with passion. For her.

"Put my daughter down." Doctor Phillip's voice echoed in the large hall. "Tamara, what do you think you are doing?"

Mara turned her head, unfortunately breaking the kiss. She glared at her father. "What does it look like I'm doing?"

"You have better things to do than canoodle with that, that animal."

She busted out laughing. "Canoodle? Really?" She tapped Indra's arm and spoke just for his ears. "Put me down, please. We can continue later."

His blinding smile was worth it. He set her down, keeping his arms around her body.

“There is much to do. I can’t process the pods all on my own.”

Mara rolled her eyes. “I know you’re not on your own, Dad. Anyone can push buttons. Have those you woke up yesterday help.”

He grumbled, “Not everyone can check the data.” He looked outraged. “And someone hit the buttons on one of the nonviable pods. It reeks in there now.”

She bit her lips to keep her giggle in.

Indra shook to keep his chuckle in. “Can you close the lid?”

“Not until it opens up all the way.” Her father’s face turned red.

“Do you still need the pod?” Indra’s nostrils flared.

Mara tried not to retch. The smell was beginning to seep from the cryo lab. A few people came stumbling out, holding their noses and looking green.

“No.”

“Stay here.” Indra shoved open the door. Mara heard him gag. A screech of metal, a curse, and banging could be heard through the door. He stuck his head out, the stench following him. “Go find Rog or Hark. Not Grace, unless she is the only one around.”

Her father ran outside.

Mara followed, wondering why Indra needed one of them specifically. She exited the cave and her father was already leading Rog back.

He waited with the door closed. "Did you find one of them?"

"Dad is coming with Rog."

"Good." He leaned against the door, keeping it closed.

"Why did you need him?"

"Fire dragon. He can burn the corpse and not set fire to anything else. The pod will be ruined though."

"Huh." She didn't know what to say to that. If it got rid of the smell, that was good. She had no idea the dragons could do something like that. "Couldn't you have done it?"

"My fire is less precise than a fire dragon, nor is it as hot. I'd prefer to contain the fire to the one pod." He scowled, looking like he'd sucked a lemon to admit that.

"Good idea. Better safe than sorry." She smiled and he relaxed. He didn't like to admit to something he wasn't good at. But he did. Her heart thumped over. Her insides kept jumping when he was around.

"What is that awful smell?" Rog waved his hand around.

“The reason I need you. We need to cremate a corpse. Someone opened the wrong pod.” Indra pushed open the door.

Mara slammed her hand over her nose.

“If it’ll stop that smell. Let’s get it done.” Rog entered after Indra.

“Mara, don’t get involved with the dragons.” Her dad pulled her back down the hall from the door.

“Why? You are involved with Grace’s mom. Or so I’ve heard. What’s the difference?” She glared at him. “Or are you the only one who can be with a dragon?”

“Grace’s mom and I are just friends. And she’s not a dragon.”

“C’mon, dad. You know that’s not possible. Unless Grace’s dad is a dragon, and she got it from him.” Mara swung her finger in his face. “No. Two different species wouldn’t even be able to have children. It’s impossible.”

“Then how do you explain shifters? They shift from animal to man. They have common ancestries. Look at the DNA. You had no clue they weren’t human. It’s possible.” He grabbed his hair in his fists. “They’ve been around long before the apocalypse.”

“It is not possible to change from one species to another.”

"They've found a way!" He glared into her face. "I don't want you to be an experiment."

"You had no problem making me one." Mara tossed up her hands. "It doesn't matter. What could be cooler than being a dragon, huh? Tell me."

"You don't mean that. Why would you want to become another species?"

"Well, they survived the apocalypse. It's more than most humans did."

"You have a job to do. You're the head doctor for the medical facility. Once we're up and running, we'll restore order. Get the government going again. We'll be in charge."

"Give it up. The government no longer exists, and if you think coming back after who knows how many years, you'll be able to restart the government and have people accept it, you're crazy." Mara clenched her fists, glaring up. He just didn't get it. She did and she hadn't met any humans yet.

But she'd met dragons and werewolves, and they didn't give a hoot about the humans. They weren't going to hide, either. She'd seen their strength. She wouldn't bet against them. Especially when the humans she knew in the facility were fairly non-confrontational. They also had chaffed against government restraints. She couldn't see anyone welcoming it back.

"You'll see." His eyes blazed. "The people will welcome back the law and order of the government."

"No, they won't. The humans have done well." Indra stepped into the hall. "No one is going to pay to support people unwilling to support themselves."

Rog stepped beside him. "And you no longer have access to the things you would use to force them. We made sure of it."

"You all don't have a clue. The government will be welcomed back with open arms." Doctor Phillip's eyes darted down the hall.

Both dragons laughed.

"The world is much bigger and smaller than you remember. Life has changed. For the better," Indra added.

Doctor Phillip stormed off, muttering under his breath. He entered a door farther down the hall.

Rog snorted. "He's going to love what he finds." He grinned. "You know, we can dispose of all the corpses so there are no other accidents with the rest of the pods."

"Eh, they'll just have to be careful. Once they're all woken up, they can decide. It's their people, not ours." Indra shrugged.

Mara was pacing and scowling. She looked down the hall where her father had disappeared. "He makes me so mad." His disapproval just pissed her off. His claims were ridiculous. Even if they were true, what would be more awesome than being a dragon? She went to her frozen sleep, determined to believe in fairy tales, and dammit, she was going to keep believing.

"How about we take a walk?" Indra grabbed her hand and tugged her closer. "Get some fresh air. I could use a bit after being in there." He inclined his head toward the cryo room.

She stopped, looked at the room and the faint smell still coming out, and Indra. "Oh my god. I'm sorry, I didn't even think. That had to be awful."

"It was." Rog ruffled her hair and, smirking, headed toward the outside door, leaving her with Indra.

Mara shook her head. She couldn't believe she had forgotten about the cryo lab like that. Her father drove her crazy. "Let's take a walk. You're right. We could both use some fresh air." She dragged Indra, heading determinedly outside. "Everything will be better outside."

Indra trotted alongside her, a grin on his face.

Mara ignored it. She just wanted to be away from people. It seemed they were everywhere. Constantly interrupting. Chattering until she thought her ears would bleed. "I need some quiet time. With you. You're quiet. Maybe in the trees far from people." It hadn't felt like a lot of people—until it did.

The dragons, the wolves, and even the humans mixed. A low buzz of noise permeated the area even when, at first, it seemed quiet.

Mara always needed refresh time. Being a doctor can be stressful. Being a doctor and working with her father was even worse. Finding a hidden group of people, not even people but *shifters,* was more than she could cope with. Especially after having words with her father.

Indra walked beside her, not saying a word. He held her hand.

Mara slowed her pace. The sounds of the camp receded. She took a deep breath and another.

Indra just squeezed her hand.

She smiled. "I'm better." She continued to walk, heading out of sight. Her goal was to hide among the trees. Let nature ease her soul.

It grew a bit cooler, the deeper into the trees they strolled. The river burbled nearby. Her shoulders relaxed. The tightness in her lungs dissipated.

Indra's hand centered her. His long fingers, entwined with hers, gave her a sense of safety. Mara stopped, closed her eyes, and breathed. Her hand radiated warmth from Indra. Tingles worked their way throughout her body. She stepped closer and lifted her mouth to him.

CHAPTER TEN

He couldn't refuse her invitation. He pressed his mouth to hers, touching just her soft lips and holding her hand. Indra tangled his tongue with Mara's, groaning at her taste.

Mara moaned and leaned into him.

Indra wrapped his arms around her, her hand still held in his, and bent her backward.

She gave him her weight, her trust.

He would never let her down. He nibbled at her throat, enjoying the salty taste of her skin. Heat rose in his body. His pheromones were kicking in. He gathered her flush to him. He lifted her so their mouths were even, the lushness urging him to explore.

Her fingers trailed from his. Her arms encircled his neck. Her legs winding around his hips.

He rubbed his tongue against hers, tasting the sides of her mouth and teeth. He thrust against her crotch, his hands holding her in place. He groaned. He could smell her arousal. Felt the heat emanating from her.

Mara writhed in his arms. The sounds from her throat encouraging him.

He grabbed her shirt but stopped from ripping it off, despite how much he wanted her naked. Instead, he let her hold on to him while he painstakingly unbuttoned her shirt. Finally, he tore it open, pulling it out of her pants and off her arms. He yanked off her bra, tossing it in the same direction as her shirt.

Indra nuzzled her neck, leaving trails of wet kisses down her throat. He boosted her up and latched onto a nipple, sucking and teasing one, then the other.

Mara squirmed, arching her back, offering herself to him.

A tiny meadow on the banks of the river offered a perfect spot to devour her. He walked over, feasting on her breasts the entire way.

Mara's sounds begged him for more.

He wouldn't disappoint. She was his. He couldn't wait anymore. He lay her in the grass, her arms trailing away while he stepped back.

She lifted her arms in entreaty, wordlessly asking him to return.

Indra grunted and stripped off his pants, tossing them aside. His cock bobbed, hitting his abdomen, yearning to fill her heat.

He kneeled and unbuttoned her slacks, ripping them down her legs. He groaned. Beneath, she wore a silky pair of panties. The center drenched with her juices.

She spread her legs. A perfect picture of enticement. His mate. Soon to be his dragoness.

Indra couldn't resist her scent. He dove toward her pussy. Slid a finger between her soaked gusset and her silken lips. He ran it up and down, watching her shudder.

"Please." Mara licked her lips. Her breasts and cheeks rosy with arousal.

He couldn't take it. Indra shredded her panties, the pieces flying everywhere. He rubbed his face in her cunt, spreading her honey all over his face. He nipped her clit, then suckled it.

Mara whined, her hands entangling in his hair, pushing his head where she wanted him.

Indra slid his tongue inside her, devouring her cream. He fingered her, then slid a creamy-coated finger into her ass.

Mara screamed and exploded.

Indra trailed his tongue from her taint to clit. He shoved two fingers inside her pussy, fucking her. He nibbled on her clit, then sucked, feeling her constrict on his fingers and throw back her head in ecstasy. Indra withdrew and slid up her body. "I'm going to make you mine, Mara. Forever and ever. Do you want that?" He took her incoherent babblings as yes.

She wrapped her legs around him, her body seeking to be filled.

Indra slammed home.

Mara's nails tore into his back, her body arching into his.

"You want more?" His tone was guttural. His dragon wild to fuck their mate.

"Yes." Her hips worked under his, keeping up a frantic rhythm, matching his thrusts. "More, more, more."

Indra bit her neck, holding her down. One hand grabbed her breast to feed it to his mouth. The other slid around her ass, holding her to his punishing pumps. One finger slid inside her pretty rosette, thrusting in counterpoint to his cock.

He felt himself swell, his erection hardening even more. He grunted, pounding Mara into the ground.

Her pussy contracted, squeezing him. Mara screamed, her nails embedding into his back.

He exploded, his seed filling her, overflowing while he helplessly pumped into her body.

Her arms dropped to the grass. Her head tilted back with her mouth open.

Indra slid from her body, once again erect. He moved to straddle her head. He admired his prints on her body as much as the sting of her scratches on his back. Her spread legs, his scent mixed with hers while their combined juices flowed from her pussy.

"Oh." Mara breathed out. "You're not done, are you?" She quirked a brow at him, a wicked gleam in her eyes.

"Never." Indra slid his dick down her throat. Adjusting when she choked. He flicked her nipples with his fingers, admiring the tightly furled buds. He deep-throated her, giving her just enough room to breathe between thrusts.

His pheromones filled the air, calling the other dragons to them.

Zeru and Hark swooped down, shifting from their dragons and strode eagerly over, each diving in and nibbling Mara's nipples.

She arched, offering her body to them.

Zeru slid a hand down to play with her pussy, petting her clit.

Mara's wiggled and eagerly arched for more.

Indra thrust harder. His jaw clenched. Nostrils flared. Her mouth worked him like she was sucking his soul from his cock.

Her whimpers were music to his ears.

Indra heard a splash and looked up, his hips still working, enjoying Mara's tight throat.

A silver dragon flowed from the river. His cock red and heavy, protruding from his scales. His tongue flickered out. He looked from Indra to Hark to Zeru. His gaze latched onto Mara. His tongue slid between her nether lips and teased.

Mara writhed beneath them.

The dragon moved to slide the tip of his dick into her cunt.

"Shift." Indra gave a guttural moan. "Now."

The water dragon hissed at him. Stuck the tip of his dick back in.

"Shift." The mating pheromones filled the air, forcing his change. Indra wouldn't let the water dragon hurt her.

"Ahh." The dragon moaned, sliding his now human dick into Mara. He pounded into her.

Indra knew her honey smoothed the way.

The water dragon shoved Hark away, latching onto Mara's nipple.

Indra grunted. His cock pulsed, pouring semen down Mara's throat.

Hark lay with his hand teasing Mara's clitoris and rhythmically squeezing the water dragon's balls. He mouthed the skin of her hip in time with his thrumming on her clit.

The water dragon grunted, thrusting until Hark shoved him away from Mara.

The water dragon's cum sprayed across Mara's pussy as he humped outside of her, covering her in his gloss.

The dragons rotated positions. Mara continued to cry out in pleasure over and over. The pheromones in their semen driving her wild.

Indra slid under Mara, holding her to him. He bucked into her rosette, breaching her between her sweet cheeks.

Each dragon crested, covering her in their jizz, rubbing it into her skin.

Indra licked his lips, the taste of cum leaking into his mouth.

They all shifted positions. The mating frenzy made them wilder each time they came.

Mara keened and writhed beneath them all. Begging for more.

Indra was once again lost in Mara, watching the beauty of her body as they performed the ritual to change his mate into a dragon.

Mara convulsed, her body clamping down on the men inside her while she screamed in pleasure.

The mating was nearing an end.

Indra thrusted wildly. His balls drew up, signaling his coming eruption. Indra shouted, Mara writhing under him. Indra pulsed, his sperm fertilizing his mate.

The other dragons rubbed their sperm into her skin. Each of them jerked off on her nubile body to ensure her change into one of their own.

Indra continued to plunder her, shooting stream after stream into her fertile, changing body. Exhausted, Indra pulled from her body, leaning up to kiss her ruby lips.

Mara smiled at him, licked her bottom lip, and dropped her head back to the ground, her eyes closing.

Indra chuckled and rolled to her side.

Finally, they all lay back. The men surrounding, protecting Mara. As it should be.

Indra sighed, his heart at peace. Mara was now his. He'd explained the process to her, even if she didn't believe him. She would. He'd heard what she said to her father. She wanted to be a dragon. He didn't know he could be this happy.

Mara's chest heaved. She lay sprawled on the grass, covered in glistening cum. Her hard nipples pointed to the sky. Her pussy pink and glossy.

The water dragon snuggled up against her, opposite Indra.

"I'm Bruno."

"Indra." Indra caressed Mara's body, amazed at her perfection.

"Zeru."

"Hark."

The clearing was silent.

Mara snorted; her eyes still closed. "I'm Mara if anyone wants to know."

Bruno choked, then laughed. It sounded rusty like he rarely let it out. "Very nice to meet you, Mara."

Indra chuckled and the others joined in.

Mara groaned. This one signaled pain rather than pleasure.

Zeru jumped up. "We'll get food."

Zeru and Hark shifted and flew off.

Bruno kissed her nipple and slid a finger through her lower lips. He winked and slid his finger in his mouth, sucking down Mara's essence. "I, too, will assist."

Indra growled while Bruno laughed and flew away.

~

Holy fuck. Mara couldn't move. She didn't want to. Every bit of her body was boneless. She didn't care she was naked. Didn't care she was sprawled out across the grass. Didn't care her hair was matted with all that sperm. She didn't even flinch when Bruno, a man she'd never met before, ran a finger through her pussy. She lay there, staring at the sky, sucking in air.

If this convinced Indra she was his mate, sign her up again. She was willing to reassure him as many times as he wanted.

A tremor ran through her. A burning started in her womb then eased. Her bones ached. A dull throb. Another tremor hit. She panted, trying to draw in air. The burning spread to every point inside her.

At some point, she was aware of the dragons returning and a fire being built. She screamed. So much pain. Even being cradled in Indra's arms hurt.

Indra walked into the river with her, peppering her face with kisses. "I had no idea. I'm sorry. I'm so sorry."

What was he talking about? The burning started again. The cool river helped the pain. She burrowed in his arms. Her bones were breaking, each one, over and over again. She'd swear to it.

Indra held her so close they seemed as one flesh. The lapping of the water against her skin relaxed her.

"My brother Crag said you'll be able to take some of the pain from her. Try to connect telepathically with her." Hark didn't make any sense.

Mara couldn't hold back her tears. She curled up, arms tightly wrapped around her middle. Fire bloomed in her womb, her stomach, and through her lungs. This must be spontaneous combustion. "It hurts."

"I'm sorry." Indra's tears dripped onto her face.

Why was he crying? "Not your fault." She tried to open her eyes, but even they hurt.

"It's the change." Indra buried his face in her hair. "I'm sorry."

She ignored him, the fire licking along her veins. She moaned, her body breaking. Every skin cell hurt. She clung to Indra, let him gather her up. She wanted to crawl inside his body and leave her broken one behind. She screamed inside, the torment intolerable.

I'll help. Indra spoke into his mate's mind. "I don't think it's working."

Mara continued to writhe in agony. At some point, they'd returned to the river bank.

Mara wept as her bones broke and reformed. Scales formed on her skin, receding and forming with each tortured breath. This couldn't be possible.

Mara's brain started working again. Sluggishly.

I'm sorry. I love you. Forgive me. Indra's voice repeated over and over in her head.

The pain lessened.

But now her stomach was growling. It was empty, ravenous to be filled. Mara roared, confused at all the sensations bombarding her.

Meat was shoved in front of her face and she gobbled it down. She ate and ate. Finally, all the pain receded. Her eyes closed, exhaustion weighing her down.

Go to sleep, my love. Indra's hands ran along her body, soothing the pain away.

"I think I lost my mind," Mara croaked out. "I'm hearing voices in my head." She ignored the chuckles around her.

My voice only, I think. Indra caressed her hair, smoothing it away from her face.

She'll hear all of us. The mating bound us all. That sounded like Zeru.

I do not wish to hear Earth, Air, and Fire. The little female is fine.

Who is that?

I am Bruno, little dragon. They are earth, air, and fire dragons. I do not need to remember their names.

Yup, she was definitely going crazy. "I'm going crazy." Mara ignored their laughter. She was too damn tired. She realized Indra was lying next to her as a dragon. Probably to protect her. She wiggled over to his side and laid her head down. She was feeling better. She stretched out and scratched the grass with her claw—

She froze. Her claw?

Mara screamed and jumped up. "What happened to me?" She turned to look at her body and spied a tail. She twisted in circles to look at it. "INDRA!"

The dragons crowded her until she stopped moving. The feel of their bodies calmed her down. This couldn't be real. There was no way.

"What happened to me?" she shrieked. She was a friggin' dragon. A dragon. Scales and everything. Mara twisted her head to see if she had wings, like Indra. She hissed. This was all his fault.

"You're a dragon. My mate." Indra tried to be reasonable. She could hear it in his voice.

"I know I'm a dragon. This is impossible." All the dragons winced at her tone. As well they should.

"Not impossible. I've seen it happen three times recently." Hark grinned. If you could call it that, with all those sharp teeth gleaming in the firelight.

She snorted. "I'm a doctor. It is not possible to become a different species." She stamped her foot. "It's not!"

"I described the process to you. You agreed. You even looked forward to it." Indra nudged her with his head.

He had actually. Mara sputtered. "Well, it sounded kind of hot." Heat climbed her neck and cheeks. Hopefully, her scales hid it. "But I never thought it was real."

"I heard you tell your father you'd like to be a dragon." Indra's whole face fell. "Did you not mean it?"

"No. It sounded cool and it pissed him off. But I never thought it could really happen." She laid her head on Indra's arm and snuggled up to him.

"There is no going back now." Indra wrapped his wing around her, pulling her in tight.

The other dragons crowded around her.

She heard the crunch of something from one of the dragons and hissed.

The crunching stopped.

A wave of exhaustion flowed through her. "I'm just so tired."

The noise started again. Someone was eating her meat. She was going to object but decided to ignore it. They could get her more later. She could barely move.

"Sleep, little mate. You need to build your strength back."

Mara closed her eyes, grumbled at the chewing and crunching, and slept. Or tried to. The male dragons were disturbing her.

Zeru shook his head. "You remember when you ate Grace's food? She almost gutted you. You just don't learn."

Hark snickered, his mouth full. *I waited until she was ready to fall asleep. I'll get her more in the morning.*

"Don't talk in my head, fire dragon." Bruno got up, snagged a carcass and tossed it to Indra. He grabbed another for himself and returned to Mara's side.

Zeru moved, his warmth gone, but he, too, came back and the crunching commenced around her.

How was a girl to sleep? She huddled up next to Indra, trying to ignore them. She snapped at the closest dragon, her jaws closing on nothing but air.

Don't bite anyone unless you want to kill them or make them very sick. Indra's tone was just enough to catch her attention.

Why?

A female dragon's bite is venomous. A human would die. It won't kill me because I'm your mate, but it won't be pleasant.

Then be quiet. I'm tired.

The noise stopped, started up, and quickly ended.

Sorry.

She didn't know who apologized and didn't really care. They were all quiet after that. Their deep breathing lulled her into a peaceful slumber.

CHAPTER ELEVEN

Indra woke slowly. His mate was burrowed under his wing. Indra couldn't help the pride bursting to be let out. His mate, HIS MATE, was gorgeous and smart. He had a mate. If he could have jumped up without disturbing her, he'd be doing aerial loops in the sky.

The sun was just beginning to rise, its rays peeking over the mountain. The day was dawning on the best day ever.

The other dragons were sprawled out, still asleep. The water dragon lay half in and half out of the river. Zeru and Hark were lying head to head. Hark somehow was sleeping on his back. They all lay loosely around Mara, protecting her.

Not that there was much out here to harm her. But Mara hadn't even walked yet. Hopefully, she loved her new life.

Hark suddenly flipped up, looking around, his eyes large and unfocused. "Wha?" He shot off a little flame and shook. "I'll go hunt."

Zeru growled and lifted his head, glaring at Hark's retreating figure. While not singed, his snout had smoke around it from Hark's flame. "What's going on?"

"Hark jumped up and flew off to hunt." Indra spoke low enough to not wake Mara. Yesterday was hard on her.

"Why did he flame me?" Zeru blew the smoke away from his face.

"No clue. He flipped out, let out a flame, and flew off."

"He is an erratic male." Zeru shook his head. "And how is the little dragoness doing?"

Indra glanced down at her. She was still sleeping. Her scales were green, with silver tips, edged in red. Her claws were black with blue talons. Each movement she made showed off her beautiful coloring.

"She is doing well. " Indra rubbed his snout along her head. "I know she has this."

Bruno lifted and slid into the river. He swam off without saying a word.

Indra wondered if they would ever see him again.

For certain Earth.

Indra looked at the water. "I'm not sure I like that dragon."

"I think he has been alone a long time." Zeru also watched the water the silver dragon returned to.

Mara stretched her legs, her claws spreading and clenching, and a big yawn hit her while she was doing so. “I had the weirdest dream.” She rubbed her head against Indra. “I dreamed I turned into a dragon.” She chuckled. “I’m too old to be sleeping on the ground. My whole body aches.”

“It wasn’t a dream.” Indra prayed she wouldn’t start screaming again.

Mara’s eyes popped open. “It had to be.”

“Nope.” He really hoped she didn’t regret this. A pissed-off dragoness was no joke.

She stretched her front legs out, looking at them. Turned her head and took as much as she could see over her shoulder. “Hmm.” She flapped her wings, causing the dying fire to flare up. “Can I fly?”

“Technically.” Zeru watched her.

“What’s that mean?” Mara sat up.

Indra missed her heat against him. “You can fly, but you’ll have to learn how.”

“When do I get to try?” She was staring at her talons. “They’re so pretty.” She clicked them. “Probably deadly, too.”

“Yes. You’ll pierce almost any living thing with them if you want to.” Indra laughed. “And I’ll teach you to fly.”

“I’ll help. It is my element, after all,” Zeru added.

A cow, followed by another, landed on the ground, making them all jump. Hark's laughter followed him as he zoomed away.

Mara pounced, tearing into the meal he'd dropped.

Zeru and Indra backed away, leaving her to feed without interference.

Mara crunched, smacked, and devoured her meal, going through both cows in no time. Just as she finished the second, another pair dropped. She snagged a third.

"I will hunt for mine." Zeru leaped into the sky.

Mara's gaze followed him.

Even when Indra lost sight of him as Zeru's camouflage kicked in, Mara seemed to still see him.

Bruno slid out from the river's banks, spewing a mass of fish in front of Mara. *Delicacies from the river, little fish.*

Thank you. Mara finished the cow she was gnawing on and started eating the fish. The wiggle in her tail showed her appreciation for the change of fare.

Indra cautiously pulled the last cow over to him. It would suffice. He needed to stay with his mate until she acclimated to her new form and could change swiftly between either. Mara eyeballed him but didn't raise a fuss when he began to eat. He could show her how to hunt later and eat a bit more.

Hark dropped down with another pair of cows. He tossed one to Bruno and another to Indra. "I ate while I hunted."

"Thanks." Indra grabbed the cow and filled his stomach.

Bruno inclined his head toward him and pulled the carcass to him. He settled in to eat.

The clearing was filled with the sounds of the dragons enjoying their meal.

Mara finished and shoved the fish she hadn't finished toward Indra and Hark. She sighed, a smile on her face. "They were delicious, Bruno."

Welcome, little fish.

Indra inwardly groaned. He felt he'd be seeing a lot of the water dragon. Mara seemed to enjoy his company, and he hers. Indra hadn't realized mating with Mara would open a pathway for all the dragons to speak to each other telepathically. He hadn't tried to talk to the others telepathically after changing Grace, so he didn't know he could. Zeru never mentioned it, and since Hark and Rog were brothers, he assumed that is why they could. If he'd known, the last couple of days would have been easier. He sighed. It would take getting used to. Not to mention teaching Mara how to keep a conversation private.

Mara wobbled over to the water to drink.

Indra chuckled, watching her carefully place one foot in front of the other. He saw her concentrating, trying to figure out how to walk with four feet instead of two.

Her legs splayed out when she plopped down to reach the water.

Bruno shook his head with a twinkle in his eyes while observing her.

Zeru landed and slaked his thirst next to Mara.

"I'm pretty sure we missed the meeting they planned to have last night." Hark wiggled his tail over the fire, dousing any glowing embers. "What do you think they decided?"

"I will wait to speculate. We'll return to the base soon enough." Zeru looked around the clearing. He shifted and started picking up Mara's clothes. He handed the bundle to Indra. "She'll probably want these."

"Thank you." Indra shook them out, folding them at his feet. He was sure Zeru was correct. Humans were funny about nudity.

Mara backed up from the water, walking a bit more easily. She turned, swiping Bruno with her tail. She looked at him wide-eyed.

Bruno chuckled and shook his head. *You'll learn.*

"Why do you keep talking in my head instead of out loud?" Mara's tail swished behind her.

To get you used to speaking telepathically. It's hard to talk out loud if you're underwater.

"Hmm. Yeah, I guess it would be." Mara nodded.

And sometimes stealth is a good thing. Bruno finished the cow and dipped his snout and talons in the water, fastidiously cleaning them.

Indra agreed. Sometimes, secrecy was necessary.

"Are all shifters able to talk telepathically? Wouldn't your brain be awful noisy hearing everyone else?" Mara stared at them, the fascination plain on her face.

"Clans can speak to each other, and so can mates," Zeru added. "Dragons involved in a mating, like we were, are a type of clan. We forge a bond during mating. It's why we can all hear each other. With time, you'll be able to converse with us without the others overhearing. We'll all have to learn since the path is so new."

Indra lifted his brows. He hadn't anticipated the connection between them all. Luckily for them, they would be able to control it. *I can speak with my cousin Randy and his family because of our blood relation, even though we are two different species. Or I could while they were still alive.* He couldn't stop the mournful note in his voice. Their loss still hurt.

"How do I change back to human?" Mara frowned. "I'll be able to, right? Go from human to dragon and back?"

"Yes. We can try that now." Indra smiled at her. "Or do you want to learn to fly first?"

Mara beamed at him. "I'd love to fly. But I think I need to learn to change back and forth first. If my lack of coordination continues in this form, learning to fly might take me a while."

Hark laughed. "Good idea."

Bruno stared at them, his tail swishing in the water.

"So, how do I do it?" Mara sat facing Indra.

"It's really simple. Just picture your human form, concentrate, and you should shift."

"That seems simple." Mara donned a look of intense concentration. "Is there any part in particular I should focus on?"

"What do you mean?" Indra flapped his wings slowly. "Here, I'll show you." He shifted in the blink of an eye. He opened his arms. "See, easy."

Mara snorted. "Yeah, that showed me nothing."

"Think about how you look as a human." Indra frowned. "It should work."

Mara closed her eyes and thought about how she looked. Her dark hair, her blue eyes. The pale color of her skin. She thought about height. Mara opened her eyes and looked at her arm. Or what should have been her arm. She grimaced. All she saw were scales. "Okay, that wasn't easy. I'm still a dragon."

Zeru shifted and placed his hand on Indra's shoulder as Indra started to open his mouth. "You don't have to close your eyes. You can if it helps. But just think to yourself, be a human. You don't have to think about anything like hair or eye color. That will come automatically."

Mara nodded. It would be easier to close her eyes, she figured. She closed them. I'm a human. She didn't feel any different. She opened her eyes and drooped a bit. She still wore scales.

"Oh, for pity's sake. It's like you've never done this before." Hark swaggered in front of the two men. "Look at all this luscious man meat." He waved at the three of them. "Just imagine you wanted to fuck your mate, and you can't as a dragon."

Mara had been trying to ignore their naked forms. She only saw most men naked on an exam table. It was hard to get turned on when they were there because of an illness or sickness. None of her patients ever turned her on. Looking at the three prime specimens before her, she knew why. They were magnificent. She checked out Hark and Zeru, but her main focus was Indra.

"No, I can't." She eyeballed him, checking Indra out from head to toe. His dark hair and his gleaming green eyes drew her in. His muscular body with the wolf tattoo on his chest. Her eyes slid down his taut abdomen, following his glory trail. She waved her hand in front of her face to cool off.

Wait. What? She looked at her hands and crowed. "I did it!" She threw her hands in the air and danced around. She faced the men again and flushed. She flopped her head into her hands. Good heavens, she was bouncing around with all her bits and pieces showing. She saw exactly what they thought of her. Every one of them saluted her below their waist.

Indra was growling at the other men. “Mine.” He leaned over, grabbed a pile of something, and stalked toward her. He blocked the men’s view and handed her the discarded clothes from yesterday.

“Did you want me to try to change into a dragon again? And back?”

Indra took back the clothes, handing her a piece at a time. “No. We probably should get back. We missed the meeting last night.”

“Oh, I forgot about that.” Mara slipped her bra on. Her shirt and finally her pants. She looked around the meadow. “Where did I leave my shoes?”

Zeru handed them to her. “Here they are.”

“I think we need to talk when we get back. I have a few questions.” Like why was he now growling at Hark and Zeru? It’s not like they hadn’t been all up and personal last night. He wasn’t growling at Bruno, but she imagined it was because he was still a dragon.

Indra leaned forward and kissed her. His lips soft yet firm. A quick nip to her bottom lip and he pulled back.

Mara groaned and reached for him.

Indra kissed her nose and stepped back. “Let’s head back. I’ll carry you.”

Mara nodded. She loved flying in his hands, er, claws. She couldn’t wait to learn to fly.

Hark and Zeru were already dragons and lifting into the sky. A splash behind her was Bruno swimming upriver toward the facility.

Indra was airborne and swooped her up in his claws.

"Woo hoo!" Mara yelled out in glee.

Indra whooped above her and they flew back to base.

Mara lay in his claws, knowing she was safe. She eagerly scrutinized the land they flew over. There were various crops other than corn. They were not in even rows but a bit haphazard. They looked healthy, with only a hint that they had been originally orderly planted. "I'm surprised the crops are still growing."

"Oh, I came here every few years and planted them from the previous year's crops. Occasionally, some humans would pass through and harvest what they needed."

"Why would you do that?"

"It made me happy to see things grow. Plus, if crops didn't grow in other areas due to weather or storms, food was always available so no one starved."

Mara wanted to hug him. His consideration for others, especially a different species, ignited a fire in her heart. Oh, she could love this man.

"You're a good man."

“Dragon.” His smug tone made her want to swat him. His angle changed downward.

Mara assumed they were close to the facility. She sat up in preparation for landing, grabbing one of Indra’s digits to steady herself.

He opened his claws, releasing her. After shifting, he snagged a pair of pants his cousin tossed and slid them on.

Such a shame. Mara smothered a giggle with her hand. It really was though. She could ogle Indra twenty-four-seven.

Randy slung his arm over her shoulders.

Indra scrambled over, sliding his arm over her and knocking Randy’s off.

Randy’s grin and wink at Mara had Indra snorting.

Mara snuggled into Indra’s side.

Hark, Zeru, and even Bruno sauntered over.

Randy looked from them to her and grinned. “So, the mating’s complete, I assume. I’ll go grab some more pants.”

“We have ours.” Zeru and Hark opened their packs and stepped into a pair of shorts.

Hark said, “We had our bags with. I don’t go anywhere without it.”

Bruno’s deep voice caught Mara’s attention. “I don’t have clothing. Is it required?”

Bruno was stockier than the other dragons. Not fat, just wider and taller. He was as muscular as the rest, not an ounce of fat to be seen. His hair gleamed white, while his eyes were a mix of green and blue. Similar to the sea she remembered as a kid. She tried to not look down but blushed because she did anyhow. His cock was at rest but even flaccid, it was impressive.

Indra poked her side. "Dragons don't share."

Her mouth dropped open. "Seriously? I recall something a bit different last night."

Bruno chuckled but didn't say a word.

"Only to make you a dragon," Hark whispered. "The change requires multiple applications of sperm to change a woman into a dragon. That's why we normally have three or more participate. But that is the only time a dragon shares his mate. Necessity."

Indra ground his teeth so loud she could hear it. "Quit looking at his cock."

Mara's eyes flew to Indra's. "Sorry. It's just there."

Bruno chuckled again.

Zeru snorted.

Randy laughed. "I'll go find you a pair of pants. Why don't you come with? You're drawing a crowd."

Bruno's cheeks pinked.

Mara bit her lips, trying not to laugh. She didn't think he could blush, but surprise, surprise. She looked around, and quite a few females looked mighty appreciative of the view.

Bruno followed Randy, but not before she saw his blush darken. Not to mention, he rose at the women ogling him, giving them even more to appreciate.

Indra sniggered.

Morgan walked over. "We postponed the meeting until this morning."

"I'm sorry." Indra sobered. "We didn't mean to delay it."

"No, the engineer and Doctor Phillip," Morgan lowered his voice, "were exhausted. We figured having them fresh would be better. Most of the humans' pods have been activated and should wake up later today. We'll have the meeting shortly after everyone finishes eating."

Mara noticed most of the wolves were in human form, with a few roaming around in fur. The humans were side-eyeing the wolves. She sniffed. She could smell their fear. She raised her nose, testing the air again. She could also tell the difference between the shifters and the humans.

Previously, she couldn't tell by looking at them if they were in human form. "That's cool," she whispered.

"What's cool?" Indra rubbed his head against hers. His fingers playing with a lock of her hair.

"I can tell the difference between humans and shifters by their smell."

"You couldn't before?"

"No. The human olfactory system is fairly inefficient."

CHAPTER TWELVE

Indra was ready to get this meeting over with. He wanted time with his mate but doubted it would happen until tonight. He admired Mara's seeming acceptance of being changed into a dragon and hoped she had truly accepted it. Unfortunately, there was nothing to be done about it.

He sniffed her hair, nuzzling her ear. She didn't reek of anxiety or panic. She seemed eager to experience everything he offered. He grimaced. She definitely enjoyed the experience last night. Hopefully, Hark's explanation nipped her desire for multiple partners again in the bud. He'd hate to tear apart any dragons who thought to share her.

"What are you growling about?" Mara tilted her head.

"I didn't realize I was." He needed to keep his thoughts under control. Mara had done nothing to set him off. It was all him. Even though he knew she only wanted him, he couldn't help his jealousy.

Doctor Phillip approached Morgan and spoke to him. His son followed behind him. He waved at Mara.

She waved back. "I'm going to have to go over all the data later. I'd like to see what triggered the loss of the people in the pods."

"Yes. I'm sure Hark or Rog will help dispose of the bodies once the rest have awakened."

"If they have family, we'll see what their wishes are. It might be a day or two until they decide."

"If they died from an illness or disease that is contagious at all, they'll need to be burned. We can't take the chance of it spreading." Indra wondered how they would know. "Will you be able to tell from the data what they died from?"

"Probably. My dad said certain things would trigger the death." Mara flattened her lips,

He approved the doctor's foresight, though Mara's tone indicated she did not.

"Can I have everyone's attention?" Morgan stood on a rock and clapped his hands together. "Once we were woken, I found out there are more facilities across the country like this." He gestured to Doctor Phillip and his son, Christopher. "The doctor will give us a bit more information."

"Hello and welcome to a new chance at life." Doctor Phillip bowed.

Indra groaned silently. The doctor was sure to drone on.

"This facility should have been woken up fifty years after the apocalypse. The dragons have told us that the time has been between one and three centuries. According to the computers, two hundred years have passed."

Indra shrugged. They didn't keep time like the humans did.

"They have said that approximately nine generations of humans have passed." He sighed. "Regardless, it has been longer than we anticipated. According to the original plan, the first facility that should have been activated was supposed to send people out to the next one and the next after that." Doctor Phillip lifted his chin. "I don't know if the other facilities were ever awakened." He sighed. "My son has been trying to set up a secondary power source to assist the solar power that runs the facility. The group working with him should have it up and running by tomorrow." The doctor paused and looked around with a smile.

There was a smattering of applause.

"We've been trying to establish radio contact with the other facilities. Unfortunately, our top two radioman were among the group that didn't wake up." He raised his hands. "One of the main engineers is working on getting the radio working, but all we receive is static. It could be the other facilities are not working or the antennas are down. I don't know if it will eventually work, but it's worth a try."

Some nodded in agreement. Mainly the humans in the group.

"However, since there was a hidden cryonic lab set up for shifters in each facility, the shifters are willing to check out the other facilities." He stopped when the crowd noise rose. He sighed. "Yes, shifters are real. In this facility, the werewo.."

Morgan loudly cleared his throat.

"Yes, yes, my bad. The wolf shifters are willing to go check on the other groups."

Hark stepped forward. "The dragons are willing to go with. We can arrange to fly a few people to cut travelling time."

"Good, good." He gestured to the humans, who were getting loud in front. "There have been shifters in the world far longer than you can imagine, living side by side with humans. The lower cryo lab contains wolves, bears, and various cat shifters."

The group in front, humans, of course, were getting louder, protesting something they couldn't do a thing about.

Indra scowled at them. They acted as if they owned the world. Wait until they figured out how the world had changed.

"Please settle down. If it wasn't for them, we would still be frozen. At some point, our bodies would have shut down, and we all would have died. They woke us up, fed us, and cleaned the passageway so we could get outside and breathe in the fresh air. Without them, we wouldn't be here."

Indra sniffed. At least the doctor told them how it was.

The group in front settled down, glancing around. Since almost everyone wore human skin, they had nothing to focus on. They turned back to listen to the doctor.

"Everyone had quarters assigned to them before we were frozen. You should all remember your assignments. If you don't, the listing is on the wall outside the lab. I printed it out this morning. You can set the locks on your quarters for your bioscan. No need for keys, of course."

He cleared his throat. "We'll go to check on the other facilities across our great nation. Hopefully, everyone else is already awake. Morgan will coordinate the team going to each facility. They will be prepared to check the cryo labs and begin the wakeup process if needed. Once that is started, they will continue to the next step. Morgan, if you will." He waved the attention back to the alpha wolf.

"Yes, Doctor Phillip covered most of it. We originally thought of sending separate teams out, but we have decided to send one team of shifters and humans." He looked over the crowd. "Indra, are there more IBC containers available?" He waved his hand at the container of corn. "How many people can you carry comfortably in those containers?"

"Depending on the weight of the people, probably four. Any more than that, and we would have to stop more often."

"So, we have five dragons that can help." He nodded.

"Six," Bruno spoke up. "I will help."

"Wonderful. If the dragons can carry four people each, we can send a team of twenty-four. We can take twelve shifters and twelve humans. Having someone who can read the information on the computers would be beneficial. Doctor Phillip suggested Doctor Tamara Phillip would be a good choice to go, along with his son, the chief engineer, to help if there are power issues at the facilities. The rest will be volunteers."

"Should I volunteer as a dragon and fly people?" Mara frowned. "What do you think?"

Indra caressed her face. “I think you need to learn how to fly first. Plus, it isn’t as easy as you think. You’ll have to build up strength to fly long distances. You can practice along the way. But you shouldn’t be burdened yet.”

“Okay.” Mara nodded. “That all makes sense.”

Indra leaned in and gave her a quick kiss. He was thrilled Mara was thinking as a dragon.

“If you’re interested and believe you can help, please come talk to me.” Morgan stepped down from the rock, giving Doctor Phillip a hand climbing down.

“I need to check the information on the deceased pods.” Mara stepped up on her toes and pulled Indra’s head down for a kiss. “I’ll see you later.”

When she left to speak to her father, he turned to Bruno. “I’m surprised you want to go. I imagine we’ll be flying across the country.”

Bruno shrugged. “I don’t mind. Water dragons don’t typically stay together unless we live in the ocean. The rivers inland are sometimes too small to support many of us.” He smirked. “Plus, I think little fish will be entertaining. Watching her learn to fly and hunt.”

Indra chuckled. “I think you are right. She took to being turned well, though. Maybe she won’t have any problems learning.”

Hark slapped a hand on Indra's shoulder, making him jump. "I can't wait to see that. My brother's mates were fun to watch and tease." He grinned and walked off.

Randy wandered over. "So, cousin, I wondered about that tattoo on your chest." His shit-eating grin told Indra he knew exactly what it was. "Did you miss me that much?"

Indra bared his teeth at him.

Randy just laughed, then sobered. He hugged Indra. "I'm sorry you had to go through that. I can't imagine it was easy."

"No, it wasn't." He squeezed Randy back. "But I'm glad to see you." He waved at his chest. "I should see about getting it removed."

Randy's jaw dropped.

Indra snickered. "Humans can't do that. I don't know of any that can anymore."

"I guess you'll just have to keep wearing my face on you then." Randy grinned.

"At least it's of your pretty face." Indra looked at his tattoo. "Or should I say your better face?" The tattoo of his cousin's wolf was from a photo they'd taken together. But he'd had them just tattoo his wolf's face. He should have had them do the two of them together, but in his grief, he decided on just his cousin. Indra rubbed it like he'd done many times in the past, when he was missing Randy.

"Shall we start waking the next group?" Rog approached with his arm around Grace. "I think we need to get them all up. Some of them might want to go with."

"Yes, since we now know they came here voluntarily," Grace added. "No one wanting to attack, like you guys thought."

"I can grab a few wolves to help. We're just waiting to head to the next facility." Randy waved at a group of people nearby. "Hey, over here."

The group came closer.

"What's up?" the woman first to reach them asked.

"We need help waking up the rest of the shifters. As many as possible to help."

"Sure." She cocked her head and went silent.

She was talking to her pack mates. Wolves always had a tell when they spoke telepathically. He should get the rest of the dragons to help too. *We need to go wake up the rest of the shifters. Can you help?*

I'll meet you there. I'm hunting for the humans that will be waking soon. Zeru must have missed the meeting.

Be right there. Hark landed near the fire, dropping his burden of cattle.

What is this waking up you are doing? Bruno asked.

The old government set up facilities like this and cryonically froze humans and shifters to wake up in the future. Unfortunately, no one woke them up until Rog, Grace, and Hark found them. Indra added, *you volunteered but didn't know what we were doing?*

It gets lonely. I haven't met other dragons in years. Bruno shrugged. *Plus, it gets me away from here and all these women looking at me.*

The dragons all laughed.

Indra slapped him on his shoulder. *Come on, then. We'll show you what to do.*

They headed into the cave and to the lower-level cryonics laboratory to finish waking the other shifters.

~

Mara rubbed her temples. She looked at the readings from the non-viable pods. Everyone inside the pods had died from a filoviridae virus. She had no clue why it wasn't detected. They probably weren't even programmed in. She didn't remember seeing it on the list or requesting it. Without further investigation, she couldn't tell if they passed from the Marburg or Ebola viruses. She needed to talk to her father. She didn't want to even open the pods. For all she knew, the pod gel was infected.

Marburg had a sixty-two percent fatality rating. Ebola ranged from twenty-five to ninety percent fatality rating. She shuddered. Being in the pod, they wouldn't have received any of the treatments that could have saved them.

She was surprised she hadn't seen any symptoms, as most of them started within a few days. Neither of these viruses were normal in the United States. But who knows what was in those missiles. They could easily have been carrying payloads with germ warfare. It could have even been in the missile that damaged the facility on the last day.

"Tamara, what have you found?" He looked at the papers she'd spread out on the desk. "Did you find out why the pods stopped working?" Doctor Phillip frowned, looking at the results. "The pods didn't shut down? This makes no sense."

"Dad. The pods didn't stop working. The people in them died. They had some type of filoviridae virus. Even with treatment, most people who catch them will die. Both have high mortality rates." She shook her head. "The pods don't provide any type of treatment. They are just for stasis."

"They were programmed to shut down in case of Category A contaminants. Are you telling me that isn't the case?"

"These viruses fall under Category C by the CDC. So, I guess not? You programmed them. You tell me."

"Then they should still be alive, shouldn't they?" He walked over and tapped on the closest pod with a non-viable subject. "But they're not."

"No. I can only assume they contaminated the gel in the pod once their bodies began to decompose. They all must have died within a month of being put in their cryo pods."

"I would like you to perform autopsies on the bodies. To double check the cause of death." He turned to her. "That won't be a problem, will it?"

"Yes, yes, it will. I won't take the chance of the disease spreading. These bodies need to be burned." Mara rubbed the back of her neck.

"No. I'm sure the families will want to bury them. We'll open the pods in the morning and take them out. The backhoe is being readied to open the graves."

"Why take them out? The pods are close enough to coffins to bury them in them." Mara's eyes bounced from pod to pod, avoiding looking at the ones still occupied and shut.

"Because I want an autopsy."

Mara flexed her hands. She realized her foot was tapping the ground and stopped.

What is wrong? Indra's voice almost had her sagging in relief.

My father wants an autopsy on the dead bodies. They died of highly contagious viruses. I don't feel comfortable doing it.

Then do not. His deep voice comforted her.

What if he opens them anyway? She clenched her jaw and glared at her father. *He just might to get his way.*

Do you think your father opened the pod that Rog had to incinerate?

Her eyes widened. *Possibly. I don't know how anyone could have mistakenly opened it like he said. I need to test everyone who was in the room to see if they were exposed. This could be catastrophic.*

Is he in there now?

Yes.

We'll be right there. Bruno, Zeru, Hark. I need all the dragons in the original cryonics room. ASAP. Randy, grab Morgan and follow the dragons in. We have a problem. Indra's frustration was evident in his tone.

Mara watched her father go from one pod to the other. He didn't touch any of the buttons. Hopefully, he remembered the stink when the one pod was opened.

The door swung open with enough force to hit the wall outside. Indra said, "Get away from the pods."

The rest of the group Indra had called followed on his heels. They must have been nearby.

"Doctor Phillip." Morgan approached him. "May I ask what is going on?"

"Nothing to concern yourself over. Just a routine procedure Doctor Tamara will perform."

Morgan glanced at her.

Mara was shaking her head.

"And what procedure is that?" He clasped his hands behind his back. "Does it involve the deceased in the room?"

"Yes." His smarmy smile said Morgan wouldn't understand. "She'll perform autopsies to determine cause of death."

"No. The fumes inside the pods are toxic. Don't you remember the smell from the one opened yesterday?"

"They died from a filoviridae virus. Those are highly contagious. I can't guarantee they aren't still active." Mara adjusted the edges of the white medical coat she'd donned upon entering the room. "I don't think it's worth the chance. Minimum casualty death rating on the most innocuous one is sixty-two percent." She shook her head. "It's not worth the chance."

"You can take them up to the infectious disease lab and review the samples from the bodies there."

Mara's draw dropped. "Parade the samples through the building? Possibly infecting everyone I see? No."

"I'm in charge. You will do as I say." Her father straightened up. "You're the lead medical officer. It's your duty."

"You have no jurisdiction over me. As lead medical officer, I deem it unsafe to remove these bodies from the pod. Therefore, it will not happen." Mara glared at him. "Not to mention, those people in here when the bad pod was opened will need to be quarantined and tested. If it's not too late."

"Doctor Phillip. There is no more infectious disease lab. It's sealed off." Rog stared at him. "It will never be opened."

"Not the dragons. We are immune," Indra whispered in her ear.

Her shoulders eased. Thank goodness she didn't have to worry about Indra. Though perhaps she should check him anyhow, just for her own piece of mind.

"Of course, it is sealed. I have the only key to open those rooms." Dr. Phillip stuck his nose in the air.

"No, you misunderstand. The rooms are welded shut by dragon fire. They will never be opened."

Doctor Phillip's jaw dropped. "You can't do that."

"It's already done. It was done before we even found this room full of coffins." Rog sniffed at him. "You will no longer have the ability to kill people with any type of germ warfare." His voice deepened. "Every facility will have the warfare room and disease labs eliminated. We cannot have the world destroyed again by foolishness."

Morgan nodded. "Indeed." He turned to the dragons. "Gentlemen, will you please dispose of the bodies?"

"No. I won't let you." Doctor Phillip threw his arms wide in a wild attempt to block them.

Morgan gestured at Randy. The two of them grabbed the doctor by the arms and carried him out of the room while he struggled.

"I'll get a sedative. Then we won't have to worry about him sneaking back in here until the bodies are disposed of." Mara hurried through the rear door of the medical lab. It was easy enough to grab what she needed. She smiled. They had taken her father down the hall toward his quarters rather than back outside. Smart, he would have tried to stir up trouble.

She marched into the room behind them. She guessed her father hadn't set up his bioscan yet. Of course not. He wouldn't imagine anyone having the guts to enter his rooms without permission.

"Don't you dare, Tamara! I have the authority to terminate your employment if you do this." Her dad's face was turning red while he struggled to get free.

"Dad, get over yourself. You only have the authority anyone here gives you. I will not endanger everyone here." She filled the needle with the sedative. "I need to get his shoulder clear. I'd rather not inject him in his buttocks." She grimaced. "He's my father, after all. No child should have to see that."

Randy chuckled. He released his arm and tore the sleeve from the shirt, ignoring her father's outraged squeak. He grabbed the doctor by the elbow, again holding him.

The doctor struggled. Shrugging, Randy grabbed him around the waist and lifted him. Morgan grinned and stepped back.

Mara cleaned him with an alcohol wipe and plunged the needle into the fleshy part of his shoulder. "I'm sorry, Dad. It just isn't safe to do autopsies on the bodies. As it is, I'll need a list of who was in the room yesterday when the one pod was opened to make sure no one has any symptoms. We can't afford an outbreak. It would defeat the purpose of us surviving."

He stilled when the needle went in. At least he had enough sense to not chance it breaking off while he struggled. "I'm not happy with you."

Mara rolled her eyes and removed the needle. She'd long ago gotten over his *not happy with you* speech. "That's too bad. It's for everyone's safety."

"So you say." He scowled at her.

"We can take a vote if you want. I'll let everyone know the infection rate and percentages of the death rate. What do you think will happen?" she chastised him. "Think they'll go along with your plan?"

The doctor sagged in Randy's arms. "Fine. I wasn't planning on telling them."

"Don't worry. I will." Morgan glared at the doctor. "If necessary."

"Go to sleep, Dad. I'll see you in the morning." Mara turned to leave.

Randy released him.

The doctor sunk onto his couch. He didn't say a word while they left.

"How long will it take for the sedative to work?" Morgan peered back at the door.

"About fifteen minutes." Mara held the needle away from her. She would dispose of it in her lab. "Dad, I'll be back later to get a sample from you."

Dr. Phillip dropped his head. "Fine."

"Randy, stay here for the next thirty minutes. Make sure the doctor doesn't leave." He waved toward the door. "Just in case."

"Gotcha, Alpha." Randy leaned against the wall next to the door.

Mara and Morgan walked back down the hallway. Mara stopped at the medical office to drop the needle in a sharps container and return the rest of the sedative to the drug cabinet. Then, she headed back to the cryo lab to see what Indra and the rest of the dragons planned.

CHAPTER THIRTEEN

Indra looked at the empty laboratory. Empty except for the dragons and the open and unopened pods. "We can't take the chance the pods carry a virus that will run through the globe again."

The others nodded in agreement.

"No, we can't." Rog took a deep breath. "We need to burn them. Pod and all."

"Can you burn them and the pod without opening the pod?" Zeru poked at one of the pods.

"Yes. It will take a while and lots of energy." Hark sighed. "I'm glad I ate recently."

"And it will have to be Hark and me doing it. Grace hasn't learned how to control her fire yet." He looked at Indra. "Does your fire get hot enough to help us burn them?"

"No." He shook his head. "I'm afraid not. I can pinpoint where to start a fire, but I can't concentrate it enough to reach the temperatures a fire dragon can. Not to totally disintegrate the pod and the body."

"Okay. Then you'll have to leave it to us." Rog turned toward the first pod. The murky gel was the key indicator that there was a problem.

"We can get food for you. We'll have the cattle out past the fire. Keep the humans from gawking too much." Zeru left.

Bruno followed him. "I'll help."

Grace stayed in the room. "You can teach me. That way, I can help."

Indra said, "I'll guard the door. I don't want anyone coming in, so let me know when you're done. Then I'll return the ashes to the earth."

"Grace, I think you should wait. It's not going to be easy. It is exhausting work." Rog growled at her. "You can guard the door."

"Don't be ridiculous. Indra doesn't need help. You do. If it's so exhausting, all the more reason to have another fire dragon help. I don't want my people to catch whatever virus or disease Mara is worried about. Let me help." Grace gave her mate her best puppy dog eyes.

Rog sighed.

Hark laughed. "You might as well give in. She's right. It will go faster with the three of us."

"Fine. But you have to do as I say. If you get tired, let us know."

Indra smothered his grin and eased the door shut. He couldn't wait for Mara to wrap him around her little finger. He saw Mara enter a door down the hall.

Morgan stopped in front of him. "You're not helping with the bodies?"

"No, my fire isn't hot enough." His gaze wandered back toward the door Mara disappeared into. "I will dispose of the ashes back into the earth. Between the burn and burying, no trace of any virus or disease should be left." He rubbed his face. "It's how we disposed of all the bodies during the apocalypse."

"So, there are no graves to return to." Morgan swallowed. "I suppose it was the wisest action."

Indra slowly nodded. He stared off into the distance. He didn't see the corridor, just the past. "Yes. There were so many bodies. After the fire, I returned them to the earth, and if it was a large area, brought the waters up to create a lake to cleanse the land." He swallowed. "There are a lot of lakes."

Morgan clasped his shoulder. "Thank you. It couldn't have been easy."

Indra shook, chasing away the memories. "No, but it was necessary. I'm a steward of the earth. She needed to be cleansed." He ignored the goosebumps on his arms and the ache in his heart.

"Still, thank you." Morgan walked away, heading back outside.

Indra took a deep breath and pushed the past behind him where it belonged. He turned at the tap of shoes coming toward him. "Is your father taken care of?"

"Yes, and Randy is guarding his door until the sedative takes effect." Mara slid her arms around his waist, resting her face on his chest. "So, what do we do now? Do we need to help burn the bodies?"

"No, the fire dragons are much more efficient. I will, however, return the ashes to the earth. In the meantime, I'll guard the door so no one enters. I don't want anyone wandering in to get accidentally burned." Indra rested his head on hers. Just having her in his arms chased away the loneliness of the years since the apocalypse. Add in reuniting with his cousin, and his world became brighter.

"Did you really change me into a dragon?" Mara whispered. "It wasn't a dream?"

Indra smiled. "I really did."

"Huh." Mara's arms tightened momentarily. "I think I can get used to it."

Indra laughed. "Well, you'd better. There's no going back now." A weight dropped from his back. He didn't realize how worried he was that Mara would reject him after finding out what he told her was true.

"I'm going to have to analyze my blood, too. Compare it to my previous sample."

Indra could hear the excitement in her voice. He kissed the top of her head and enjoyed her in his arms. "You do that."

Mara reared her head back to squint at him. “You sound just a bit patronizing.”

“Nope. Not me. I’m happy you’re so excited to experiment on yourself.”

Mara sniffed but laid her head back on his chest. She sighed. “I need to start getting blood from everyone.”

“We’ll worry about it after the bodies are disposed of."

They stood there, guarding the door against no one.

“Hey, we’re done.” Hark stuck his head out. “Now, it’s your turn.”

Indra released Mara and escorted her into the room. “I’d like to show you how this is done. It’s easier as a dragon but not necessary.” He pointed to the gray piles of ash scattered all over the room. “Earth dragons are familiar with using air, earth, fire, and water. In this instant, we’ll just use the earth. Luckily for us, the floor is made from polished stone. You see this pile here?”

Mara rolled her eyes and nodded.

Indra refused to chuckle at her sassiness, even if he wanted to. It was time to start teaching her the powers a dragon could wield. “I’m going to touch the floor and have it absorb the ash.” Indra crouched and touched the stone. The stone became permeable, and the ash moved into it, becoming solid.

"Holy cow." Mara reached down and rubbed her hand over where the ash had been. She looked at her palm. "There's not even a trace left. How did you do that?"

"It's like talking telepathically. I touch the substance I want to change and ask it to do as I request." Indra stood. "Try the next pile."

Mara looked around the room. "This is going to take a while."

"You've got this." Rog waved and left, Grace and Hark following.

"No, I'll show you a trick once you can do it a couple of times." His eyes sparkled in amusement. "But you have to walk before you can run."

"Pfft." Mara attempted to follow his directions. She pressed her hand against the floor, closing her eyes tight. Nothing was happening.

Indra placed his hand against hers. *Do you feel how alive the earth is? The cool presence drawing you in?*

Maybe. Oh. Oh, yes. I think so.

Just ask her to take back the ash.

Just like that?

Yes. His mate was adorable.

Please take the ash into the stone. Oh! I feel it.

You can see it if you open your eyes.

Mara opened her eyes. The pile was gone. "Can I do it again? See if I can do it by myself?"

"Sure." Indra pointed to the next couple of piles. "Do all of those. I'll work over here." He watched Mara do each pile, a wide smile of pure joy on her face. When she headed to her last pile, Indra stepped to the area he would do. He touched the stone. All the rest of the piles disappeared.

"Hey, that's cheating." Mara scowled at him. "Why couldn't I do that?"

"You can. But you wanted to learn. I didn't want to spend the rest of the day cleaning up pile by pile." Indra pointed to her. "Didn't you say something about wanting to take your blood sample?"

"Yes." Mara grabbed the sample tubes and needle from the store room. She tied a tourniquet on her arm and put the needle in her elbow. Once the needle was in place, she removed the tourniquet.

"Let me help." Indra placed the little vacuum attachment to the needle.

She filled two tubes, handed them to Indra, and removed the needle. She grabbed a small pad to stop the bleeding. "I can't wait to see the results and compare them." Mara put the tubes in the machine and pressed a button.

Indra watched them spin. He had no clue what the machine was doing to check the sample. He enjoyed the sparkle in Mara's eyes. Her total absorption in what she was doing. "How long will that take?"

"Just a minute, the centrifuge doesn't take long. Then I'll put it in the Thermo Cycler. That will take a while." Mara straightened when the fuge stopped. She moved the tubes, turned it on, and smiled. "Now what?"

"I think we need to take you flying. I have to get four more containers set up for the voyage to the other government facilities. You can learn to fly on the way to my cabin." He held out his hands for her.

Mara slipped her hands into his, giggling when he wrapped their hands behind her, effectively immobilizing her, subject to his mercy. Indra leaned over and nibbled on her neck.

"Now what are you going to do?" Mara's eyes sparkled.

Indra could fall into them forever. He continued nibbling, enjoying her squirming against him. He pulled her tighter against him, slipping a leg between hers.

Her moan sent shivers down his spine.

Indra breathed in her arousal. The delicious odor spiked his need. Indra picked Mara up, loving the strength of her legs as they wrapped around him. He walked forward, stopping only when he had Mara pressed against a wall.

Indra pulled at her waistband, the button flying. Her shoes plopped to the floor. He unzipped and tugged at her pants until they slid to the floor along with her panties. He quickly undid his and slid inside her. He shuddered at her tight canal encasing him.

Mara groaned. Her arms around his neck, her tongue tangled with his.

He frantically plunged in and out, wild for the release his mate could give him.

She thrust down, impaling herself with each of his movements, rubbing her breasts against his chest.

Pressing her against the wall, Indra tore her shirt open with both hands, buttons scattering across the lab. He grabbed her mounds, plumping them up and tugging her nipples. He lifted her to taste the tightened buds, sucking while she frantically rode his cock. He prodded her, teasing her with just his tip while feasting on her bounty.

Mara groaned in frustration.

Indra grunted, let go of her nipple with a pop and fully seated Mara on his length.

Her cry of ecstasy echoed around the chamber. She bounced on him, her boobs bobbing against his chest, the brush of her nipples sending shocks of electricity straight to his heart. Her nails drew blood from his scalp. She was magnificent.

He grunted with each lunge, his length plumbing the depths of her body. He had no words; sounds of bliss erupted from his mouth. His hands held her steady while she screamed against his neck.

Her pussy pulsed and squeezed his cock.

Indra thrust, pounding inside her. He cried out, groaning, his climax torn from his body. He leaned against her, squishing her against the wall. He didn't want to move. Mara fit perfectly in his arms.

"Move." Mara pushed weakly at him. "Can't breathe."

Indra chuckled and gave her just a bit of room.

"More." She snickered. "Let me down."

Indra nuzzled her neck, enjoying her squirming. "Mmm." Then he pulled free, his cum dripping from her body.

She wobbled but stayed upright, still within his arms. "So, I thought you meant a different flying lesson."

Indra snickered. "I did indeed."

"But first, I need to get samples of everyone's blood." Mara sighed, dropping her head against his chest.

~

Tedious but necessary, Mara finally had a blood sample from everyone. Since those in the room had been mingling with the rest, everyone was being tested. Not even the wolves escaped, as quite a few had been helping in the cryonics room when the bad pod was opened. The samples had been centrifuged and the rest were in the VirScan.

She'd left her father to watch for results. A truce, so to speak. Being able to give the results of the tests was just up his alley and mollified him from not having so much control over her life. He wasn't happy about her becoming a dragon but had no choice. It was done. Nor could she tamp down her happiness. He'd eventually forgive her.

She'd also left her father to monitor the DNA samples from the dragons, including hers. He was busy matching the shifter's results with the stored DNA. Since the dragons proved immune to every disease that wiped out pretty much the rest of the world, he was trying to isolate why.

Christopher shrugged and high-fived her and continued checking the facility systems. So, all was good on her familial front for the moment.

Then she'd escaped with Indra to learn to fly, but this flying was harder than she figured. Mara flailed after Indra dropped her into the sky. It freaked her out until she shifted into her dragon. Her wings wobbled and caught the air currents. Tears ran down her face from the wind. She blinked, trying to clear them away. It wasn't like she had hands to wipe them. If she used her claws, she would probably blind herself. She blinked and realized her eyes stopped tearing up. She had double eyelids. She blinked and her vision changed. Wow, if she wasn't mistaken, the first set of eyelids allowed her to see infrared. Awesome! She flickered her lids again, checking each phenomenon. Being a dragon was amazing.

Below her, one of the dragons flew. To each of her sides, she also had a flying guard.

Mara twisted her head, looking up, and began scrambling. She plunged down, flailing her wings to steady out.

Don't panic. You've got this. Indra's smooth tones comforted her.

If not, I'll try to catch you. The teasing voice could only be Hark.

Ignoring Hark, Mara let Indra's confidence seep into her mind. She could do this. She watched the dragons next to her.

The silver one spread his wings and glided through the sky.

Mara spread her wings instead of flapping them like a madwoman. She grinned. The air current buoyed and steadied her.

Good girl. Bruno's deep tone of approval had her preening.

With the dragons surrounding her, it was like she had her own harem.

If you click your talons together, you will become invisible, Zeru said.

But don't do it until you're more comfortable flying. Indra's concern was evident.

True, only another air dragon could see you. If you fall, the others can't catch you, only I.

Hmm. Mara clicked her nails. She could still see herself. She did it again. Still there. Maybe it didn't work.

Dammit, Mara. Don't do that again. Indra's momentary panic made her realize Zeru was right; she could turn invisible.

The chuckles from the other dragons had Indra scowling.

I just wanted to see if it worked. She couldn't help the pleased tones in her voice.

Well, it did. Indra lowered above her, forcing her lower. *Let's try landing now. We're at our destination.*

They were approaching the cabin with the container units.

Indra stayed above her, and she matched his speed and descent.

The rest of the dragons were landing in the clearing.

Slow up. Indra did something to slow, but she couldn't figure it out.

Mara tried to imitate what Bruno, Zeru, and Hark did. Unfortunately, it didn't work out so well. Instead of smoothly slowing and basically walking onto the ground, she tumbled. Mara squawked, tripped over her claws, and slid, landing on her back. She ignored the snorts and laughter from the other dragons. Jerks.

Indra nudged her, helping her get back on her feet.

"I could've done it." Mara shook and glared at the male dragons.

"I know. You did pretty good for your first landing." Indra rubbed his nuzzle across her jaw.

"You should have seen my sister-in-law the first time we dropped her into the sky. She fell. Good thing her mate was around to catch her." Hark shook his head, grinning. "It took her a while to learn to fly."

Indra shifted. "I need to get the rest of the containers. It seemed like a good idea to help Mara learn to fly on the way to pick them up."

The rest of the men shifted.

Mara goggled at them. So much naked eye candy. She could practically feel the drool forming. But Indra was the handsomest of all.

"Mara, you need to practice shifting. Why don't you do that while we get the containers cut and ready." Indra waved the three to come along with him.

She sighed. She didn't have any clothes with, but supposed it didn't really matter. They'd seen all of her. As a doctor, she was familiar with bodies in many forms of undress, but not usually herself. Mara closed her eyes and pictured herself. Again, nothing happened. She caught a glimpse of Indra, watched the play of his muscles and pictured touching him. She saw her hand reaching for him. Her cheeks heated and she dropped her hand.

"Can't we just rip out the plastic all together?" Bruno stared at Indra's container, watching him slice the top of it.

"No, the humans won't be able to travel well without it. I don't want to break any legs. Plus, the plastic will reduce the wind blowing through it, keeping them warmer." Indra continued to slice the top, walking around all the sides.

Zeru and Hark followed his actions, each starting to cut a container.

"Fine." Bruno worked on the container in front of him.

Mara thought about being a dragon. She didn't change. She stamped her foot. This was getting her nowhere. She didn't want to be dropped midair to have to change again. Then she thought about the feel of the air on her wings. Of soaring over the ground and how small everything looked. She preened when her scales appeared. And, yes, she had a tail. She twisted and her tail swung in counterpoint. She thought about being human, the feel of her skin against Indra's.

"I did it!" Mara checked out her arms with a smile. It was getting easier. She thought about flying over the mountain, her mate alongside her. "Woo Hoo!" Her scales appeared. One more time. She imagined her hand wrapped in Indra's. She did a happy dance, wiggling her booty and waving her hands in the air.

Indra's arms slid around her, sending electric shocks through her body. "Good job."

She threw her arms around him, lifting her mouth to his. The warm touch of his firm lips sent liquid to her core and beaded her nipples against his hard chest. She squirmed at the grip of his strong hands on her ass. She loved the feel of his body, hard to her soft.

Bruno's groan and Hark and Zeru's whispers pulled them apart.

Indra growled and bared his teeth at them. His hard cock leaked at the tip.

"It's not like they haven't seen it all before." Mara tugged at his arm, bringing his attention back to her.

"Why don't you gather some corn? We can bring some back in the containers." Indra's flashing eyes had them grumbling, shifting, and flying away. "It doesn't matter if they've seen it before. You're mine."

"I'm confused. You had no problem sharing me before." Mara slid a finger along his abdomen, smiling at the goosebumps following its wake.

"That was a special occasion. You had to become a dragon to live as long as me. Plus, it's the only way to ensure we are compatible for hatchlings."

"Hatchlings? Will I lay eggs when we decide to have children? Or will they be human?"

"Eggs, of course."

Mara's jaw dropped. "Say, what?"

"You'll be in dragon form when it's time to lay them. We will both help nurture them in that state."

Mara just gaped at him.

"They are growing even now." Indra stroked her belly. "It'll be a while before they need to be laid in the hatching ground."

"I'm pregnant?" She shook her head. "What if I'm not ready to have children? Hatchlings?"

"You don't want hatchlings?" Indra's face froze, his eyes pools of sorrow.

"Yes. You never mentioned getting me pregnant, though." Mara gritted her teeth. "So, in nine months, I'll be laying eggs. According to you."

"Nine months? No, you should lay the eggs in three months."

"I'll have children in THREE months?" Her voice climbed, ending on a screech. She stomped her foot. "THREE MONTHS?" She ran her hands through her hair and paced, muttering under her breath.

Indra winced. "No. You'll lay the eggs in three months. They won't hatch for close to a year."

Mara stilled and turned to look at him. "So, we'll have a hatchling, as you called it, in a year and a quarter."

"Yeees." Indra stepped back. "Hatchlings."

"An *s*." Mara stalked toward him. "You added an s."

She could see his Adam's apple bob.

He backed up just a little farther. "I did say eggs. You did say children."

Mara stopped. She took a deep breath. "How many?"

Indra straightened, lifting his head. “Usually about six. It can be as little as one, but up to…” Indra took a deep breath, “a dozen.”

Her brain stopped working at that point. She just looked at him, and her jaw dropped.

CHAPTER FOURTEEN

Indra swore to sleep with one eye open. He stood firm. He couldn't keep backing up from his mate. Surely, she wouldn't kill him. Though from the look on her face, he had his doubts. He swallowed. He couldn't decide whether he was afraid or... He nodded. He was afraid of her.

At this point, he wouldn't have reminded her that the bite of a female dragon was venomous. She just might bite him. It wouldn't kill him since he was her mate, but it would not be pleasant. Thank goodness it was only effective in dragon form.

Her eyes came back into focus. The sharp intelligence normally in them returning. She shook her head. "I can't even."

"Even what?" Indra wasn't sure what she was saying. "Of course, you can. It's a simple process. In your dragon form you lay the eggs in the hatching ground. We and the rest of our clan nurture the eggs until the hatchlings crack the shells."

Mara was just shaking her head.

Indra stopped. He sighed. "What would you like to know?" Maybe Mara needed to get her thoughts together. As a doctor, she was sure to have questions. He could answer them.

"Can we just shelve this?" She gestured to her abdomen. "Just get me up to speed on being a dragon and then discuss it?"

Indra slowly nodded. It wouldn't change anything, but he could do that. "Yes. If that is what you wish."

"It is." She walked farther into the meadow. "I think I'm just going to keep practicing shifting."

Indra watched her move away.

Suddenly, she was a dragon. Then human. Then dragon.

Can one of you get food for Mara? She's...upset.

Why would she need to eat because she is upset? Zeru inquired.

Why is little fish upset? Even Bruno's telepathic voice was deep.

She just found out that she is going to have hatchlings.

Oh. Hark's snicker came through loud and clear. *Why does she need food, though?*

Mara is shifting. And she's not stopping. Over and over.

Zeru flew overhead. *I will hunt.*

Sure, leave me and Bruno to carry the corn back. Harks chortling was getting a bit irritating.

Just go bring the container to the corn, Indra added, distracted for a moment.

Hopefully, Mara would calm down soon. He knew better than to say it, though. Growing up with his sisters assured him of that.

Maybe they should leave for the mission as soon as possible. It might distract her. Maybe she just needed to fly. That always helped him.

Regardless, she needed a distraction. They had plenty of time before the hatchlings came. "Mara." Indra walked over to her. She was human, and he could see how tired she was. "Would you like to go flying? I can show you how to start from the ground."

"Rather than toss me out in the sky?" Mara snarked. She had a right to be upset.

He hadn't told her everything, plus she hadn't even believed him. "Yes."

She stared at him and shifted. Her beautiful dragon looked ready to bite him.

"You will have to start by running and flapping your wings. Watch me." Indra shifted and ran, his powerful wings taking him to the sky in no time. *Try it. It might be hard at first. You'll have to gain wing strength to fly from standing. This is the way we teach hatchlings.*

Mara bared her teeth at him, then snorted and ran, flapping her wings. She was able to gain a little air before hitting the ground again.

Good job! Indra was pleased that she managed to get off the ground a bit. *Keep trying.*

She didn't answer but did try it again. Each time, she gained altitude. Her expression slowly cleared, looking happier each time she succeeded. *Look, I'm flying!*

I'm proud of you. Indra's heart raced, looking at Mara. She was taking being a dragon wonderfully. Except for the part about the hatchlings, but there was plenty of time before they came.

Excellent, little fish.

Awesome. You're doing much better than my new sister Hope had, Hark added.

Time to build your strength again. Eat. Two cattle dropped from Zeru's claws to the ground.

Hark and Bruno finished placing corn into one of the containers and took off. Presumably to hunt.

Zeru settled down with his catch.

Mara contentedly munched her food.

"I'm going to hunt. I'll be back shortly. Zeru is here if you need anything while I'm gone." Indra kissed her on her snout, shifted, and flew off.

"Show off," Mara grumbled and went back to eating.

Indra looped in the sky, unable to contain his joy.

Mara's giggle made the sun shine brighter.

He spied a deer in the trees, having trouble climbing the mountainside. From its looks, the whitetail was elderly and not long for the earth. Indra didn't see any fawns. He watched it for a bit, then swooped down. They couldn't sustainably eat just cows. It would thin the herd too much. He ate the deer while he searched for more prey.

He found more cattle, more deer, and a herd of bison on his flight. He grabbed one of the bison from the outskirts of the herd. He quickly took off with it while a few gave chase. They were fast. Indra headed back to find Mara still shifted.

She was napping.

He figured she was tired from shifting and trying to fly. Not to mention, she'd been a bit of an emotional mess after finding out she was carrying hatchlings. With a full belly, it wasn't surprising she slept.

"Took you long enough." Hark finished cutting the top off of his container. "We're almost ready to go back." He looked around. "Did you live in the cabin?"

"Occasionally. I found it years ago and came back. Didn't realize my mate was right under my nose." Indra's gaze softened, looking at Mara.

"That has to burn." Hark looked back at the mountains. "Did you do much exploring?"

"A bit." Indra looked at all the mountains circling the valley. "Where specifically?"

“The mountains on this side of the valley. Are there caves?”

“A few. I didn’t really explore them. Why?”

Hark sighed. “Our other brothers built their weyr near their mates’ family. They mated sisters.” Hark smiled. “Quite a pair. But Rog and I never made one. I guess we were waiting to find our mates. And we don’t really want to live with all the humans.”

Neither did he, but he would for Mara.

“But I know Grace wants to stay near her family, and this mountain range is just as close to her family as the government facility. I was going to suggest to Rog that we check it out.”

“Good idea. I’ll stay wherever Mara wants.” She was staring at him. What a wonder. Smart and beautiful, he loved how adventurous she was. His heart raced just looking at her. He wanted nothing more than her in his arms.

Bruno lumbered out of the trees. *Are we done here?*

Yes. All the containers were cut and ready. Hark and Bruno had filled one container with ears of corn.

Zeru came across the meadow. *Are we leaving?*

Yes. Indra wandered over and scratched Mara’s head. “Mara, do you want to ride in a container?”

"Can't I fly?" She fluttered her lashes at him.

Indra snorted. "Yes. Let me shift and I'll grab you so you can get off the ground." He shifted, took off, circled back, and carefully took Mara in his claws. Dragons didn't usually carry each other. Normally, they'd only be this close as dragons during the mating ritual. He had to be careful not to damage her wings. *Now, run and try to fly. I'll lift you and get you in the air.*

Mara ran with a smile on her snout, jumped, and flapped her wings.

Indra grabbed her at her wing joints so as not to interfere and assisted her in the air. He slowly released her and watched her fly.

The joy on her face was amazing.

Indra circled back down and latched onto a container.

Bruno grabbed one and flew. He soared under Mara and sniffed her.

Hark and Indra each grabbed a container, racing back toward the facility.

When did you complete your mating flight? Bruno slid next to Indra.

We haven't yet. She's just learning to fly.

She is not carrying hatchlings.

What? Of course, she is.

You don't hang out with other dragons much, do you? Bruno shook his head. *You fertilize the female's eggs during the mating flight.*

I thought it was when we all turned her?

No. It changes the female's reproductive system, along with her DNA. The change enables her to carry hatchlings.

Oh. Indra chewed the inside of his cheek. *I suppose I need to tell her.*

Yes, you do.

Indra sighed. Bruno was right. He'd have to tell her even if he didn't want to. *I will. I was just looking forward to having hatchlings.*

Little fish didn't seem to have the same reaction.

No, no, she didn't. Indra gazed at Mara, wishing she'd have been excited instead of upset.

Does that mean I can't complete the mating flight? His wings drooped.

No. Just don't fertilize her.

Like I can control that. He couldn't help the bitter tone in his words.

You can control that. Bruno's exasperated tone had Indra wincing.

Um, okay. He could figure it out.

Just block your glands. Bruno snorted and zipped away, following the river back.

Indra's eyes widened. *I never thought of that. Thank you.*

Bruno's wing dipped in acknowledgment as he continued his flight.

Indra soared over to next to Mara. He may not be thrilled about Mara's reaction, but she had been through a lot in just a short amount of time. He should be glad she was taking it so well. He rubbed his snout against Mara's, staying out of her wingspan. *Can we talk when we get back? In your rooms?*

~

Mara's stomach flipped. *Sure*. She wondered if he had something else to tell her that he hadn't yet. After all, he'd given her one shock after another since she'd met him. The last one the biggest so far.

Indra glided in the air, scales gleaming in the sun. He was magnificent beast in dragon or human form.

Her life as a human, before she was frozen, seemed like a dream. She wondered if the chemical gel she'd been frozen in somehow affected her. Was it the gel or the extended time they'd spent in it? She'd have to analyze the gel to see if it had broken down in any way. Nope, it didn't matter. No one had any side effects she could see and it's not like anyone would be frozen again. Nor did she want to spend her life inside a lab. There was a whole new world for her to explore. It was hard to believe it was real.

The silver of Bruno's scales flickered in a stray sunbeam. Kind of like a dragon-shaped disco ball.

Mara chuckled, imagining it. Some nineteen seventies disco playing while Bruno circled the room sparkling. She watched him fly above the river, his scales and the gleaming water cheering her up. So, what if she was going to lay eggs? She scrunched her nose. Yeah, bravado didn't help. She was totally unprepared. Maybe she could see herself holding an adorable copy of Indra in her arms. But laying eggs? Lizards hatching and being told she was their mother? Would three months be enough to lay that ick factor to rest? She wasn't sure it would. Or would her maternal instinct kick in at some point? She could only hope.

A black blur zipped by, so close she felt the change in air along her wings.

Mara wobbled and straightened out, once again stable. *Watch it!* She hissed at Hark.

Sorry! Just checking your response to turbulence. The gleaming of his teeth in a grin didn't ring true with his statement.

Indra circled back around to check on Mara. *Are you fine?*

Yes.

He's not wrong, but a little warning would be good. Indra's eyes narrowed, following the black figure playing in the sky.

It's not like bad weather or air flows can be expected. Hark zipped by them again, but not as close. His good humor wasn't dampened in the least by Indra's admonishment.

Weather can be predicted. Besides becoming invisible in the air thanks to my gene contribution, I hope Mara can also sense any storms coming like most air dragons. Zeru eased next to Mara. *Just let your senses roam.*

Indra hummed next to her. *Zeru gave you invisibility in the sky and, hopefully, some weather radar. I gave her the ability to manipulate earth. Hark, what do you think you gave Mara?*

Hopefully a sense of humor. Hark chortled and looped in front of them.

Mara snorted, rolled her eyes, clicked her throat, and blew fire at him. *Whoa!*

Ack! Hark bobbled in the air, almost dropping the container he carried. *I guess the fire dragon's ability to throw fire. Luckily, fire dragons are immune to each other's fire.*

I wonder what I got from Bruno?

We will see little fish. Bruno's voice seemed distant.

Mara couldn't even see him anymore.

I can't wait to find out. You are a beautiful mixture of all of us. Indra beamed, his pride for her plain on his face.

They flew back to the facility with no other incidents. The males set the containers down.

Mara landed a bit awkwardly, tumbling, but luckily, not head over heels like last time. She ignored Hark's laugh. He was a bit of a tease. She shifted, leaving the containers between her and most humans wandering outside. She grabbed the pile of her clothes she'd left waiting and dressed.

She slipped on her shoes and straightened up. She pulled her shoulders back, her normal confidence returned. Huh. Slacks, a blouse, and shoes were her human armor. She strutted toward Indra. Give her a lab coat and she'd be invincible. She snickered. Maybe Hark did give her a sense of humor.

"Mara." Indra grabbed her hands and drew her to him. "May we go talk?"

"Yes." She looked carefully into his face, ignoring the tingles his touch sent through her body. Indra sounded serious, more so than she expected. Hopefully, he wasn't going to drop more bombs on her. The last one was quite enough.

Releasing one hand, he walked side by side with her. His arm brushed along hers, sending pleasant zaps and the ever-present buzz from holding his hand.

At her quarters, she pressed her thumb to the biometric lock and heard the click of the lock opening. She pushed the door in and released Indra's hand. She slipped off her shoes, placing them inside next to the door.

Indra sat on her couch.

Mara sat on one of the recliners, kitty-corner to the couch. His serious expression made her nervous. She clasped her hands to keep them from giving away how anxious she was.

"I'm sorry." Indra's deep voice rolled through her.

She cocked her head, frowning. "For what?" She couldn't help dragging out the phrase. He hadn't done anything that she knew of.

"For saying you were expecting."

Mara straightened up. "Did you lie?" What was going on? She didn't know how many more surprises she could take. Though the lightness in her heart hoped he had. But, if so, why?

Indra's sad eyes looked into hers. He scooted closer to her without leaving the couch. "Unintentionally." He sighed. "I thought the process of changing you into a dragon also impregnated you."

"You never mentioned that part. Not at all." Anger flickered inside her, but she stuffed it down. She wasn't pregnant. She had no reason to be mad about it now.

"I never even thought of it. But when I told you, and you were so upset, I realized you had no way of knowing. You didn't even think I could change you." He gave her an outraged look but wrestled it down.

Mara sighed and shrugged. "Seriously? I could barely believe dragons existed even when I saw you change. They didn't in my world before."

"Oh, we did. We just knew better than to expose ourselves in front of humans."

Mara narrowed her eyes at his arrogant tone. Then she thought about it. Shifters would have been massacred. She had no doubt about that. Humans were not the most accepting creatures. "Understandably."

He grabbed her hands. "When you were willing to go through with the ceremony to change you, I was ecstatic." His fingers tightened on hers. "How could I know you didn't think it was real?"

Mara winced. "Well, it sounded like a fantasy come true. Multiple men giving me pleasure? I figured once in my life, I could throw caution to the wind and just enjoy." She remembered the frenzy and the pleasure. "It was everything I had fantasized about." She laughed, squeezing his hands. "Just not the end result."

"I ignored my doubts about your skepticism. You were willing and I took advantage of it."

Mara couldn't stand the look on his face. "I was willing. It's not your fault I didn't believe you. Even Grace tried to explain it."

Indra chuckled. "I heard. She made little sense at all."

Mara's laughter joined his. "I don't regret it. You have to know that. I love flying." She winked at him. "I loved flaming Hark's butt. I'm sure I'll find many things to love about being a dragon. It only added to my life. It hasn't taken anything away from me."

Indra blew out a deep breath. He straightened and smiled, the twinkle coming back to his eyes. "Thank you."

"Now, how about you tell me about this pregnancy scare." Back to the worst part about being turned into a dragon.

"Well, we haven't completed the mating yet."

"We haven't? Does that mean another bout with all of you?" Mara didn't want to be too eager, but she wouldn't turn it down. It had been the hottest experience of her life.

"No." His lip curled. "That happens only once." A low growl escaped his throat.

Bummer, but that was okay. It's not like she could become a dragon again. After all, she had the hottest dragon of all. She stroked his hands with her thumbs.

He continued. "We still have to complete a mating flight as dragons. It is during the mating flight you can become pregnant."

Mara gazed at him, at his hopeful look. But she knew, deep down, at the pit threatening her stomach, she wasn't ready to carry what sounded like a litter. Someday, but not now.

"So, we can hold off on the mating flight?" She winced at his growl.

"Bruno told me how to prevent impregnating you. We'll still have our mating flight." He sighed, casting puppy dog eyes at her. "We can wait until you're ready to have hatchlings."

Mara threw herself onto him, tumbling Indra back into the cushions. She covered his face with kisses. Her heart filled with joy. "Thank you, thank you."

Indra rumbled beneath her. His arms wrapped around her, pulling her snugly to his body. He took control.

Mara's hands tightened in his hair, keeping his lips against hers. Already in the short time she'd known him, she was addicted to his flavor on her lips and the feel of his body on hers, in hers.

His hands were busy divesting them of their clothing.

They rolled and hit the floor, landing between the couch and the coffee table. He'd managed to flip to hit the floor first.

Mara gazed down at him, affection in her eyes. "I'm becoming addicted to you."

"Good." Indra groped her ass, sliding a finger inward to test her readiness.

She could have told him. She was so ready. She rocked on his pelvis, teasing herself against his penis. The slick petals of her sex spread, ready to accept him. She loved his hands, kneading her bottom, controlling her movements.

Indra leaned forward, tongue tracing the contours of her breasts.

She arched into him, offering them to his hot mouth.

Indra flicked his tongue, teasing her nipples.

She shoved forward. "More."

Indra chuckled.

Mara groaned. She needed more. She needed...

Indra sucked her nipple into his mouth, giving her everything she needed. Each draw sent contractions to her pussy. She needed him in her.

Mara whined, undulating against his cock, his head hitting her clit with each slide.

His fingers flicked her clit and grabbed her hips. He lunged upward with his cock, spearing her.

Mara cried out, filled with him. Fire raced through her veins.

His suction on her nipple, his fingers bruising against her hips, sent her spinning. His hands moved her up and down, slamming into her with each thrust. His groans and grunts with each plunge into her body had an unending babble of nonsense burbling from her mouth.

The slap of their bodies echoed in the room.

Indra shoved the table away and rolled over, trapping Mara beneath him. He dove into her neck, nibbling and sucking on her sensitive skin.

Mara wiggled and wove her arms around his body, nails digging into his back. The cool floor against the heat of her body electrified her. She shook, her body out of control.

Indra stuttered, moving erratically.

Her body quivered. Her legs wrapped tightly around him. She threw her head back. Mara keened, fire streaming to every nerve end. Her sex squeezed his shaft, dragging his essence from his body.

He grunted. The pulse of his ejaculation filled her and drove her crazy. His hips pinned her to the floor. He collapsed on top of her, his hands in her hair. His mouth suckled beneath her ear. “I can’t get enough of you.”

“Me either.” Her arms and legs wrapped around him, holding him tight to her. Mara whispered. “Someday, I want babies.”

He bit her neck and followed it up with a sweet kiss to her lips. "And I'll let you have them." His eyes twinkled. His mischievous look and answer had her giggling.

Banging on her door had them both groaning.

Indra kneeled, dragging his cock from her warm depths. He stood, and the heat in his eyes made her squirm.

Mara stretched and wrinkled her nose at the rush of fluids from her body.

Someone banged on the door again. "Indy, I know you're in there. Answer the door." It was Randy.

"Hold your horses. I'll be right there." Indra grabbed a towel from the sink and cleaned himself off.

"I'm hopping in the shower." Mara got up and grabbed her clothes on the way to the bedroom. She felt Indra's eyes and added a swing to her steps. She snickered at his groan. She closed the bathroom door and jumped into the shower. She hoped he would hurry up and join her soon.

CHAPTER FIFTEEN

Indra slid his pants on, shoving his once again hard cock to the side to prevent injuring himself on the zipper. He opened the door to Randy's grinning face.

"Sorry to interrupt." He so wasn't.

"Right. So, what brings you knocking on our door?"

"The other shifters are waking up."

"And? Why would that concern me?"

"Don't you want to be there to greet them? Like you did me?" Randy's eyes sparkled with mischievousness.

Indra narrowed his eyes. "Is there a reason for me to?"

"Maybe a couple." Randy's smile widened. "A couple and their cubs."

Indra froze. "Family?"

Randy beamed. "Yes." His face fell. "I wish mine had made it." His nose reddened. He glanced at his hands. "I don't even have anything to remember them by." He looked at Indra's chest and snickered. "Not like you do."

"Shut up."

Randy laughed. "I'm glad you found me." He bit his lip. "But I don't know why we weren't woken up like they said we would be."

Indra shrugged. He walked over to his bag and pulled out a piece of paper. "They were all together at the end." He cleared his throat, his eyes stinging. "I took this." He held out the photograph. "So, I didn't forget."

Randy's eyes went wide. He ripped it from Indra's hand, gazing at it. "Thank you." He tossed his head back, blinking furiously. "Must be the dust."

"Yeah, all the stone." Indra clasped his shoulder, holding tight.

"I can keep it?" Randy had the photo held to his chest.

"Of course." He pulled Randy to him. "I missed you."

"Yeah, me too, ya pansy."

Indra chuckled. He didn't have words. Randy had been his closest friend his whole life. And now, he had him back.

"Is that a pickle in your pocket? Or are you glad to see me?" Randy chortled, stepping back. "I didn't think you swung that way."

Indra tossed his hands up. "Ass." His erection deflated the moment Randy mentioned it.

Randy's crooked grin soothed his soul.

He had missed the asshole. "That's all for my mate."

"Whatever you need to tell yourself." Randy jumped back when Indra swung halfheartedly at him. "Seriously. The Pats are there, along with Teddy, Olly, and Noah. And part of their clan."

"That's great." Indra heard the shower turn off. "When do you think they'll wake up?"

"From what the other dragons said, in probably a couple of hours. We did start the process first thing this morning." Randy sniffed the air. "I'll meet you outside. Your mate smells clean, but you stink." He danced back out of Indra's reach. "Ta-ta." Randy turned and ran out the door.

Indra shook his head, a smile on his face. Randy still acted like a pup.

He made sure the door was completely shut and headed to the hall bathroom. He grabbed his bag on the way. He stripped, dropping his jeans in a hamper against the wall. Randy hadn't been wrong. He did stink. Turning the water on, he was happy it warmed up quickly.

Indra stepped into the hot water, groaning as it pummeled his back muscles. He'd missed hot showers. He generally cleaned in the rivers. When he was in his cabin, which wasn't often, the solar-powered water heater was enjoyable, but the hot water ran out quickly. This was great. Indra stood under the spray, luxuriating in the heat.

He groaned and finally grabbed the shampoo on the shelf. He poured a bit in his hand and sniffed. It was a bit thick but still usable. He lathered his hair, grabbed the soap bar, and scrubbed every bit of his body. He stretched, rinsing off. It felt good to be clean. He wouldn't mind if Mara wanted to live here. He stepped out and dried off.

If she did want to stay here, they would need a weyr. He placed his hand against the back wall and looked.

The mountain revealed itself to him. He saw the layout of the whole facility. Beyond that were unexplored caverns. He smiled. The mountain's structure would sustain a weyr. He could easily connect it to Mara's space. Then they'd have hot showers whenever they wanted. There was a large enough space that could be prepped for hatchlings when Mara was ready. And enough chambers for any dragons, wolves, or bears.

He could make separate entrances for all the shifters if they wanted. The mountain range was large enough, with enough natural caverns, to give all of them homes if they desired. It would be up to them. The humans would probably be staying. It seemed they had apartments ready for them.

"What are you doing?" Mara's voice came from the now open door. "More earth dragon stuff?"

"Yes. I was looking at the structure of the mountain range." He glanced at her. "Would you like to see?"

"Yes!" Mara slid next to him. "Show me how."

"Place your hand on the wall and close your eyes." Indra wrapped his arm around her and whispered. "It's like when we talk, but we can see also." Indra opened his mind to the mountain, sharing it with Mara.

"Oh, it's like when we talked to the stones." Mara's excitement shown in her voice. "But a bit different." She leaned, resting her forehead against the wall.

"Yes. Here, look. This is the layout of the facility. Look a bit farther, these are the natural caverns in the mountain." He tightened his arm around her. "Now look farther. You can see the mountain range."

"Oh, wow. That's amazing."

"It is. But you can't stretch your senses too far. It will all just run together." He smiled at the joy on her face. He loved showing her there was more to the world than what she knew as a human. Her appreciation made it all new again to him. His world was once more filled with wonder, all because of Mara.

He released her to open his bag. He put on a clean pair of jeans. He rummaged in the vanity drawers and pulled out toothpaste and a new toothbrush. “Good thing plastic is forever.” He brushed, enjoying the minty flavor.

Mara laughed. “I never was so glad for some of it. So, why did Randy come by?”

“There were a few more surprises in the rest of the shifters. It seems our aunt, uncle, and three of our cousins are being unfrozen today.”

“That’s awesome.” Mara threw her arms around his waist and hugged him. “I bet you’re excited.”

He rinsed the toothbrush and set it down. He pulled Mara’s arms to his front, enjoying the sensation of being in her arms. “I am. I had given up on seeing my family again. At least, the ones that aren’t dragons.” He turned in her arms, wrapping his around her waist. He hugged her tight against him. Words didn’t really express the turmoil inside him. He’d always been closer to the furry branch of the family. He loved his brothers and sisters, but they’d spread across the continent before the apocalypse.

The wolves needed a pack, and the bears needed their sleuth. Both groups, but especially the wolves, treated him like one of their own. Bears were a tad bit more independent but still lived near each other. The wolves practically lived on top of each other. Indra had loved it. Finding out part of his family still lived was wonderful. He just didn't know how to express it.

"I'm happy for you."

Indra buried his face in Mara's hair, holding her to him, breathing in the strawberry fragrance of her shampoo. He squeezed his eyes shut, willing his tears to not fall. He'd been given a gift, multiple times over. First Mara, then Randy, and now his bear clan.

Mara snuggled into him, her hands running soothingly up and down his back. She didn't say anything else, just held him.

Feeling a bit like the pansy Randy had called him, Indra let her comfort him. He'd be good momentarily. Swallowing, Indra eased back. He cleared his throat. "You know, the bears will need someplace to live."

"They're bears. Can't they live anywhere?" Mara grimaced. "But they're people too. I guess they might take some of the apartments of those who died."

Indra chuckled. "Let's get out of the bathroom."

Mara led them back to the living room. She settled on the couch.

Indra eased down beside her, tugging her tight. “I don’t think they’d want to mingle with so many humans.”

“Right.” Mara nodded her head. “You’re cabin’s not big enough?”

“No, but you saw the inside of the mountain. The cavern system up the mountain would be perfect. More trees for privacy. If you’d like to help, we can fly up there and get it ready. At least get it started.”

“Um, sure. I’m not sure what I can do.” Mara frowned. “I can sweep, I guess.”

Indra cracked up. “How about I show you some more earth dragon powers?”

Mara bounced up and down on the couch. “Yes. Can we go now?”

He grinned and stood, pulling her to her feet. “Yes. One thing we usually do is bring a bag with. If we need to shift, it’s good to always have a change of clothes, at least. Do you have a small duffle?”

Mara scrambled to her bedroom. “Yes. I’ll get it ready.”

Indra heard drawers opening and shutting and Mara muttering. He retrieved his bag from the bathroom. He glanced through the vanity drawers and found a case for the toothbrush. He dumped the toothpaste and toothbrush in there. He met Mara back in the living room. “All done?”

“Yes. Should I bring any food?”

“No, we can catch our food.” He glanced at the kitchen cabinets. “I’m sure there is something decades old here, but I prefer my food a bit fresher.”

Mara gurgled. Her face alight with amusement. “I get your point. Then let’s head out.”

Indra grinned, holding the door open for Mara and making sure the door shut behind him.

~

Mara spit her bag out of her teeth. She’d have to figure out a better way to carry her bag. She shifted and pulled her clothes out, hurriedly dressing in the cooler air. She watched Indra do the same, admiring the movement of his muscles. The man had muscles on muscles. She’d always dated pale, skinny men before. Looking at Indra had shoved them out of her mind without even trying.

His dark brown hair was messy but short enough that it looked contrived. She knew it wasn't though. It was the result of the wind and his fingers running through it. His eyes deepen from blue to green with his emotions. They were endlessly fascinating.

"So, what are we doing?" Mara zipped up her bag, slinging it over her shoulder.

"We're going to set up the caverns for the bears."

"How will we do that?"

Indra grabbed his bag and her hand. "I'll show you." They walked into the cave entrance. "Touch the walls with me. Look into your mind. Do you see the cave system?"

"I do." It was mindboggling.

"Good."

She ignored the amusement in his tone. "Now what?"

"Okay, just beyond the bend, there is a larger cave and a couple of smaller ones."

"Okay."

"I'll merge two of the small caves together. Watch and feel what I do. Make sure the ceiling heights are big enough for a dragon."

Mara's jaw dropped. The caves slowly widened until they were one big cave. "Wow."

Indra grinned. "Now, try to do the same to the two on the other side of the large cave."

Mara gritted her teeth, thinking hard at the rock. She squealed when they slowly started enlarging. “It’s working!”

“Good girl.” She heard the smile in his voice. “Keep going. Once they match mine, create a large entrance to the big cave.”

She worked until they looked about the same size. “But they have an entrance on the other side. Do I need to block that off?”

“Only one. Leave the other.”

Mara nodded and concentrated on following his commands. She slowly created a large entrance. “Big enough for a dragon?”

“Indeed.”

This was fun. While she worked, Indra was smoothing out the floors in the rooms. In the central cave, he built a large pit and a shaft leading to the outside of the mountain.

He created another shaft in the room she’d enlarged. “Good job.”

Mara wiped her brow. Until she finished, she hadn’t realized she was sweating. “Wow, I never imagined moving rock with my mind was such hard work.”

“Now, watch this.”

Mara did as he said, amazed at what he was doing.

Indra formed the rock into countertop-height cabinets, smoothing the top into a beautiful countertop with stone faucets over a large stone sink, all seamless.

He coaxed water through the stone, creating a tiny river to flow into the sink and down a drain system he had also created. She opened her eyes, blinking at only what was now in front of her.

"Let's go farther in." Indra grabbed her hand, tugging her behind him.

Seeing him manipulate the earth was a huge turn-on. She shivered but ignored it. She wanted to learn all she could and then maybe jump his bones.

"Look at this." Indra beamed at her. "This is perfect so far." He leaned over to touch the floor. Around the giant pit, he created large seating areas. The first row circled the pit with breaks for access. Behind that, he created another. In each of the corners, he built long tables with benches. "This side space will be the council room for the sleuth. They'll need a large table with benches, a counter, and shelving along the wall. Do you want to try?"

"Oh, yes." Mara swore her grin was permanent by this time. She walked to the entrance Indra had built, touching the doorway. She closed her eyes and slowly formed a giant table with plenty of room to walk around. She formed a counter along the wall similar to the one Indra had built in the other room. She was panting by the time she was done. "What do you think?"

"You're a natural." The pride in his voice had her preening.

"Thank you."

"Now do a long bench on either side. Make sure to give it plenty of support. Bears are heavy."

Mara followed his directions. She looked at the table and concentrated on finishing the top until it shined.

"Show-off." Indra gave her a quick hug. "Now, we need to form sleeping quarters. Let's get a little closer to where I want them to go. The closer we are, the easier it is."

"The proximity helps? Could we have done it from the facility?"

"We could have, but we would have more strain and wouldn't be able to do as much." Indra's hand slipped back into hers. "I'd like to at least get as many apartments done as possible."

"How will we do them? Any specific configurations?"

"Yes." Indra explained exactly what was needed, then showed her before sending her off on her own.

They continued making blocks of units until Mara slumped against a wall. "I'm pooped."

Indra gathered her in his arms, rubbing his cheek against her head. "I think we've done enough. Ready to go back down the mountain?"

Her stomach growled. Mara rubbed it. "If there's food down there, you can't stop me."

Indra laughed and kissed her head. "Let's go then."

Mara let Indra turn her and walked back toward the entrance with his arm around her shoulders. "How many units did we do?"

"I'd guess twenty-four or twenty-eight." He smiled down at her. "You were a big help."

Mara beamed at him. "It was fun."

"Good. We'll need to do more tomorrow."

Mara groaned. "Then we'll bring food with too."

He laughed. "You got it." At the entrance, Indra stripped off his clothing and shifted.

Mara admired the work of art his body was. For such a solid-looking man, he moved with such ease. When he shifted, her inner dragon drooled.

"I can carry you back if you'd like." He gave her a toothy smile. "This way, you don't have to try to take off from the ground."

Mara sniffed, but he wasn't wrong. Plus, she was beat. The mental strain of working rock might as well have been physical. "Fine. Toss me your bag."

Indra grabbed his bag with his teeth, tossing it her way. Then he lifted in the air and she scrambled into his claw, careful not to accidentally be scratched by his sharp talons.

She really needed to learn how to take off properly and fly. Not bunny hop like she was doing earlier. Yes, the guys had laughed. Honestly, she would have too, if it wasn't so frustrating. Being a dragon and subjected to the indignity of being carried like a hatchling was humiliating. Mara chuckled. Those thoughts obviously were her dragon's. She'd not worried about such things before.

Indra moved his claws to hold her securely, and off they flew back down the mountain.

Mara smelled the meat cooking over the fire, awakening her appetite. Her stomach grumbled louder the closer they came. She pressed her hand against it. The gnawing hunger getting worse by the minute.

Indra opened one claw, letting her scramble down.

She tugged their bags out and watched Indra land and shift. She tossed his bag to him, tossed hers to the side, and sprinted toward the spit. She grabbed two makeshift plates, and a person she vaguely recognized filled them with meat and corn. She tried to place them, but her attention centered on her food, salivating at the scent. She turned and jumped, startled. Indra stood close behind her. She shrugged and smirked, handing one of the plates to him.

"I thought you were planning on eating both servings," he winked.

"I may have to go back for seconds." Mara stuffed a hunk of meat in her mouth. She sat on one of the rocks surrounding the fire. Indra settled next to her, his body heat keeping her warm.

"Mm-hm." His mouth was full. He shoveled the food in, trying to feed the beast growling in his stomach. It was as loud as hers. The mental work definitely depleted their bodies.

Indra quickly cleaned his plate and headed back for more.

Mara wasn't far behind. Eating so much surprised her, but she figured the dragon needed a lot of grub to keep healthy. She slowed nearing the end of the second serving. With a last bite, she groaned. The pressure in her belly let her know not to eat another bite. Her jaw cracked in a giant yawn. She shivered. Now she just needed sleep, asap.

"Give it to me." Indra grabbed her plate and took it with his to wash in the barrel someone had set out and filled just for that purpose. He washed them and placed them with the other clean pile of rocks. He glanced at the pile and back to Mara, placing his hand on the top one. He gave her a wink.

She snorted as the pile of rocks turned into a stack of beautiful stoneware plates. Emphasis on the stone. She laughed. She was getting punchy. She struggled to her feet.

Suddenly, Indra was in front of her, pulling her up. He wrapped his arms around her. "Let's get you to bed."

Mara groaned. "As much as I'd like to do more, I'm dead on my feet." Even the tingles she got every time they touched were low-key.

Indra swung her up in his arms and kissed her forehead. "Understandable." He strode toward the cave entrance, through the door, and up the stairs to her rooms. He jiggled her a bit and pressed his finger to the biometric lock, opening the door.

Mara sighed. His chest made for a wonderful pillow.

Indra pulled back the blankets on the bed, laid her down, and stripped her. He tucked her in then leaned over and gave her the sweetest kiss. “Sleep. I’ll be back in a bit. Just going to check on my family.”

She closed her eyes and drifted off.

CHAPTER SIXTEEN

Judging by the amount of meat being roasted, they were preparing for the next batch of shifters and humans to wake up. With more shifters now, they could revive more at a time. The bears were being woken up, and he wondered if the cats were too. It would make it easier, but he hadn't had a chance to finish the dens for the bear sleuth yet. Doing it for the cats would be more work. Of course, they may not want to live in caves or near the other shifters, to be honest. Cats were a curious group.

He should have asked the wolves. He could clear out spots if they wanted. So far, it hadn't been an issue. But that was a problem for another day. He knew the bears would want them.

He headed toward the shifter cryo lab. Indra couldn't wait to see more of his family.

The dragons and a few wolves were checking on the pods in the lab. It looked like the bears were almost ready to emerge.

Randy stood by a few pods, watching intently.

"Are they almost ready?" Indra peered into the pods. He couldn't stop his smile. Sure enough, Patricia, Patrick, Teddy, Olly, and Noah were stirring. The lids on the pods were up, nothing to impede their way once they were fully conscious. The gel drained from the feet, leaving them with just a thin layer.

"I think so. It's a good thing we weren't frozen in our animals. That gel is hard to get out. Can you imagine it all stuck to our fur? Yuck." Randy's disgust was evident on his face.

"Yup. We'd of had to shave your ass." Indra snickered.

Randy elbowed him, gesturing to their aunt. "Look. She's starting to come out of it." He wrinkled his nose. "It's a bit disorienting at first."

Suddenly, everyone around them, including their family, was moving.

Randy helped their aunt and uncle, while Indra helped their cousins. Randy led them all toward the shower room. They seemed in a daze, going along with whatever was suggested.

Indra wondered why they weren't surprised to see him and Randy. He continued helping the others out of their pods and directing them toward the showers.

Randy joined him a few minutes later, assisting those who looked especially woozy.

"Are the cats also being woken up?"

"Sort of. Once we started waking the bears, we decided to give it a few hours before we woke up the next group."

Emma, the wolf doctor, sidled up next to Randy. "We didn't want to overwhelm them. The shower rooms are limited and we need to feed everyone." She sighed. "Plus, there's the problem of housing. None of us have any idea of what the world is like."

"I can help with housing. I need to finish the bears' den I started. I know their preference. They'll want to feel secure." Indra stretched. "Mara and I started on them today. We'll finish tomorrow. I can work on something for the wolves after. I suppose it depends on when we'll leave for the other facilities."

"How are you making the shelters?" Emma stared at him, her eyes intent.

"I'm an earth dragon. So is my mate. We can shape the dens from caves." Indra shrugged. "Admittedly, it's easier if they already exist. We just kind of mold them how we want."

"We can scout and find a cave system for us. Though I'd prefer cabins. I don't like being closed in," Emma added.

"I can find a system without scouting. Let me show you." Indra took her hand. "Just concentrate."

"This is so cool." Randy added his hand to theirs.

Indra shared the picture in his mind. It was easier with Randy since the mental pathways had been there since they were born. It was a bit harder with Emma, but he knew he'd succeeded when he heard her gasp. He made sure to zoom out to show them the caves in the surrounding areas.

"Unbelievable." Morgan's voice drew Indra back. "How is that possible?"

Indra blinked and dropped the hands on his. "How were you able to see that?"

"I don't know. I think you were on the pack link." Morgan gestured around him.

The wolves were all staring at Indra in surprise.

Indra's neck turned hot, the heat creeping toward his face. "I'm a dragon." He got a few nods and a couple of thoughtful looks, then they returned to what they were doing. "Did all the wolves see that?"

"Pretty sure." Morgan laughed. "So, if you can do that again, where did you put the bears? I overheard you. I'd like to see what is free."

Indra touched his hand and shared the image. “The one higher up this mountain is the bear’s den.” He focused on it. “Here. The lower caves of this mountain range are available and the higher and lower ones in the other range are also free. Well, other than any natural critters living there.”

“What about the central ones here?” Morgan frowned. “That might be too close to the humans for us.”

“That one will be my weyr. The dragons will nest there. It is the perfect conditions for us for a hatching ground.” Indra moved the picture to the other mountain. “Hark mentioned he and his brother were going to probably build their weyr there.”

Morgan laughed. “We won’t fight dragons for a home. That would be a losing battle.” He looked around the room. “Lower would probably be better. It should stay a little warmer and the cats like high ground.”

“There’s a huge unpopulated world out there. Not even a tenth of the humans around when you were frozen.” Indra dropped Morgan’s hand. “If that much.”

“How advanced are the humans?” Morgan leaned against an empty pod.

Indra noticed most of the shifters, wolves, and bears who'd come out of the shower room leaned in to listen. "They have no more planes. Very few vehicles beyond solar-powered ones. If they were able to get horses, they use those again. There are few doctors. Most of those were trained as apprentices. No major hospitals." He thought for a minute. "Are you familiar with the Amish?"

Most of the room nodded.

Indra smiled. "That is about the sum of their technology. This place can help improve their lives." He looked at all of their faces, meeting their eyes. He couldn't emphasize this enough. "But we can't let them get the upper hand. We need to live side by side with them. The dragons will not hide ever again. Some of our species can hibernate for decades, coming out to check the world around them. But not all of us do. I refuse to hide ever again. While you were all frozen, the dragons helped the humans. We brought them together so individuals didn't die. Babies had someone to care for them and children didn't starve. Humans are social animals, and we made sure those who lived beyond diseases and missiles can start over. Most of the humans know about dragons." He shrugged. "But they tend to not believe until they see us."

"You were always a good boy." Aunt Pat stepped over and gave him a hug.

Indra rolled his eyes, cheeks heating again. He hugged her back. “It’s Pat. I’m so glad to see you again.” He chuckled when she swatted him. Randy and he always teased her. Back when technology was taking over the world, they’d watched a show called Saturday Night Live. It had a skit about a character named Pat. They never figured out if they were a man or woman. And since his aunt and uncle were named Pat, it was too irresistible not to tease them.

“Howdy, boy.” Uncle Pat joined the hug. “Still up to your shenanigans?”

Indra chuckled. “No more than usual.” It felt wonderful to be embraced by them. “How did you end up here?” From the corner of his eye, he saw the other bears heading out, directed by the wolves and dragons. The cats would be up by the morning.

“Randy. His hunting group was visiting us when the government contacted him. A bunch of our sleuth opted to come. Especially as the illnesses hit the young and the old. Once we buried them, the rest of us headed here.”

“Thank god.” Indra squeezed them one more time before letting go. “There’s food at the fire outside. Once you’re done, I’ll show you the way to your den.” He stretched, yawning. “It’s not completed, but it should work until I finish it.”

"A day sleeping outside won't kill any of us. We can just *bear* up." Pat chuckled.

Indra, Randy, and Aunt Pat groaned. Uncle Pat always thought he was the dad joke and pun king.

"Coz!" Teddy, Olly, and Noah crashed into him. Teddy squeezed him, lifting and swinging him around. "Glad to see you survived."

Indra tried to take a deep breath but had to elbow his way free. "Dragons appeared to be immune to everything that was released."

"Everything? How many diseases were there?" Olly frowned.

"Multiple waves were sent in missiles across the country. We were devastated. Once it seemed like it was over, something else was sent." Indra shook his head. "It was only a year, but it was one that changed the world." He cleared his throat, the thickness forming despite his desire to remain stoic. "The humans refer to it as the apocalypse. I have to agree. It changed the face of the world."

"I thought we were targeted. I worried we'd be woken up to a country occupied by another." Teddy folded his arms together.

"No. Well, maybe it started out that way. But the diseases travelled rapidly. Hell, the government tried to bring our troops back home from wherever they were deployed. Good thing, too. The overseas bases were targeted and decimated. No one really knows whether they all made it or not." Indra shrugged.

"Well, the government promised to help us get set back up when we were woken. How long were we asleep?"

Indra laughed. "Good luck with that. There's no more government. And it's been about nine generations, give or take, since the apocalypse."

They stared at him. Jaws dropped and mouths opened and moved, but no words made it out.

Indra scratched his chin and yawned. He was exhausted. It had been a long day preparing the bear dens, and he wanted to snuggle with Mara. "Come on, let's get you some food. Then you can pick a nice piece of ground to sleep on. Aunt Patty, you and Uncle Pat can sleep in my mate's spare room." He looked at his cousins. "The rest of you can crash on the floor there, or sleep out here."

Indra yawned again, noticing they were practically the last ones here.

"Yeah, let's feed those bellies." Randy rubbed a hand over Noah's abs. "So skinny." He laughed and jumped back from Noah's swat. "Never going to be faster than a wolf."

Indra grabbed Randy and gave him a noogie. "Or you a dragon. Let's go. I'm beat."

They all ate around the fire. After that, they went to Mara's apartment and got the Pats settled in a spare room. He realized there was one more, and Teddy and Olly opted to share it. Noah and Randy, because of course he followed, each took a couch. It reminded Indra of old times. He ignored the ache in his heart, knowing it would never be quite the same. He'd mourned his other cousins, but he'd never stop missing them. His happiness was just a touch bittersweet.

"Night." Indra eased open the bedroom door, then shut it, blocking out the rest of the world. He crawled in beside Mara and breathed in her fresh scent, spooning against her. He rumbled in contentment and quickly fell asleep.

~

Mara wiggled from Indra's tight embrace. He was snoring away, a low hum that soothed her. Luckily, he wasn't loud. She'd bet it was from exhaustion, having no idea when he came to bed. She'd laid down and was out for the night.

Mara ran to the bathroom, her bladder begging for relief. She finished and brushed her teeth, running a brush through her hair and splashing water on her face. Scrubbing dry, she stretched. Twisting brought a satisfying pop to her spine.

Tossing on a bathrobe from the back of her door, Mara snuck past a snoozing Indra and eased the bedroom door open. She glanced at his body, a hum in her blood at the sight. He was everything she'd hoped to find in a man. She never thought her dream man would be a dragon or that they even existed. She was awfully glad, though. Stepping lightly into the hall, she closed the door.

She stepped into the living room, heading to the kitchen. She kept her fingers crossed that the mylar-wrapped, dehydrated food was still good. She really wanted pancakes.

She hummed, opening the pantry and looking for the package she wanted. Finding it, she opened the bag. Inside were multiple smaller bags. She pulled one out and resealed the outside. Now for the true test. Mara grabbed a bowl, the frying pan, and a measuring cup. She made the mix and poured the circles onto the nonstick pan. Her stomach growled at the smell.

"That smells good," a male voice spoke behind her.

Mara screamed, waving the spatula in front of her. "Get back! Who are you?" Her heart raced.

Indra ran into the room, roaring, followed by a bunch of other people she didn't know. He slid in front of Mara, turning to face the intruder. "Oh, Noah. Why are you scaring my mate?"

"You know these people? How did they get in here?" Her pulse steadied. Indra obviously knew them.

"Mara, the idiot next to Randy, is my cousin Noah." Indra glared at him.

Mara blushed. She hadn't noticed Randy in the surprise. "Hi."

Noah smiled and waved.

Randy just stood there grinning.

"This is my Aunt Patty and Uncle Patrick. My other cousins, Theodore and Oliver." Indra gave her a sheepish look. "I didn't want to wake you last night, and since they needed a place to sleep, I invited them in. I didn't know where else might be available."

She gave a tentative smile, flushing at her overreaction. Of course, they couldn't have got in here except with Indra. The doors required a bioscan, and she was pretty sure Indra had no idea how to program one. "Well, I'm hoping the pancakes turn out. Who knows if they managed to stay good all this time."

"They sure smell good." Randy sniffed the air.

Mara heard a few grumbles from bellies in the room. "Well, let me just get them ready." She added more mix and water. There would be a lot of people to feed.

"Let me get plates out." Indra opened and shut the cabinets until he found what he wanted. "Teddy, can you set them out?" He passed the plates to Theodore and started opening drawers. He grabbed silverware and set them out on the table.

"I'll go grab some meat from the fire outside." Randy sniffed. "Make sure you save me some."

"Don't take too long." Indra made his way over to the pantry. "Do you have coffee in here?"

"Yes. It should be labeled. And creamer." Mara flipped the done pancakes onto a platter and added more to the frying pan.

"Aha." Indra waved around the coffee and creamer. He opened the bags and grabbed out a pouch of each. He stared at the coffee maker. "I wonder if it still works."

"Here. Let me help. You can go get dressed," Aunt Patty said. "You act like you've never used a coffee maker before."

"Not in at least a century." He shoved the coffee into Patty's hands. He headed into the bedroom, slipping on pants before returning.

"Look for filters." Aunt Patty rinsed out the coffee pot, pouring water through the machine.

"They'd be in the cabinet above the coffee maker." Mara wondered if Indra even drank coffee. Where would he get it from? "How did you make coffee then, Indra?"

"I haven't had any for years. When I travelled to the southern continent, they still grew it there and I'd get some beans to grind, but I haven't been there in..." Indra shrugged, "a while."

"Well, it seems like I just made some a couple of days ago, so move out of my way." Patty's smile lit up her whole face.

Mara chuckled. It really did seem like a couple of days ago. It was unfathomable that centuries had passed. Her mind spun when she thought about it. She finished the rest of the pancakes, placing them on the platter. “What’s today’s plan?”

A knock at the door stopped the conversation. One of Indra’s cousins, Noah, she thought, opened the door.

Randy carried in a bucket of meat. He dropped it on the center of the table. “Freshly cooked and hot off the spit.”

Mara added the pancakes to the table. She heard the coffee hissing and pouring into the pot. “Coffee should be done soon.” She pulled out a bottle of syrup from the pantry. The whole pantry was some type of specialized self-sealing storage container. Her brother explained that it was like a super mylar bag cabinet. He swore it would last centuries and keep the food fresh. She really hoped he was right.

She sat next to Indra, and the food was passed around. The sound of cutlery and chewing filled the room.

Teddy grabbed the pot of coffee. He brought over a bunch of cups and the creamer. The pot was emptied, and Aunt Patty refilled it. The hissing and tinkle of water began all over again. Finally, everyone was done. The huge mound of meat was gone, and not even a crumb was left on the platter.

"Thank you," a chorus of voices joined in.

Mara wiggled in her seat. Her cheeks heated. "You're welcome."

"Mara and I will finish up the bear den. You can watch where we go and follow us up. We made a cave for the alpha's family and finished more units. Do you know how many families there are?"

"We'll have to check with the alpha. We didn't all come in one group. As we arrived, we were put under."

"You didn't seem surprised to see me." Indra rubbed his hand on Mara's thigh.

"You were usually hanging around Randy, so no. Why would I be?" Uncle Patrick frowned. "Weren't you frozen too?"

"No. I searched for you guys. For years. The diseases hit the shifter community bad. Most were wiped out." He rested his chin in his hands, steepled on the table. "If you hadn't come here, the only shifters still left would be the dragons. I often wondered if the diseases were targeted."

The silence at the table was stunning.

Mara grabbed Indra's arm. "You can't believe that. Who even knew about shifters?"

"The governments did." Oliver waved his arm around the room. "Obviously, as they froze us."

Mara worried her bottom lip. "But they saved you."

"I think, since we are all part human, we were susceptible to the diseases, just like humans." Teddy leaned back in his chair. "From what you were saying, even the humans were decimated."

"Yes." Indra sighed. "I suppose you're right. The humans didn't fare any better."

"Don't forget, they outnumbered us," Noah added. "Probably still do."

"They do." Indra nodded.

"Well, let's get started on the day." Uncle Pat stood, finishing off his coffee. "After just one more cup." He went into the kitchen to refill.

"I'm going to get dressed. I'll be back in a minute." Mara said.

"We'll clear off the table, dear." Patty had all the men clearing the table in one gesture. One of the men filled the sink and started cleaning.

Mara smiled and went to get dressed. Her quarters had never had so much life in them. She could get used to it. She slipped on clean clothes and headed back out, grabbing her bag and Indra's.

They were definitely efficient. The table was cleaned off and wiped. The dishes were done. Even the coffee pot was empty and cleaned.

"Ready?" Indra pulled her into his arms.

Mara lifted her lips to his. She shivered as a fire lit in her blood at the touch of their lips. She moaned and wrapped her arms around his neck, going onto her tiptoes. She'd never get used to this. She wouldn't go back in time if she could. Not knowing Indra was here. She dropped to her feet, breaking the kiss. They'd never get anything done if they didn't stop. "Yes."

Indra grinned. The cockiness shined in his eyes. He knew exactly what he did to her. "Let's go then."

"Where is everyone?" Mara looked around the room. It was quiet. Too quiet to still hold any of Indra's family.

"They're waiting outside." Indra grabbed her hand and took the bags from her. He walked with her out of her quarters and to the outside.

His family was with a large group. She'd assume it was the bears. "What do you call a group of bears?" She assumed wolves were a pack and even heard that term, but not a clue about bears.

"A Sleuth." Indra's smile reached his eyes as he watched them.

"Hmm." There were plenty of people sitting around.

Indra walked to the largest group. His family was there also.

"Indra, this is the alpha Arthur," Patrick introduced them. "Indra is finishing up the den."

Arthur shook his hand. "Thank you. We all appreciate your thoughtfulness. Pat was saying we can head up and start getting settled."

"Yes. My mate and I will finish them up, but we need to know how many individual dens to make."

Arthur growled, the distress in his tone clear. "I believe we only have thirty family groups. And maybe six singles."

Indra bowed his head. His hand tightened on Mara's. He cleared his throat. "We have twenty-four units done. We can easily have them completed today." He pointed up the mountain. "We'll fly up; just watch where we land."

"There's a storeroom here with supplies. You'll need pots to cook. Plates, silverware, mattresses. If they are still good, you can use what you need." Mara looked around. *Hark, can you take some of the bears to get supplies? And use the containers to bring the supplies up?* She figured she might as well use the communication she had at her fingertips. It was kind of awesome.

Sure. I'm by the fire. Send them my way.

"One of the dragons, Hark, will take a few of the bears to get supplies. He'll fly them up when it's loaded." Mara smiled. She couldn't imagine having nothing. Since the shifters were frozen too, it made sense there would be supplies.

"Thank you, that will help." Arthur sent a handful of bears over to meet Hark.

"We'll go and head on up. I'll have to go finish some type of septic system. What I have set up should work. I just need to make sure I don't cross the water system and contaminate it."

"I can double-check that." Bruno came over. "I'll make sure it's flowing as needed and remains safe."

Indra clasped him on the shoulder. "Thank you. That would be awesome."

"If you want, I could check with my brother. He set up solar and hydroelectric power for the whole place here. He can see if he can rig up the cave system for you."

Arthur's smile widened. "I would be grateful for all of it. Thank you."

"Let's get going." Indra dropped his pants and shifted. He lifted a wing, hiding Mara from view.

She stripped, stuffing her clothes in her bag along with Indra's and shifted. Indra rose and grabbed her in his claws. Her talons hit something. Bruno was beneath her, assisting Indra in gaining height. She flapped her wings.

Indra let her go and Bruno moved.

Mara sank before she caught a breeze under her wings. She chortled and swooped through the air, racing Indra and Bruno to the cave system.

They landed and shifted back. The cave entrance was large enough even for dragons. But it would be tight with three of them.

Indra led Bruno to the bathrooms they'd created near the main hall entrance. "If you can, check the flow? I don't want to contaminate the water for the mountain." He waved toward the hall where the individual apartments were. "And if you can do the same for the units? Each unit has one bathroom. It would go a lot faster if we could just form the units and you do the plumbing, essentially."

Bruno chuckled. "So, now I'm a plumber again."

"You were a plumber?" Mara raised her brows. Huh, she wondered how many supernatural creatures she'd had contact with before.

"Long ago. I was in the US Navy as an HT. A turd chaser." He snickered. "A long, long time ago." He shrugged. "It helped being a water dragon. I didn't end up with a face full of water like many of my colleagues." Bruno put his hand in the water. His eyes closed and his face tensed. "I'll let you know where I need the piping formed. I'll mark the routes with running water, but you'll need to form a permanent path around it."

"Will do. Just let me know." Indra pulled her away. "Let's get finished. We've at least another ten units." He sighed. "I'd rather do fifty apartments. Give the bears room for growth."

"Especially if we find more in the other facilities," Mara added.

"Exactly."

CHAPTER SEVENTEEN

A couple of days later, they were ready to check on the other facilities. They were enroute to the closest one. It was a beautiful day to fly, with clear skies and the wind streaming in the direction of their first destination.

Indra checked on Mara's progress. She opted to fly rather than be carried in the container. Her scales glinted in the sun, showing off every beautiful inch of her form. He brimmed with happiness.

They had to be quite a sight to see. Hark, Zeru, Bruno, and the ice dragon, Blanc, carried a container holding two humans and two shifters. Indra and Rog's containers had an empty spot for their mates should they get tired.

Grace and Mara were busy testing out their wings. Wheeling through the sky, circling the other dragons, and generally being pests.

It was only a matter of time before they got too tired to fly.

Blanc had been sent at Hark's request for Indra's mating, but the ice dragon had managed to get lost on the way. Luckily, Bruno had answered the mating call.

They were worried that since they hadn't been woken up, perhaps none of the other facilities were. The human and shifter populations were low enough that they could easily be absorbed. The shifters actually needed the boost to stay viable as a species on this continent. He hoped they would find more.

Indra figured somewhere, somehow, a snafu occurred. The facility they were going to was originally assigned to send people to wake up the other facilities. Doctor Phillip had tried to send messages to the other installations, but got no response. It had been a long shot, but they wouldn't be making this trek if they had gotten a response.

He grinned, watching Grace and Mara chase each other. The little black dragon flew away, and the little green dragon streaked after her. Once she tagged her, with fire no less, they reversed, and Grace chased Mara. They would tire out soon enough. Both women were small enough to fit in his container. Carrying five would be nothing.

Watching her made it hard to control his urge to complete their mating flight as a dragon. It did give him a chance to learn how to subvert his urge to fertilize Mara. It wouldn't be easy, but since she was not ready to have hatchlings, he wouldn't force them on her.

The mountains were far behind them. They were heading north, and the land was stretching out before them. Grassy, untouched lands as far as the eye could see. Knowing how fertile these lands once were, it looked odd to see they had reverted to a natural state. If any humans farmed them, he couldn't see it. Perhaps they hunted; the game seemed plentiful.

They had been flying all morning and the humans probably needed to make a pitstop. They had begun to shift restlessly in the containers. Indra double-checked the area. He blinked his lids, checking for any heat signatures. Only animals.

It might be a good chance to stop and hunt. I don't see any humans around. Indra spoke to the other dragons.

Sounds good. I'm hungry. I'll let Rog and Blanc know. You should really connect with them. It would be easier since we'll probably end up neighbors. Hark went silent, hopefully letting them know.

Indra realized Hark was right. The male dragons started angling down toward the ground. *Hark, what path are they on? Can you bridge me to it?*

Sure. Just follow this path.

Indra concentrated, following the mental pathways to the other dragons. *This is Indra*. They could communicate a lot easier now using a general pathway.

The other dragons nodded.

Thank you!

You're welcome. Hark dove, the first to catch a meal.

Indra followed the mental pathways and realized Mara and Grace had already been communicating. *Mara, we're landing to eat.* Indra knew she heard him, but the two females were busy chasing each other. *Now.*

Fine. Mara snarled at him. *I'm not a child, you know.*

Grace headed down, abandoning their game.

I'm sorry, you're right. But stay in the air. I'll show you how to hunt. I just need to set the container down so the rest of the group can eat and relieve themselves.

Indra set it down in the wide field and flew back up. *Randy, can you let them know to eat and rest? We're going to hunt.*

The other dragons also deposited their burdens and returned to seek sustenance.

Will do. Don't worry about us. We brought enough food to make it through a couple of days. It would take too long to set up a fire before the evening. Randy saluted him and talked to the rest of the passengers, helping the humans climb out. The shifters easily disembarked, turning to assist the less agile humans.

There's a herd of some slow-moving creatures over this way. Hark shot a flame for their attention. *Some type of cow, I believe*.

Mara, head toward Hark. He found prey for us. Indra chuckled at her big sigh.

I heard him. So, do I just grab them? If they fight me and I drop them, what then? Mara swooped above him, her tail flicking his underbelly when she passed.

Indra followed, his desire for food switching to a desire for her. The teasing waggle of her tail and the flirty looks she was tossing him sent his blood boiling. His loins throbbed, ready to extend. His eyes narrowed. He sped up, ready to lock her to him.

Mara looked back and squawked. She darted away.

Indra rolled, circling her.

Mara dodged, her tail flicking his belly again.

Fudge. His erection slid free. The wind barely cooled the heat in his blood. He grabbed for her and missed.

Her laughter trailed behind her as she spun away.

Indra followed, swooping to her swirls. The chase inflamed his senses.

They played, mirroring each other.

Mara spun, flying upside down beneath him.

Indra moved closer, grasping her and sliding his cock inside her welcoming body.

Mara gasped, her wings trembling. Her talons scrambled.

Indra locked his talons to hers, pulling her in closer. His larger wings pumping to keep them alight. She tightened on him, milking him.

Control your glands. Bruno's admonishment brought him back from the brink.

He didn't bother responding, but he sought and found how to not fertilize his mate. Her scales brushing against his drove him wild. His blood sang through his veins. His penis throbbed in the scalding heat of her.

Her squirming and shimmying quickly drove him mad.

Indra bit her neck, holding her as still as possible.

Mara shivered and her cloaca locked, squeezing, tugging his ejaculation from him.

Indra thrust, holding her throat in his jaws as he flooded her heated passage. He slowed his speed, his wings pumping just enough to keep them in the air. His body relaxed and his penis retracted, once more nestled in his body. He released Mara's neck, twinning his neck and tail around hers. He slowly released her, making sure she steadied.

Now, I'm really hungry. Show me what to do. Mara flipped over, flying above a large herd of cattle.

Indra chuckled. *Watch me.* He plummeted, aiming for one of the beasts. He grabbed it with both claws, snapping the creature's neck. *Always snap the neck to kill it instantly. It will prevent its suffering and keep you from dropping it, which might not kill it.* He set the carcass down, grabbing another. With all the energy expended carrying the containers and then his mating flight, he needed to feed.

Mara dove, grabbing a smaller cow and winced when she twisted the neck, effectively killing it. She dropped it and grabbed a second. She struggled but finished the job. *Are we taking these back to the group?*

No, Randy said they brought food, so we don't have to cook until the evening. These are for us. Go ahead and eat your kills. I'm going to eat mine. Carrying the containers takes a lot of energy. Indra settled down, munching and crunching. He kept an eye on Mara.

Mara was daintily eating her first cow.

He chuckled, watching her squeeze her eyes shut before she took a bite. Luckily, the dragon in her happily devoured the meat in front of her. The bones of the animal would help keep her bones and teeth healthy. She would eventually become used to it.

He ate both his kills while Mara was still finishing her last. "I'm going to grab more. I'll be right back." He flew up and noticed the other dragons were grabbing more game. If, for some, game was hard to find elsewhere on their journey, at least they would have reserves if they ate their fill. And from the looks of the area around here, there were no humans or shifters to help cull the herds.

He grabbed two more, just in case Mara wanted more. He landed next to her. She was still slowly eating her last kill. "Do you want more?"

"Oh no, I'm full. Will you be able to eat both?"

"Yes. I'm hungrier than I expected." Indra dove right in, enjoying the crunch of the bones. He quickly finished. His belly was stretched just on the good side of being too full. Ideally, he'd find a nice sunny spot and nap the afternoon away. Instead, they would be expending energy carrying the containers full of people.

They finished and flew back toward the other shifters and humans.

~

Mara loved being a dragon. Admittedly, she wasn't carrying a large burden like the male dragons. Of course, neither was Grace. She sped forward alongside Indra. She stretched out, trying to make herself as long as he was. Compared to him, she was tiny. Mara flew and hesitated next to Bruno. Nope, not as big as him, either. She arrowed through the air and compared herself to Hark, Rog, Zeru, and even the new dragon. The white one. She forgot his name.

He was just a bit smaller than the other males.

She spun and looked for Grace.

Grace was riding an air current, wings spread with a happy smile.

Mara glided alongside her. She measured herself against Grace. Maybe it was just that the females were smaller than the males. It made sense. She'd heard Hark mention sisters-in-law and that they were small also. Female dragons also didn't have the spikes running down their spines. She wondered how female dragons defended themselves in a fight. Sure, they were bigger than humans, and the scales appeared to be wonderful protection, like a built-in bullet-proof vest, but over the whole body.

Hmmm. Were they bulletproof? Would that even be an issue? The facility had a weapons room, probably filled with guns.

What little fish? Bruno's endearment and the deep tone of his voice, even in her head, told her who was speaking.

Are our scales bulletproof? Mara really hoped they were. It would be awesome if they were.

It all depends on the bullet. Armor-piercing can take down a dragon. A normal bullet, no, we're good. Why did you want to know? Indra glanced at her, the heat in his eye sending tingles to her tummy. He was so hot. Even her dragon knew it.

How do female dragons protect themselves? We don't have the strength or even the size of a male dragon. She really wanted to know. It would suck if they always had to depend on the males.

Good question! Grace chimed in. *I throw a mean axe but don't normally carry one around.*

The scandalized look on Rog's face had Mara and Grace giggling.

The bite of a female dragon is venomous. Hark grinned. *It will kill a human and can put a male dragon down in minutes. It won't kill him, but he'll wish it did. It can easily kill other shifters.*

Mara and Grace looked at each other, eyes wide.

For real? Like if I bite you, you'll almost die? Grace snapped her teeth at Hark, then doubled up laughing when he backed away.

I shouldn't have told you. Hark glared at Grace's snickering.

That's good to know. But what if we accidentally bite you? Grace fluttered her lashes at him. *Because I would only bite you on accident.*

Mara stifled a laugh, but she could see instances where it could cause a problem, especially with Hark.

You have to activate your poison glands. I'm not sure how to do it. We can have our sisters show you how. They bit us enough that Rog and I are partially immune. Hark's disgruntled tone had Mara and Grace laughing at him.

And you probably deserved it. Grace smacked him with her tail as she flew by him.

I plead the fifth.

All the dragons laughed. Hark's behavior already proved why he was partially immune. Mara could easily see why his sisters had bitten him.

Mara found an airstream and rode it to save a bit of energy. She didn't want to admit she was tired, but playing through the morning with Grace and eating a large meal had her blinking her eyes. Maybe she'd ride in the container for the rest of the afternoon. She wasn't sure what would happen if she fell asleep flying. Would she fall to the ground? Would she glide? Or would she float to the ground? Her guess would be that, no matter what, it would be painful and embarrassing. She wasn't sure she wanted to find out.

They arrived back at the containers. The people were stretched out, waiting. Everyone had brought some type of a bag for clothing and toiletries. Each of the containers had a cooler from the storeroom. It was stuffed with cooked meat and MREs, plus bottles of water they could refill.

Randy, can you toss Mara's bag to her? Indra's words caught her attention.

Why? Do I look tired? Mara hadn't said anything to Indra, even though she just wanted a nap at this point.

Sure. Randy tossed her bag, hitting her on the snout. He didn't successfully hide his smile.

Mara hissed at him.

Indra chuckled. *Your thoughts weren't quite thoughts. And yes, you'll fall from the sky if you fall asleep. Every little dragon has done it at some point or another. No need to test it out today.*

Grace, want to ride for the rest of the afternoon? Mara figured she might as well have company. It would be her, Grace, Emma, Randy, and another female wolf. She shifted and grabbed her bag for her clothes.

Grace shifted, walking over to the basket for her clothing. "Might as well. I could use a nap."

"Me too."

Rog and Indra growled. All the male heads shifted away from her and Grace. *They said shifters didn't care about nudity but tell that to those two*. Mara snickered and Grace joined in. Mara dressed and slipped on her hiking boots. "I'm going to step away for a second. I'll be right back." She didn't want to announce she needed what amounted to a bathroom. She grabbed a bit of toilet paper and a small shovel. Leave no trace from her Girl Scout days had stuck with her whenever she went hiking.

"I'll be right behind you." Grace walked over to Rog, kissed him, and swatted his rear leg.

Rog snorted and licked her.

Grace jumped back. "Eww. Now I have to wash."

Mara laughed and headed into the nearby bushes. She heard Grace trailing behind. She dug a quick hole and filled it in when she was done.

"Why are you doing that?" Grace stood near her.

"So, the toilet paper decomposes."

"You don't just use leaves?" Grace peered at her. "Is that what that is?"

Mara held it out. "Yes. Don't you use it?"

Grace shrugged. "I've never seen it before. How is it made?"

"It's mostly made from recycled paper. Mara looked at the roll. "Don't you have toilet paper?"

Grace looked at it. "We don't even really have paper anymore. Just in books in the library. And those are all from before." She fingered the end. "I don't have a clue how you could even make it."

"Huh. It is made from trees and processed in a paper factory."

"Well, since we don't have factories, we don't have paper." Grace smiled and headed back to the group.

Mara looked at the roll. She was just beginning to see what the world had lost. Flying this far, she'd been playing with Grace. Now she realized the landscape below them had shown no sign of habitation. Not since they'd flown over a small town near the foot of the mountains. It must have been the town Grace was from. There'd been nothing since then, and that had been hours ago.

No farms, no roads, no buildings. Yes, the area had been rural, but roads connected the towns easily. Flying in airplanes, you could still see how many and how close even those isolated rural communities were. Now, nothingness. The land was wild and animals ran free. Her stomach twisted, and not in a good way. This wasn't a dream and the lack of devastation told louder than words how much time had passed.

Unsettled, Mara looked around. She hurried back to the group. Getting lost here and now would probably be a death sentence.

"It's time to move on. Let's get ready to load up. Fill your water bottles and relieve your bladders," Morgan announced. He might be the current alpha of the wolf pack, but his confidence had even the humans obeying.

Mara grabbed her water bottle and filled it from the small stream.

Grace did the same.

The male dragons drank from the stream.

Mara realized dragons took care of business like the birds while flying. She hadn't been conscious of it, but she realized it now.

She climbed into her designated container, resting against her bag and snuggling under a blanket. The dragons had deemed the weight of coolers, blankets, and a pillow for each person, including the dragons, worth it. Mara had to agree. There wasn't much room for five people, but as each climbed in, they fit well enough.

Randy was the largest, but the dragons insisted on at least one man in their basket.

Mara snorted. As if they would need protection when the dragons were flying them.

Morgan glanced around. "Are all the containers full?" Each affirmative had him nodding. "Okay, time to fly." He settled down.

The dragons grabbed the sides of the containers and lifted off.

The slight rocking had Mara yawning. She noticed Grace doing the same. Her eyes drifted shut, lulled to sleep by the movement and the murmured whispers of the wolves.

CHAPTER EIGHTEEN

Indra frowned. “Are you sure this is the right location?” They’d travelled for just under a week to get here. He stared at the flat overgrown fields. Or what used to be fields. The centuries of growth created woods that hid most of the ground from view.

“According to Doctor Phillip's latitude and longitude, it should be somewhere around here.” Morgan checked the sextant he held. “It’s probably hidden in the trees.”

Anyone see a spot to land? Indra looked near him, but it was just trees.

Over here. There is a small clearing. Zeru was a bit north of the rest of them. *And it’s near a stream.*

Good. Let’s land.

Zeru dropped his load and shifted.

Each dragon followed suit.

Indra was the last to land. He rotated his shoulders. It would be good to not carry the containers for a few days. He grabbed Mara’s hands and helped her out of the container.

Rog helped Grace.

Randy was being his charming self and helped both the female wolves out.

Emma rolled her eyes, but the other she-wolf fluttered her lashes and let him assist her.

Randy ate it up.

Indra snickered.

"Are these the correct coordinates?" Mara frowned.

"According to Morgan. These are what your dad gave him," Indra said. "But I don't see any mountains."

"Oh no, this facility was probably built underground using a silo." Mara stretched, catching his eye with a teasing smile.

She knew exactly what she did to him. He cursed under his breath, willing his body not to react, but it did no good.

They hadn't had any alone time, and he was desperate to have her under him again. Or over. He didn't care as long as he had her.

Mara giggled and tossed his clothes at him. "I think you need to put that away. Before someone else takes it as an invitation."

Indra rolled his eyes and pulled on the jeans she tossed him. He had to move around and grunted to close them, but he did it.

Mara rubbing against him didn't help.

He just wanted to devour her.

"A silo? Are you sure? I don't see evidence of one." Morgan frowned. "It doesn't even look like a farm could have ever been here."

"Let me check." Indra kneeled and pressed against the earth. A picture of the area took form. He looked deeper into the ground. Off to his right was a depression. Below the years of dirt, a man-made object. Some type of door or manhole cover buried by years. Beneath that, an unmistakable man-made bunker leading deep into the earth.

They had found it. Now, to see what happened to it.

"It's here." It was actually in the middle of the clearing. The thick cement and possibly steel walls below the ground prohibited the trees from taking proper root. Even centuries later, humans left scars upon the world that Mother Nature couldn't fix.

"Here? Really?" Hark looked at the slight depression. "Are you sure?"

"Yes. We'll have to dig for the door. It is under a lot of dirt." Even with Indra's abilities, the dirt would refill the hole because it was so fine. "I think we can leave it until the morning."

"Agreed. We need to hunt and replenish our food. Since we'll be here a while, we can start smoking meat." Morgan pointed to the shifters. "Bring back enough for everyone."

"The dragons will hunt for their suppers. The humans can start gathering wood and setting up a large fire pit." Zeru shifted into his dragon, with the rest of the unmated dragons following suit.

Rog and Indra stripped and waited for their mates to undress and join them. They took off, followed by their mates. The days of flying across the country had finally strengthened their wings so they could fly from the ground without assistance.

The rest of the shifters went to hunt.

The trip had been tiring for everyone. Wolves hated being cooped up and enjoyed the chase, as did the few feline shifters that had joined them. The bears, while preferring to roam, had had no issue sleeping their way across the country. The dragons, who could have traversed the same distance in a couple of days, took almost a week with the burdens they carried.

The dragons found plenty of game and flushed some prey toward the earthbound shifters. A few brought back carcasses to spit over the fire for the humans and then joined the hunt once again. When everyone had food, the dragons ate their catches. The sound of crunching was heard throughout the woods. More life in it than probably for decades.

A couple of the more enterprising humans had found edible tubers and onions along the stream and were roasting them over the fire.

Indra sniffed, enjoying the smell of the cooking food. His belly was full though. *I will see if I can dig out the area around the door.*

Can't we just ask the dirt to move? Mara wiggled up next to him, snuggling beneath his wing.

We could but this kind of dirt won't be easy to shift around. It's too fine. It's easier to dig.

Indra rubbed his face against hers. *You can try it if you want.*

Yes! Mara perked up and concentrated.

Indra could practically see her brain working.

The dirt moved, a little bit clearing to settle next to a small hole. The wind blew it around, and most of it landed in the hole. Mara growled. She prowled closer. Squinting at the spot of dirt she aimed at, it just settled back again. She made a noise of disgust. *I see what you mean. It's like trying to catch water in your hand.*

Indra chuckled. *An apt expression. Dirt is just...dirt. Stone is a lot easier to control. Back up, I'm going to dig.*

Mara moved.

Indra checked to make sure he didn't fling the dirt at anyone. He used his front claws and started digging. The loose dirt flew behind him. Hopefully enough, it wouldn't get in anyone's face. It was fine and loose. No clay to help keep it together. The deeper he dug, the more the condensed dirt clumped together. He backed up and moved the dirt, adding it to the pile behind him. Mara assisted, making the job easier.

The clearing was dark by the time they had the concrete slab exposed. The flickering light from the fire illuminated a large hatch in the center of the concrete. A speed wheel connected to latches sealed it in place. Edges on the concrete showed some walls or a roof once covered the area. They were damaged and chipped, like an explosion had destroyed it.

"It looks like they used a door from a Navy ship. Or something similar." Bruno peered over the edge, looking at it.

Mara slid down the side of the hole and gingerly tapped the concrete. She moved toward the door.

To Indra, she flickered in the light from the fire. He adjusted his sight to better see her and the door in the dark. "Try the wheel. See if it will move."

Mara leaned down to touch the wheel. She tried to turn it. “It’s stuck, or maybe it’s locked from the inside.” She tried a couple of more times. Nothing moved. “It could just be age.”

“We’ll attempt it in the morning. I’d rather see it clearly. Maybe we’re missing something.” Indra held his hand out to help her up. He really didn’t want to see it crumble beneath her feet. He doubted it would, but Indra didn’t want any chances taken with his mate. He’d just found her and didn’t plan to ever let her go.

Once back up top, they settled around the fire with everyone. Morgan and the others were making a plan to guard the entrance while a group went into the space. He set guards up for the night. They didn’t know this area and didn’t want to become victims of anyone who thought they might have something they wanted. He assigned different shifters, as the humans would test any systems in the facility if they were faulty.

Indra cuddled up with Mara. Their bodies wrapped together as dragons. Just the size of the dragons should discourage anyone with bad intentions. They hadn’t seen a nearby town like the one Grace was from, but it could be farther away, so it didn’t draw attention to it.

~

The dawn brought increased activity. The few bears with them offered to guard the top of the facility while the rest went below. The humans needed to do the jobs they'd trained for. The doctors among them were there to wake anyone still frozen while the shifters would search for a shifter cryonics lab and do the same.

Indra and Bruno hopped down.

Indra laid his hand on the cement. There was a tunnel leading straight down. It was wider than the door, and branches led farther down the tunnel. Indra assumed there would be some sort of ladder. As far as he knew, humans couldn't fly. And they'd have to go in human. This opening was too small to go in shifted.

"Be careful. We found booby traps at the entrance of the other facility. It may not be the same here, but look out." Rog hopped down with them. "We had to basically break in the other door." He looked at the hatch. "But it was locked from the outside and the inside. Hopefully, this isn't locked."

"Let's find out." Bruno leaned over and grabbed the wheel. "Does this twist?" He tried spinning it. Nothing happened.

"We'll both do it." Indra grabbed the wheel across from Bruno. Another set of hands landed on it.

"Might as well have all three of us try." Rog grinned.

Indra's muscles strained. "Again."

They pulled, twisting the wheel or trying to. All of them swore.

"I think I felt it move." Bruno grunted, still pulling.

Indra and Rog continued. "Are we turning it the right way?"

Hark dropped into the hole. "Move over, I'm here to save the day."

Rog snorted and shifted so Hark had his hands on the wheel too.

Indra knew they'd have to do something else if this didn't work. There was no more room for another dragon and they were the only ones with enough strength to do this. "Turn it the other way."

They tried it the other way.

"Yes." Indra felt a slight movement. "Now the other way."

They worked the wheel back and forth in increments. The squeal of the wheel was deafening with each twist.

Indra noticed the wolves and felines were gone. Their ears had to hurt from the noise. Dirt had gotten into every crack and crevice. Years of disuse, as evidenced by the amount of earth needed to excavate the opening, would have to be worked out.

No one had any idea if there was another entrance. Until they actually got in, they wouldn't know. Any more than they knew their mountain that had been hit by a missile was actually an entrance to an underground forgotten government facility.

With a shriek, the wheel turned freely and the latches grudgingly gave way. They all looked at each other and down at the hatch.

"What do you think?" Zeru eyed the hatch as if monsters would erupt.

As if they weren't monstrous enough. Dragons were basically the toughest monsters left in the world. On ground, at least. There were things in the sea that humans had never known about. Some of Bruno's stories were interesting, to say the least.

"I think we open it. It's why we are here." Indra reached for the hatch.

"Stand back. It's hard to kill a fire dragon. I'll go first." Rog stepped forward, but Hark's arm shot out, blocking him.

"Brother, I'll do it this time. You have your mate, after all." Hark didn't wear his grin for once. "I haven't found mine yet." He shrugged. "Plus, I wouldn't want to have Grace pissed at me if something happened to you."

Indra rolled his eyes. There it was, Hark's sly grin crossing his face.

Rog snorted and stepped back. “Fine. You can have the glory this time.”

Indra shook his head at their back and forth. “Ready?” He tugged at the hatch. “The mechanism is open, but…” He pulled again and the hatch swung up, dirt flying from around the circle. The gasket was stuck half on and half off the hatch. Bits of its debris flying with the dirt.

“Huh, there are no lights.” Hark peered down the hole.

“What? There should be.” Christopher, Mara’s brother, jumped into the hole. “My schematics for solar power should have been implemented at all three facilities.” He moved to go down the hatch, but Rog and Hark grabbed him.

“Wait. Let us make sure there aren’t any boobytraps here.” Rog pulled him back.

“There shouldn’t be. That was something my father set in place. He was paranoid another country would come in and destroy us.” Christopher shook his head. “He had me design them.”

“Maybe he shared them.” Bruno peered down the hole.

“No. He would love nothing more than to be the last facility standing. He’d try to run the world.” Christopher laughed. “He had no clue the world would change so much.”

"Still. Let me go first. I'm a lot tougher than a human." Hark leaned into the hole. "There's a ladder here." He lifted his head up and swiftly lowered into the hole. He shouted back up. "Looks like there is another hatch down here."

A grating noise indicated the hatch below was in better shape than the first one, but still, the years of non-use were evident. A clank told them it was now open. The dragons and Christopher peered inside. Still, no lights could be seen.

"There should be ambient lighting in the halls," Christopher muttered. "This doesn't look good."

They could hear Hark scrambling down the ladder.

Indra saw Hark move off the ladder to the side. There was a small platform with a door sealed like the hatches. "Why would they use watertight doors underground?"

"Too seal rooms off if needed. Don't forget, the military had a lot of input into the facilities." Christopher squinted into the darkness. "I wish there was light."

Oh yeah, he was human and couldn't see in the dark. Indra couldn't do anything about that. He was just glad it wasn't a handicap dragons had. "We can use a torch if you'd like. Once we go down."

There were plenty of pine trees in the area. *Randy, can you get a couple of branches cut for torches? And tree sap.*

Will do.

Indra wasn't sure where he was but knew he was close.

"Nothing here yet," Hark yelled, tugging at the individual handles on the door off the platform's side. He banged on them. From the clanging, he must have partially shifted. The sound changed to something heavier hitting the metal. A shriek of metal followed by more banging each time he opened a handle and started on a new one. "Finally." He pulled on the door, grunting at the effort. It flung open, banging against the wall.

Indra saw him stick his head in.

Hark stepped into the room and a low hum began. Lights flickered and then began to glow. "I wonder what the rest of the buttons do?" he hollered up.

Christopher pushed through and descended the ladder. "Don't touch anything else."

Don't light the torches. Hark got some lights working. Indra sent the message to Randy. There was no response, but he knew he got it.

Christopher jumped on the platform and disappeared into the room with Hark.

Rog followed.

Bruno and Zeru glanced at each other and shrugged, following.

Indra looked at Mara. She was so gorgeous. He'd rather find a nice private area, but they had things to do. "Shall we?" He climbed down with Mara just above him.

They stopped at the platform. There was another hatch below them.

"We'll work on the next hatch." Indra dropped down to the hatch. It too, sat on a concrete slab similar to the entrance. He watched Mara climb down the ladder, her heart-shaped bottom wiggling from side to side. He groaned and adjusted himself. He had to keep reminding himself they didn't have time for sex. His body didn't appreciate the message, but he'd live.

Mara stepped off the ladder, giving him a sly smile.

Indra narrowed his eyes. The little minx knew exactly what she was doing to him. Her quick glance down and smirk sent his pulse racing. Two could play at that game. It would be a delicious bit of foreplay.

Indra crouched to open the hatch.

Mara peeked over his shoulder. Her breasts brushed against his back.

Indra rubbed his ass against her pelvis and made sure his elbow caressed her breast. Her intake of breath had him smothering a grin. He turned the hatch, the squeal of the metal loud in the enclosed space.

Mara jumped back, covering her ears. “Wow, that’s loud.”

He tugged the hatch open, keeping Mara behind him, just in case. A woosh of stale air and dust swirled around them. They both coughed. Once it cleared, they scrambled up the ladder where the air was fresher.

“It’s nasty air down there.” Mara wiped her eyes.

“This isn’t right.” Christopher was checking the computer in front of him. It wasn’t working. “Why isn’t there power?” He turned to the door. “I need to check below. There should be power. The solar should have had the lights on.”

“Are you sure the solar is working?” Hark poked at the button he’d turned to get the lights on.

“I don’t know how else there could be power here.” Christopher grimaced. “But it sounds and smells like a generator. I don’t even know how it could be working.”

“Well, we opened the hatch below and it stunk.” Mara scrunched up her nose. “I have a bad feeling about this.”

Indra did too. From the looks of the other dragons, it was mutual.

"Were there lights?"

"No. I don't think so. Maybe we should go first?" The siblings might not like that idea, but who knew what they would find below.

"No, if I have an issue for any reason, I'll leave right away." Christopher eyed up Mara. "But maybe Tamara should wait here."

Her glare let Indra know what she thought of that idea. "I'll be fine." She stuck her nose up in the air. "I am a dragon, after all. I can handle it."

Christopher frowned. "I know. I'd like to know how that happened. It shouldn't be possible."

Mara's cheeks reddened. She turned away. "Let's go down."

Indra heard more people descending the ladder. "It's going to get crowded real soon. We need to explore."

Morgan stepped off the ladder. A couple of wolves were reluctant to get off the ladder. They were sniffing the air.

"What have you found?" Morgan peered into the small room. "What is this?"

"Overrides." Christopher grimaced. "And power switches. A generator of some type. Makes no sense at all." He continued to grumble, poking and prodding the switches and buttons in front of him.

Morgan sniffed the air. “Maybe the dragons should explore. The wolves and felines will not like the smells down here.” He started climbing the ladder, shooing his men to return to the top. “Let me know what you find.”

Indra sighed and watched him clamber up. “We might as well start. Christopher, do you want to go with?”

“Yes. I need to see what’s going on.”

The dragons looked at the hatch below.

Hark jumped down. “I’ll lead the way. Just in case of boobytraps.” He took a deep breath and disappeared down the hatch.

Randy, send down the torches. Indra was glad he’d had Randy get them ready.

A couple of branches dropped down the hole.

Rog grabbed one and lit it, handing it to Christopher. He took the other. “I’ll carry this until or when we need it.”

Indra grimaced and climbed down. The ladder ended on a long corridor similar to the one from the mountain facility. It was pitch dark and the stale smell filled the air. He moved away from the ladder and waited.

The rest of the team followed him, one after the other until they all stared down the long hallway.

Indra growled. “Let’s get started looking for the cryonics room.”

CHAPTER NINETEEN

Mara stared at the long ladder in front of her. She tried not to think of the rows Hark, Rog, and Grace incinerated in the cryonics room. The rows she and Indra absorbed back into the stone. Ashes to ashes and dust to dust. Every muscle in her body was tight. Her nose was stuffed and her eyes were tight and stinging, holding back the tears she wanted to shed.

They'd found a second exit, but it had been destroyed by a blast a long time ago. They'd searched but found no evidence of a secondary cryonics chamber. This appeared to be a human-only facility.

They'd explored using blueprints they found in a conference room. This base appeared much more military than civilian. They'd even found a huge armory. Hark and Rog had melted every piece into a large pile of metal.

Indra had used his powers to check underground. But the earth surrounding the facility wasn't as easy to read as the mountains were. The concrete left an unmistakable form though. He still found no evidence of any hidden chambers.

They did find out why the power failed. Missiles had detonated on the solar array, destroying any chance of the facility working. The room leading to it had been filled with evidence of a large blast. Large enough to destroy part of the facility.

Mara thought about how close they had been to being in this same position. The missile that detonated near their facility damaged only their entrance. She fisted her hands. Her nails dug painfully into her palm, just enough to let her know she was alive. Unlike the poor souls here.

A room of backup generators had never kicked in. They should have been fed from natural gas. Since none of the old power plants were working, according to the dragons who'd been alive this whole time, they probably stopped working. The lines were cut off long ago, and the gas was not sent to the facility. They'd probably never know.

Arms slid around her waist, pulling her in tight.

Mara turned, burying her head into Indra's chest and slipping her arms around his waist. "Such a waste." Her voice was thick. Her eyes stung and her nose barely pulled in air.

"Oh, sweetheart." Indra's love enveloped her. "I doubt they even knew what happened."

She knew he was right. The people in the pods looked undisturbed. What was left of them. They'd decayed, probably never waking up. "I hope so." She shuddered. "My one big fear was dying in a pod, waking up with no way to fight free of the gel. Slowly suffocating."

It seemed impossible, but Indra's arms tightened even more.

It brought her a bit of peace. Like he was keeping her pieces from flying apart.

"You never have to get in one again. I won't let you." He growled.

The protective tone, his hard arms, and the care that emanated from him sent inappropriate tingles through her. Mara rubbed her face against his chest. "Thank you." She stayed still in his arms, soaking up his comfort. Letting it wash away the emotions from this awful day.

"Ready to go up?" Indra asked.

Mara sighed. "Yes." She was more than ready.

Indra's arms released her. He turned her and tapped her butt. "Up."

She snorted, a bit of a giggle escaping. "Going." She climbed the ladder back to the surface. She wondered what would happen to this place.

Randy was at the top, reaching out to help her exit. He pulled her up and out. His strength was more than she'd imagined by looking at him.

The same could probably be said for her now. She still looked like she always did, but it belied an inner strength her dragon contributed. She headed toward the camp, climbing stone stairs some enterprising soul had put in to make getting in and out of the pit easier.

The rest of the dragons and Christopher followed behind. The clang of the hatch being shut echoed across the clearing.

"So, what did you find?" Morgan waited until everyone had taken a seat around the fire. All the people they'd come with were within hearing range.

Christopher took the lead. "The power here was gone. We had to use torches to see."

"There was no second cryonic chamber," Indra added.

"Did you find a first chamber?" Morgan asked slowly. He'd heard the hatch close. He wasn't a stupid man by any means.

"We did. There were no viable subjects." Mara's heart hurt. It was easier to speak as if it was a science experiment gone wrong rather than saying everyone had died.

Silence settled over the group. One of the bears stood. "Well, there's no reason to stay here anymore." He looked over at the pit. "Should we cover it back up or leave it?"

Zeru followed his gaze. "Leave it. It would make a good home for a group if the power could ever be restored."

The felines perked up. The leader of clowder, Lane, spoke. "We need a place to live." He looked over at the wolves. "We'd really like a bit of space from the other shifters." He turned to Christopher. "Would you be willing to show us how to fix it?"

"Yes, I would be happy to. There should be supplies in the storerooms to fix the solar panels."

"Good. We'll continue to the next facility and return here with all our people." Lane smiled, looking distinctly catlike in his satisfaction. "Hopefully, we will find even more at our last stop."

Morgan sighed. "Well, let's eat up, pack what we can tonight, and leave in the morning."

At that, everyone broke away. The felines gathered together, speaking in whispers Mara couldn't even hear. She saw them all glance at the hatch. She had a feeling they'd be exploring shortly. Not that she'd blame them. The area in the mountains could easily get crowded if everyone stayed nearby.

Bruno walked up to the group of felines. She sidled closer to listen.

"When you want to settle here, I can help bring water where you need it. A natural spring is nearby; I can enlarge it so you have a lake if you'd like." Bruno gestured to his right. "It's in the trees that way. There is also water going to the chambers below. It should work once there is power for the pumps."

Lane shook his hand. "Thank you, friend. We'll take you up on that."

Bruno smiled. "It's good to see shifters again. I haven't met any in a long while."

"When was the last time you saw any?" Lane frowned.

"I've met a few here and there. There are not many left in this country. Overseas, you can find packs, clowders, tribes, and clans." He leaned closer to Lane. "There are more shifters than humans overseas. Down in the southern continent in the jungles. And in Africa, for example. On the plains."

Lane froze. "More? Like me?"

Mara wondered what he meant. He was a feline shifter. She didn't know what kind, but what difference would it make? She studied him. His blonde hair was shaggy, and his eyes were blue, but so were Zeru's. And he was a dragon.

"Eavesdropping?" Indra's voice made her jump in fright.

Mara had been intent on the conversation, not paying attention to her surroundings.

Indra had snuck right up on her. “Naughty girl.”

Mara snorted. “What did he mean?”

“Did who mean?” Indra grasped her hand, pulling her away from Bruno and Lane’s conversation.

“Lane, when he said like me?”

“He’s a lion shifter.” Indra shrugged. “Why?”

“Bruno said he’d seen shifters on the plains in Africa.”

“Maybe he has. I never ran into any, but I was looking for wolves and bears.”

Mara didn’t have to ask why. Indra had spent more than a century looking for his family. Speaking of family. “Why don’t you ever talk about your dragon family? It seems like you spent more time with your cousins.”

Indra shrugged and laughed. “Because all the siblings my age are female. They drive me crazy. My brothers are older than me. They have hatchlings my age, so I rarely saw them. They established weyrs around the country. But my sisters all stayed close. Close enough to constantly bug me. I escaped to my aunts and uncles whenever I could slip away.” He tickled her. “Girls have cooties, you know.”

Mara giggled and moved away. "Can't have you catching cooties." She ran toward the trees. Her pulse thrummed, anticipating Indra catching her.

"You go, girl." Grace's chuckle followed her.

Indra's low laugh spurred her faster.

The trees were in front of her. Mara slipped between them, effortlessly dodging while she ran. Definitely her dragon's influence. As a human, she'd have slipped on the first root or run face-first into a tree.

A growl right behind her twisted her nerves tighter. Her body reacted—nipples tightening, her pussy throbbing—making her panties damp. She scooted behind a tree, Indra's hand just missing her. "Too late." She laughed and ran.

"Just wait." Indra's chuckle was close. Too close.

Mara screeched.

Indra swung her into his arms. "I have you now." He buried his face in her neck, sucking her flesh.

"Oh." Goosebumps covered her body. Her arms wrapped around his shoulders. He could have her any way he wanted her.

Indra carried Mara deeper into the trees. They'd be flying and exhausted for the next couple of days until they reached the last facility. The farther they moved from the others for a bit of private time, the better.

Mara teased Indra's ear. She caught her breath when he hitched her higher so she had better access. She felt his shiver when her tongue ran along his ear's edge.

"You're playing with fire." His arms tightened beneath her.

He didn't change his hold though. She was enjoying her snack. Little nibbles to tease and entice him.

"It's far enough." Indra let go of her legs, holding her to him. He eased her to the ground and stripped.

Mara watched every move. His muscular chest, with his tattoos rippled with each movement, led down to a yummy six-pack and his adonis belt aimed the way to his impressive package. She licked her lips, imagining the ways he could pleasure her. He grew harder and longer under her gaze. Beneath his appendage, thick thighs and calves supported him on well-shaped feet. Who knew feet could even be sexy?

Mara's attention slid back up, stalling on his erection. She forced herself to continue past all that impressive muscle to his face. His brown hair tumbled in the slight breeze. His green eyes blazed down at her. The look on his face, smug.

He knew she liked what she saw.

Mara wanted more than just eye candy. She raised her arms to him. "Indra." It was enough.

He dropped down, stripping her. Then stretched out across her body. His hardness to her softness.

She rubbed her nipples across his chest, enjoying the feel of him. The pressure of his body, flush against hers, sent her senses spinning. “More.” Her pussy dripped with desire. Grasping at nothing. She needed him inside her.

Indra grunted. “I can’t wait. I need you.” He flexed and slid smoothly inside her. “Ah.”

Mara arched, the pleasure of him overwhelming her.

He began to move, faster and faster. Deeper and deeper into her welcoming body.

Her hands grasped his firm buttocks, urging him on. Smooth and hard and she wanted to hold him inside her forever. The noises from her mouth encouraging him meant nothing and everything.

He grunted with each thrust, deep, erratic breaths making his chest heave.

Nothing was in sync, yet the yearning for him built in her blood. Her thoughts swirled. She never wanted anything more than this man, this dragon. Her everything. Pleasure built inside her, and with a final thrust from Indra, Mara exploded.

She clenched on him and he stilled, his cock coating her insides with cum.

Indra dropped down on her. His body pressed hers to the ground. His lungs heaved.

She wrapped her legs and arms around him, holding him to her. She'd need to breathe shortly, but wasn't breathing overrated? She just needed him, anchoring her body to the here and now. Forever. She needed forever with him. "Can we just stay here?"

Indra moved, sliding to her side, letting air fill her lungs again.

She would have rather he stayed on her and in her.

"Probably not. For one thing, I guarantee our families would come looking for us."

Mara snickered. "You're right."

"Of course I am." He grunted. "My family is annoying."

Mara choked back a laugh. "You love your family."

"Doesn't mean they're not annoying." Indra nuzzled her ear with little licks along her neck. "Mmm. I could eat you up."

Sated, Mara lay sprawled along the ground. She doubted her legs would hold her up. She ignored the crackle of leaves beneath her, the little sticks beginning to poke her backside. What she couldn't ignore was the sound of footsteps cracking branches and scattering leaves. She sighed. The soft giggle and hushed voices indicated Grace and Rog were also looking for a bit of privacy.

"We'll soon have company." Indra groaned. He kissed her and stretched, pulling their clothes to them. "Better get dressed."

Mara grumbled and sat up with Indra's help. Now, the ground was uncomfortable. They dressed and slid on shoes over their bare feet.

Mara shook her head. It sounded like leaves had taken up a home in her hair.

"Let me." Indra plucked a couple out, holding them up for her inspection with a grin. He dropped them and grabbed her hand. "We might as well head back."

~

Three days later, they landed at the final coordinates.

The mountains were different from the ones of their facility. The coordinates here led to a defunct mine. The signs were no longer legible. Too much time and not enough care had passed.

Indra eased the container onto the ground. The other dragons did the same. There was a small town here. The people in it stared when they arrived, followed, and watched while they landed. He wondered if they were going to have any trouble. They didn't appear hostile, but you never knew. There was no escaping the town. The coordinates didn't give them a choice.

Mara, stay as a dragon. I want to make sure we're able to fly away if there are any problems.

He figured the other dragons felt the same as no one shifted. Changing would make everyone more vulnerable, without a way to fly out.

Morgan hopped out of his container and approached the people. "Hello. Do you know anything about an old government facility here?"

A man said, "There was an old mine here." He shrugged. "The stories say the government used it, mined it for sapphires for different uses."

"We've come to check it out. Has anyone explored it?" Morgan looked over the small crowd.

The man waved forward another man. "Bob here used to go all over in the mine." He laughed. "He used to tell quite the tall tales about what he found down there. You can ask him."

Bob nervously looked around. "I don't go down there anymore. What did you want to know?"

"Walk with me?" Morgan gestured toward the dragons and containers. "When was the last time you were in the mine?"

Bob followed him.

The crowd drifted to follow, but Indra and Zeru stepped forward, blocking their path.

The farther Bob walked from the crowd, the taller he stood. He glanced back and saw the people no longer following, and he exhaled, puffing out his chest.

Indra figured in relief.

"I was in there the other day. I found an entrance on the other side of the mountains. I don't go in this way. I made sure it was blocked off."

"Why?"

Bob made a scoffing sound. "I know these people. Jerry, there, he likes to rule the roost. Once I told them there were dead bodies down there, they stayed away." He looked toward the mine.

"Are there dead bodies in there? What else is in there?" Morgan pressed him.

"There's a bunch of coffins. Above ground, like they were preserving them." Bob grimaced.

Indra and Mara looked at each other. They could hear the discussion easily. Mara's smile had the people from the town backing up. A dragon's smile was a little disturbing if you weren't a dragon.

"Could you take us to the other entrance? Or show us the one you blocked here?"

Bob scratched his head. “I could. But at night. I don’t want them to see there’s another way in.” He nodded toward the group of people watching them. “Maybe just go in this way and check it out. Then leave. I’ll meet you in a couple of days.”

“That won’t work for us.” Morgan looked at him, the convivial expression he usually wore dropping. “How did you block the entrance?”

Bob shrugged. “I rigged an explosion. Covered it with a bunch of the tunnel.” He looked away again.

Indra wondered if he was hiding anything. He could just be nervous with all the dragons here. No doubt there was another exit, but it would be hard to find without knowing where it was. He could check the earth, but that didn’t always show him exact locations.

He would be able to see the facility from the inside, but he couldn’t see what it looked like from the outside. Making it harder to find from the air.

I’m going to check and see if a facility is here. No need to waste our time if it’s not. He sidled over to the side of the mine entrance. He leaned against the stone.

I want to talk to the people. Mara glanced at him.

Don’t shift in front of these people yet.

Why? They seem harmless.

We don't know if they would attack or not. This might not even be the whole town. They could have people hiding with rifles. As dragons, we can keep everybody safe and fly off as needed.

Okay. I wanted to talk to them though. See what life is like now.

We can do that later. But as humans.

Fine.

It's safer that way. We don't know these people.

Okay, I get it.

Indra turned his concentration to the back of the mine, down a vertical shaft. A hatch similar to the last one lay at the bottom. There appeared to be a couple of tunnel collapses before the hatch, effectively blocking it off.

Below the hatch, a larger facility was laid out. Indra found the entrance. This one appeared to be an escape hatch. The compound was multiple layers as large or larger than the facility he'd found Mara in.

He found a second entrance in another mine. The facility went on for quite a way. Hopefully, the cryo chambers were intact. He thought there might even be two. They wouldn't know until they checked it out in person.

He concentrated on *seeing* where the other entrances were. He thought he could guide them near one of the entrances. Indra stood, looking to orient himself with the inside of the mountain. One of the entrances was lower and could very well have been compromised. The other was higher in the mountains. He'd prefer to check it out from there. There would be less chance for the people to follow.

Morgan was following Bob into the mine.

Indra knew none of the dragons would fit at the entrance. It was carved out for humans and not much bigger.

Randy, why don't you and a couple of wolves or bears follow Morgan.

I don't trust these people either. Randy got the attention of a couple of shifters and they followed Morgan in.

The crowd glanced at each other and a couple stepped forward but were stopped. Quick touches to get their attention without trying to draw the dragons' attention. Too bad it didn't work. Indra moved in front of their people, subtly moving Mara behind him. Rog moved Grace behind him.

Mara, quietly let someone know to pass the word to get back in the containers. I think we're going to leave here.

Will do.

Indra saw her drop her head to a couple of people. They, in turn, spoke to the others. Bit by bit, they climbed back into the containers. Ready for the dragons to pick them up. Two containers stood empty. Morgan, Randy, and the men with him would use those when they were done. Zeru and Hark would fly them.

An explosion and a shout came from in the mine. The dragons grabbed the full containers and flew farther up the mountain, keeping their people from the guns suddenly appearing in the hands of the people below.

Morgan, Randy, and the other shifters ran out of the mine.

Get in the container! Indra shouted to Randy. *What happened?*

The idiot taking us in set off an explosion, trying to trap us. No clue why.

He didn't say anything?

He was just rambling about how we were there to steal the jewels. Like we had any interest in them.

Did he die?

Nah, we just left him to find his own way out. So now what?

There's another entrance, two, actually. They may know about the one, so we'll check out the other. We'll have to set up watches to make sure no one sneaks up on us.

Randy snorted and jumped in. *That's not likely.*

Indra grabbed a container once the rest of the shifters jumped in, ignoring the shouting from the townspeople. He flew toward the hidden entrance, hoping he was correct. Indra figured the town rejected any outsiders, like some towns he'd run across before. It could just be that they were too large a group and, therefore, a threat. They hadn't actually fired any of the guns. Or they'd never seen dragons before. Hard to believe, though. But the dragons were a ferocious-looking group, enough to make any puny humans nervous. As long as no one started shooting, relocating was the smartest move. They'd be days trying to locate them.

Indra landed with his container. "If you need to relieve yourselves, now's a good time." The town couldn't reach them anytime soon. Indra concentrated, checking the area. It was a little disorienting seeing the facility from this angle. He finally found the entrance he was searching for. He opened his eyes, still looking at the inside of the mountain and trying to orient himself.

The entrance was a couple of peaks over.

Mara stood next to him. She pressed against his side, her arms attempting to hug him. He chuckled and watched her smile.

"You can shift, you know."

“I know. But where we need to go is a couple of peaks over. There is an entrance there. I’d like to get there today.” It would take a bit of time to fly there. Not too much, but he’d rather get there during daylight.

“You need to eat though.” She stood back. “Shift and let’s eat. Everyone else is.”

She was right. And she already had his clothes. “Alright.” He shifted, enjoyed her drooling and slowly got dressed.

Mara giggled.

He buttoned and swooped down on her, tickling her. He tossed his arm around her shoulders, kissed her cheek, and headed over to grab something to eat. “Let’s do this.”

Zeru handed him a rock and a slab of meat. A few green things sat on the edge. “Can we make it to an entrance today?”

“I think we have to. There are two entrances. We need to get in before the townspeople do.”

A hand clapped on his shoulder. “I think you’re right. How far do we have to go?” Morgan was stuffing his mouth. “I think we need to leave after we eat.”

Indra nodded. “It shouldn’t take too long. It is just a couple of peaks over.”

“Good.” Morgan walked away, stopping to speak to the few groups.

"I'm going to ride in the basket. I don't want to change again," Mara added, stuffing a bite in her mouth before swallowing. "Once there, we can head straight to the cryonics room and start."

"We'll need to look around and see if there's a second chamber. Hopefully, we'll find more shifters." Bruno joined their group.

"I'll work with the bears to set up security at all the entrances. You said there were two?" Randy came over, and a group of shifters came with him.

"Actually, there are three. There's one in the mines, but it might have a collapse blocking it. However, there still could be access. I can't tell for sure." Indra took another bite and finished his food.

"Then I'll get guards arranged. The humans may not be a threat, but I'd rather make sure. I'll put three on each entry. We have enough bears and wolves. That will leave, what, twenty-two people to search the facility and start waking up anyone still alive." Randy nodded. "That should work."

"We can have ten people start the process on the first cryo chamber while the other group looks for another chamber." Mara nibbled on her lip, obviously thinking. "Indra, can you tell if there is a second chamber?"

"No, I just see the size and shapes of the rooms, nothing in them."

"I'll log into the computer systems if it's working. I can check the blueprints for another room," Christopher said. "Rather than waste time. The sooner we wake up everyone, if there is anyone to wake, the better." He shrugged. "They could all be non-viable subjects like the last place. Or they could be empty. With a town so close by, they could be the descendants of the original group frozen here."

"Well, it sounds like you all have a plan." Morgan laughed. "I'm not needed. If you're done eating, time to find a bush if you need it, and let's head out."

Mara and Grace headed for some privacy. Rog followed at a distance to keep an eye on them.

Indra and the other dragons stripped, put their clothes away, and shifted. The rest of the group climbed back into the containers.

"Follow me. I'll lead the way." Indra waited for Mara and Grace. They came running back and nimbly jumped in the container.

Rog stripped, tossed his clothes to Grace and shifted.

Indra grabbed his container and flew off, allowing the rest to catch up. He looked around and visualized the entrance. Following the picture in his mind as close as he could, he flew over another peak and landed. *Let me make sure this is the place.*

He put his claw against the nearest rock. Yes! *It's here. Go ahead and land.*

Indra shifted and went to get his clothes from Mara.

She ogled him while he walked toward her. A sly smile on her face. She could see what she did to him and so could anyone else.

Her pink cheeks could be from embarrassment or arousal. If she didn't like him getting visibly aroused, she needed to stop eye fucking him. He reached the container and leaned over. "Like what you see?"

Grace giggled and elbowed her.

Mara's cheeks deepened in color. "Wouldn't you like to know?"

Oh, he knew. Indra chuckled. "May I have my clothes? Though I have no problem walking around naked."

Mara tossed his clothes at him, including his shoes.

He did a reverse strip tease, which had Mara practically drooling. He preened at her appreciation.

Rog lifted Grace from the container. “You should be watching me.” The teasing note in his voice had Grace rolling her eyes.

“Indra, can you show us where the entrance is?” Morgan waved him over.

Randy stationed three shifters at the tunnel entrance. Bruno had opted to stay outside in his dragon as one of the guards. The rest were going in to guard the other accesses.

Indra touched the wall and kept his hand on it, walking toward the entrance he saw in his mind. Mara guided his steps. He walked up to a wall of stone. “It’s here. I just have to find a way to open it.” He checked, looking for a mechanism in the almost seamless rock. He narrowed it down and was able to find the location of it. He used his claws and tore the stone, leaving a bioscan lock the previously hinged rock was hiding. It was in an odd spot. Higher than a thumbprint scanner would be.

“Let me try it. I should have access.” Christopher put his eye to the scanner. And with a grinding noise, the wall in front of them shifted.

Indra’s brows rose.

Christopher appeared to have a high level of access. The door led into a hallway. Once there, he keyed something into a tablet on the wall. Doors slid from the side, covering the large stone wall they'd passed through. "There. Now, we can just use the doors. The stone will stay open unless we close it." He quickly showed the guards how to set it if they needed to shut the door. "At least there's power here."

"Can you lock the other entrances? From that pad? There are more entrances, correct?" Morgan asked.

Indra nodded. "Three total. It would make it a lot easier to keep out the town's people if they try to interfere."

"Sure thing." Christopher typed in more information. "That should do it." He checked the tablet. "Power is working great." He pressed a button by the next set of doors. "Let's see if there is anyone to save."

The group moved forward, checking each room they passed.

Christopher found an office and quickly went into the computer system. He found a list of rooms and a map and printed five copies. He handed one to each set of guards, pointing out their current location and the exits where they needed to go. The two groups left. He gave a set to Morgan and each group looking for the cryo chambers.

"There are two cryonic chambers." He pointed them out on the maps. "They are our priority, aren't they?"

With everyone's nod, they headed out. Their group went up one floor, and the other went down.

It was a mixed group of humans and shifters.

Emma, the shifter doctor, and Morgan went with the group going down.

Indra led their group. He didn't want Mara or any of the humans to run into problems. He was big enough to deal with almost anything. Zeru and the quiet ice dragon also protected the group.

The room was right where Christopher said.

Indra took a deep breath and entered the room. He glanced around and stepped away to let the rest enter the room.

Mara started bossing people around right away. “Okay, if the gel is cloudy, call me to check it. Don’t start opening it. If it’s still blueish, go ahead and start opening the pod. Does anyone have any questions on how to do it?” She moved to the closest pod. “Watch me do this one. If everyone starts with a different row and the same column, we’ll make sure no one is missed.”

Mara described the procedure as she opened the pod. “Any questions?”

No one had any, and they moved per her suggestion. Soon enough, the creaks of the pods and the beep of buttons filled the rooms.

Mara logged into the computer to check the information. Once she was done, she began the process of opening pods again.

Indra stayed near the door, guarding it. Yes, there were guards at the entrances, and yes, they were locked, according to Christopher. But his sexy mate was in here and he would make sure she and the rest of them were okay. He looked over the room. This facility was bigger than the others. It may take them a couple of days to get everyone woken up. His gaze slid to Mara.

“Are you going to help?” Mara stood with her arms akimbo, glaring at him.

“I was guarding the door.”

She snorted. "I don't want to be here forever. We're fine. Bruno's at the tunnel entrance. The other entrances also have guards. We could use every hand."

Indra turned to the door and checked it out. There was a lock. He snicked it closed, chuckling at Mara's huffing. "I'll help now."

"Good, start over there." She pointed rows down away from her.

"I would rather stay by you."

"Then you should have done that in the first place. Now go." She scowled at him until he reluctantly went where she pointed.

Indra stopped, glanced at her glare, and started opening a pod. Zeru was laughing at him. *You just wait until you find your mate.*

I can hardly wait. Zeru puffed out his chest. *I will not let her dictate to me. She will know who has the final word.*

Indra laughed. *I can't wait to see that.*

CHAPTER TWENTY

Mara stared at the group of people. It had taken a full day of opening pods. Now, two days later, they were all awake. She knew a couple of them from meetings and going over the medical procedures to start the process of freezing them. They all looked surprised that so much time had passed. To be honest, they all looked a little lost.

Morgan had finished a briefing with all the humans. They had woken up five hundred people. Five hundred. At least double, if not more, the amount from their facility. That didn't even include the shifters.

"What are we going to do with all of them?" Mara really wondered. They were all adults, but she doubted most had even stepped out of a city their whole lives.

Indra shrugged. "Nothing. Wasn't there a whole plan for when they woke up?"

"Well, yes. But so much time has passed." Mara frowned and then leaned against Indra's strength. She needed it.

"They still have power. They still have their homes set up inside the mountain. They still have their plan. They should be fine." Indra wrapped his arms around her. "What else can we do?"

Morgan said, "The man in charge wants to meet with the townspeople. Want to follow?"

Mara perked up. Huh, that might be interesting.

"No. I'll check on the shifters in the other cryo chamber." Indra shook Morgan's hand. "Good luck."

Morgan laughed and walked away.

"I wouldn't have minded going," Mara said.

"You can, but I'd love you to stay nearby. I don't know that I trust the townspeople." He set his head on top of hers, wrapping her in his arms.

Mara wavered. She loved being surrounded by him. She was curious about the shifters. She'd spent the last two days with the humans, reviewing their records to ensure they were healthy and getting them fed.

The last of the shifters were also awake. She had to admit, she was curious. "Well, let's go see the shifters."

Indra smiled and released her, grabbing her hand. "This is just as large a group as the humans. It's wonderful news."

They took the stairs down. Similar to their facility, except there were three floors. All the apartments were located on the middle floor. There was room for all the humans they'd woken up. Unfortunately, no such provisions were made for the shifters. There were, however, storerooms of gear for them. At least they had that.

She guessed the government figured they could make it on their own.

Indra led her to a large room filled with seats and a stage.

Every seat was filled. The dragons were answering questions.

"What kind of shifters were here?" Mara whispered.

Wolves, of course. Bears, felines, and a few dragons, and about fifty refused to say anything. But Zeru swears they are badgers. Says he's been around them before. Indra used the telepathy thing since there was a question-and-answer session, and it was certainly politer. Wait a minute. *Dragons?*

Yes. It turns out that not all of the shifters were volunteers. They're pissed, but the ones who captured them are long gone. We know because we caught them stalking the humans, and they claim they're not here.

Well, it could be true. It was probably the military, and the last compound looked exclusively military.

True. Indra frowned, obviously thinking about it. *Anyway, this is why I wanted to be here. The humans are taken care of. The shifters were not really thought about other than capturing them here. The supplies will help, but it is a different world than they were used to.*

Mara nodded and tuned into the conversation.

"What are we supposed to do?" Someone shouted from the seats to be heard.

Zeru sighed. He seemed to be the one with the most patience. "Decide where you want to live. Two dragon weyrs are willing to take you in. The bears have a den being built. If the earth dragons are willing and available, more could be built. The felines are planning on taking over the compound south in what used to be Kansas. The wolves..." He turned to look around. "Huh, Morgan can tell you what the wolves are planning, but he's not here right now."

Randy stood up in the front. "I might be able to help with that. Morgan is taking steps to set up multiple packs. He has been sending scouts to search for locations to give enough territory to each pack. We'll have a pack-only meeting to see how we want to do this. Once the number of packs is established, those interested in being alpha will compete until we have one alpha per pack. Then each alpha will choose a beta and omega. Any other questions?"

The wolves grumbled but settled down.

"Where is the bear den?" A large man stood up.

“It’s in the mountains. Plenty of game and a small human town. Near the dragon weyrs and plenty of fertile soil and a large forested area.” Zeru looked at Indra. “Indra can tell you more about it.”

Indra, dragging Mara with him. He lifted Mara onto the stage and jumped up, turning to face the people. “I built it halfway up a mountain. It’s natural caves. You enter into a combo lounge and dining area. We built a meeting room to the side. Across from there is a communal kitchen, which leads to individual apartments. The alpha bear's room is first and we built fifty units. Each has a large living room, three bedrooms, and a bathroom. We can adjust them if needed. The living area section has enough room for a small kitchen if desired.

We can look into a second toilet area in some apartments. But we made huge communal restrooms off the lounge area. Showers, toilets, and sinks. We even added changing tables in each one.”

“It has running water? Flushable toilets?”

"Running water, yes. The toilets are not flushable, unfortunately. The engineers are looking into it, but there are not many around. Don't forget, there are no more manufacturing plants." He shrugged. "Our water dragon worked it out with some engineers; it's sanitary, and we've done what we could to keep the smell down."

"What if we don't want to live there?" the man asked. He looked a bit belligerent but this had to be a shock.

"You don't have to live there," Zeru said. "We are just offering options."

"Who is the alpha bear you expect us to live under?" The man glared up at Zeru.

Zeru shrugged. "I have no idea. That's up to you bears to decide."

The man looked surprised. "We get to decide?"

"If that is how bears choose your alpha, yes," Zeru answered. "The world is different than when you were all frozen."

"Humans are small and few in number," Indra added. "Dragons will no longer hide in the shadows. I would suggest that each of your groups do the same." He looked at the group, who refused to name their animals. "There is no reason to hide. Shifters should be helping shifters. All of the humans should know about dragons by now."

"Well, maybe not all of us want to be out." The group Indra was looking at all nodded.

He sighed. “Then it is, of course, your choice. There is no government to regulate us, or anyone even.” Indra laughed. “The humans will have the hardest time with this. Each town or village you come across has different rules by which they live. Unfortunately, some are unfriendly to anyone. They will shoot first and ask questions later. If you manage to survive.”

“Why do the humans know about dragons?” One of the badger shifters jumped up. “What did you do?”

Indra looked at Zeru, both of them sighing. “We saved humanity. A lot of it anyway. Without stepping in, there would be even fewer humans.”

A few grumbles and a few *you should have stayed out of it* floated through the room.

Rog grinned. “Think about it. Many of our mates were human. If we let them die, we would die out too.”

The grumbles died down, though a few shrugged, not worried about the humans.

Zeru waved his hands to get their attention back. “We will leave tomorrow to return to our homes. The dragons we woke up are also willing to help transport. Not everyone will be able to fly.” He nodded down at Randy. “The wolves agreed to go overland to bring anyone that wants to come with us. Morgan recommends all the wolves come so your hierarchy can be established.”

"If any of the bears would like a den made here, though the humans nearby don't seem the friendly type, I can contact a couple of earth dragons to build a den. Or if you know of a location, they can take you there to establish one."

The one man stood up again. "Would one of you dragons be willing to take us to check on an old den? To see if it is still there and livable?"

Hark raised his hand. "I would be happy to. I don't have a mate, so that would be no problem. We have enough dragons to take home the original group, plus more."

"I could contact an earth dragon to go with if that's okay. If there's damage to the den, they might be able to solve it with minimal effort," Indra added.

Mara squeezed Indra's hand. She wanted to show support, but since she hadn't been a dragon that long, she didn't even know how to help other than following Indra's lead. She watched him concentrate. He was talking to someone. He didn't let her in on the conversation. Probably another earth dragon she hadn't met.

"If you can wait a couple of days, one of my sisters will meet you here. She'll go with to rework the den to see if it can be saved."

"That would be acceptable." The man sat and began conversing with the people around him.

Mara guessed he was an alpha bear from his air of authority. She had so much to learn about this new world. Sliding her arm around Indra's waist, she hugged her body to his. Thank goodness she had her mate. His reciprocating hug filled her with warmth. "Will we stay to see your sister?"

"No. We're leaving tomorrow. She knows where to find me. I'm sure she'll stop in to meet you when she can." He sighed. "They never leave me alone."

Mara snickered. Poor baby. She squirmed when his fingers tickled her side. Giggling, she pulled away. "No."

Indra looked down at her. The adoration in his eyes warmed her soul. He pulled her into a giant bear hug, or should she say dragon hug, lifting her from her feet.

On second thought, Mara couldn't wait to get home. She wrapped her arms around his neck. The idea of hatchlings had grown on her, especially since Grace was expecting. She fluttered her lashes at Indra, loving his naughty grin. Mara wiggled from his hold and grabbed his hand, pulling him away from the group.

Indra's plans for a weyr built near her quarters and a hatching ground were too tempting to delay. "Let's go have a proper mating flight."

Indra's eyes lit up. "By proper, you mean..." He whispered, "hatchlings?"

Mara nodded. "Hatchlings." Life was too short and she wanted to experience every bit of joy with her mate.

Indra swung her around, his embrace stealing her breath away. Just like his kiss.

THE END

Other titles by Beverly Ovalle:

A Dragon's Fated Heart Series:
Rise of the Dragons
Stealing Hope
Finding Faith
Saving Grace
Waking Tamara

The Santiago Series:
A Saint's Salvation
A Sailor's Delight

The Glen Series:
Lightning Strike
Willow's Cry

Standalones:
A Dragon's Treasure
Dragons' Mate
Touched by the Sandman
Love Me Forever
Triple D Dude Ranch

Anthology:
Destiny Whispers
A Gift of Sensuality

Thank you for reading my book. If you liked it, consider leaving a review. You can leave a review on Amazon, Barnes & Noble, Kobo, Goodreads or anywhere you purchased Waking Tamara.

Author Bio:

Beverly Ovalle has been obsessed with dragons and romance since she was a young girl, collecting dragon books and reading everything she could find on them even down to the care of real-life dragons. She's always been slightly panicked that the world as we know it will end, so has prepped for it, haunting survivalist pages and prepper projects she felt she needed in the event SHTF (shit hit the fan).

An avid fan of all romance, Beverly's goal is to share her love of the written word and write the spicy romances that she enjoys. She writes what she loves to read and it was only a matter of time before her obsessions crept into her writing for her to share. She hopes you enjoy her tales as much as she loves writing them.

www.ingramcontent.com/pod-product-compliance
Lightning Source LLC
LaVergne TN
LVHW010050110826
845155LV00028B/274

9781952525032